BOOK FOUR IN THE RECKLESS SERIES

Reckless FAITH

NYSSA KATHRYN

An NW Partners Book
Cover by Deranged Doctor Design
Developmentally and Copy Edited by Kelli Collins
Line Edited by Jessica Snyder
Proofread by Amanda Cuff and Jen Katemi
Cover Photography by Regina Wamba

❁ Created with Vellum

Letting him go was the hardest thing she'd ever done...until he returns, and letting him back in proves even harder.

Elle Marshal has spent most of her life pining for the same boy. A boy she's known since she was eight. A boy with beautiful blue eyes who's never been interested in anything more than friendship. For years he's been away, and she's been able to convince herself that she can live without him—until Jace returns. And every emotion she's spent a decade and a half denying comes crashing back with a single look. All throughout high school, she watched him date everyone but her, and while she's no longer that girl, deep down, a small part of her still doubts she'll ever be enough for the boy she's loved forever.

Jace Walker is the youngest of six siblings, including four military hero brothers. Following in their footsteps was a rite of passage, but leaving the small town of Misty Peak also meant leaving his best friend. A woman he's always wanted but never allowed himself to have. Not when he had so much to prove, when Elle deserved someone better...and when he has a habit of losing people he loves. But he's older now. Wiser. And when he realizes he can't deny what's between them any longer, Jace will do whatever it takes to have her.

Getting Elle to trust he's a safe bet proves harder than Jace thought. And when his past misfortune of losing those closest to him threatens his present—including his happiness with Elle—he'll have to speed up his timeline if he wants to keep them both safe long enough to have a future.

ACKNOWLEDGMENTS

A big thank you to my team—Kelli, Jessica, Amanda and Jen—you're the dream team. You helped me make this book ready for the world and I'm so grateful for that.

Thank you to my ARC team and readers. Your support and willingness to step into every world I write about makes sure the next book is written.

And to my family—you're my world. My reason. And you inspire me every day to work hard and keep writing.

PROLOGUE

ifteen Years Ago

Elle Marshal stared at the scatter of stars in the dark night sky. They were beautiful. Like small drops of silver on a black canvas. There was no moon tonight, but there didn't need to be. The stars cast a dim glow over her as she sat on a log in the forest.

The dull thud of music vibrated the ground beneath her, the distant sound of laughter and shouting cutting through the quiet.

Why was she here? She should be at home, tucked into bed with a book or a movie. She never enjoyed these parties. They were loud and messy and full of drunken idiots.

A set of beautiful blue eyes flashed in her mind.

Him. He was the reason. He was the reason she *always* came to these things. Every time she told him she wasn't coming, he'd step close, maybe touch her arm as his ocean-blue eyes bore into her, claiming he *needed* her to come. That he needed his best friend.

She shook her head. And silly her, she always said yes, even when she knew girls would paw all over him and she'd quickly be forgotten. Beautiful girls with perfect hair and makeup and hour-glass figures…basically her exact opposite.

She tugged the sides of her cardigan together, hating that she continued to compare herself to girls she'd never look like. Hating that for the millionth time, she didn't feel good enough.

A rustling noise sounded behind her, causing her back to straighten and hope to seize her chest. Was it him? Had Jace seen her slip away and come to find her?

The hope died as a very drunk, very unstable-looking Casper stepped out of the tree line. Or maybe he wasn't drunk. Maybe he'd taken something. It wouldn't be the first time. He and his friends were all the same—idiots who took drugs and acted like assholes.

"What do you want, Casper?"

"Jeez, way to be friendly, Marshal."

She rolled her eyes and looked away. He was a jock. A jock who was rarely kind to anyone unless he had something to gain. "Go back to the party."

He dropped onto the log beside her. "*Or*…I could keep you company."

"And why would you do that?"

He lifted a shoulder. "Because I'm a nice guy. Some would even call me charming."

She snorted. It was the least ladylike sound she'd ever made, and she absolutely didn't care. "No one has ever called you charming."

His brows slashed together. "You know, you're a real a bitch sometimes."

Anyone else, and she might have been offended. Casper? No. "Why are you sitting with me then?"

He lifted a shoulder. "I wasn't looking for you. But now that I'm here, you can tell me what Walker sees in you."

Something hard kicked in Elle's belly at the mention of Jace. "We're friends."

He scoffed. "Yeah right. He may have his arm around Alana right now, but he's always with *you*. You follow him around like a puppy dog, and he lets you."

Pain skittered through her veins. Was that how people saw it? Like she was the pathetic, lovesick girl who followed Jace around?

Casper squinted at her like he was looking for something. "You're friends with benefits, yeah? You give him what he wants, whenever he wants it..."

"Argh. You're disgusting!" She tried to rise, but he grabbed her arm and tugged her back down so her butt hit the wood.

"Come on, everyone wants to know. Just tell me why someone like him would want to spend so much time with someone like you."

His words hit like a physical blow. She shouldn't let what he said affect her. But weren't they the same words that whispered in her head every day?

Someone like her...someone plain and chubby and unremarkable. Probably why her mother had left her and, a couple years later, her father. Jace was the only person who seemed to stick around...for now.

She forced her features to remain blank. "Get your hand off me, Casper. I'm leaving."

"Just tell me. You good in bed? You good at—"

"*Now.*"

His eyes narrowed, and instead of releasing her arm, he yanked her closer. "If you're gonna be a bitch, I—"

"You fucking deaf, White?"

A shudder coursed down Elle's spine at the sound of Jace's voice. At the rage that slid through every word.

Both she and Casper turned their heads to see Jace storming toward them from the break in the trees. Even though it was dark, there was no missing the fury in his gaze. It made his blue eyes look almost black.

"Get your hand the fuck off her," he growled. "Unless you want a broken fucking nose."

Casper unclasped her wrist and stumbled to his feet, almost falling backward. The jerk was scared. Because even though he played a tough game, he wasn't stupid. Jace was bigger than him. Stronger.

Casper lifted his hands. "I—"

Jace shoved him. "You what? Couldn't understand plain fucking English?"

Elle's pulse sped up. Jace may only be seventeen, but she'd seen him hit a bag. He was fierce, and she didn't want him to get in trouble for her.

"Come on, Walker," Casper tried. "Elle and I were just having a conversation."

Jace took a threatening step forward. "Didn't look that way."

"Jace." Elle kept her voice soft, even though fear filled her. Fear that Jace would hurt Casper. He deserved it, but she didn't want Jace to do something he'd regret.

A beat of silence passed before—finally—Jace looked down at her.

"It's fine," she whispered.

For a moment, his intense gaze just held hers, making her heart pound that bit faster and her skin tingle. It was only when he looked back to Casper that she realized she hadn't taken a single breath.

"*Go,*" Jace said in a low, dangerous voice.

Casper did. He ran back toward the party like something was chasing him.

For a few seconds, Jace watched him go, as if daring the guy to come back. Then his jaw clenched, and he once again turned his gaze to her as he lowered to the log. He sat so close that his warmth soaked into her side, causing a tingling sensation to run through every limb.

"Are you okay?" he asked quietly, some of the anger still there.

"Because if you're not, I'll go back and pound the fucker. Hell, I want to pound him anyway just for touching you."

He said things like that a lot. And sometimes she allowed herself to buy into the fantasy that it was because he cared about her, not as a friend but as more.

Images of him with Alana tonight flashed in her mind, and she dropped her gaze to the dirt in front of her. "I'm fine. He was just being stupid. He was clearly on something."

"He *is* stupid. Doesn't give him the right to touch you though."

Another clench of her heart. "Where's Alana?"

He lifted a shoulder. "I don't know. I saw you were missing and came to find you."

Why did he have to say things like that? Things that gave her just a bit of hope, when in reality, she knew there wasn't any.

She loved him. It was a secret that lived deep inside her. A secret she would never, not if she lived a hundred years, release into the world. How could she when it was so one-sided?

He cleared his throat. "What are you doing out here by yourself?"

"Getting away from the noise and watching the stars. Dreaming about being back in my bed."

His lips twitched. "Liar."

"I'm not a liar."

"Yeah, you are. You like the noise because your home is too quiet."

It was true. Usually, she did find her house too quiet, something only he knew. Exactly why the second she'd turned sixteen and gotten her driver's license, she'd spent so many nights driving to his place and spending her evenings with him. His family was big and loud and fun...and he was there.

"Fine, I like being out of the house. But I don't like this party."

"Me neither. Fuck, I can't wait to get out of this town."

His words cut into her flesh. Was this the last party they'd attend together? They were about to graduate high school, and he'd already been accepted into the Air Force. She wouldn't see him every day anymore. She wouldn't hear his voice or be able to sneak into his room when her aunt became too much.

It shouldn't affect her the way it did. She shouldn't *need* him the way she did. She'd always known he'd leave. He was the youngest of six siblings, four of them brothers, and all the older boys had already left for the military. It was always going to happen.

The letter she'd written for him burned a hole in her pocket. She'd had it with her every day for the last month, never knowing the right time to give it to him.

Was it now?

"Is it really so bad here?" she asked quietly.

* * *

Jace Walker let the question sit in the air for a moment. It should be a simple one, right? Was life here in Misty Peak so bad?

If anyone else had asked, he'd make a joke so they didn't see the complex layers beneath his surface. The ones he tried to keep hidden.

"It's not that it's bad…just that there's this thing inside me that needs to get out. To make something of myself like my brothers have." He'd never said those words out loud before, but fuck, they were true.

At Elle's silence, he looked at her to see the small pinch in her brow. She was so damn cute when she did that. It meant she was thinking. Pulling little pieces of him together in her head to figure him out in a way no one else did.

"This isn't about Lawson, is it?" she asked.

The thought of his former best friend felt like a dagger to his chest. It took every ounce of strength to not hunch over and let the heaviness of that name suffocate him.

"Because his death wasn't your fault," she whispered.

She'd whispered those words to him so many times, he almost believed them…almost. "I wanted to go out that night. And he paid the price for that."

Elle gripped his arm, and he had no choice but to turn to her. To let the gray shades of her eyes sear into him like they always did. "A drunk driver ran a red light. Lawson's death is *not* on you."

Then why did the weight of his death feel so heavy? Why did every breath feel like a battle? Every second feel like he was fighting an enemy he couldn't see?

"You couldn't have saved him," she said softly.

Her voice slipped inside him, making the part of him that had hurt for so long almost feel normal. For a moment, he ached to touch her. To let himself buy into the idea that had toyed with his mind for so long…that he could have her. That they could have each other.

But they couldn't. Because he needed to get out of here. Away from the memory of his friend's death. His mother's death. He needed to become *more*.

He clenched his fists, forcing his usual half grin to his face. "You gonna be okay without me, Tink?"

There was a flash of disappointment in her eyes. She hated when he defaulted to humor, but it was what he did. "Of course, because we'll stay friends, right?"

"Yeah, we'll stay friends. You can't get rid of me that easily."

"Promise me."

His brows flickered—and for some reason, he didn't want to. He didn't know what his life was going to be like once he left Misty Peak. But her eyes…*fuck*, those perfect grays…they bore into him, and he couldn't say no.

"I promise, Tink."

"Good." She slowly reached into her pocket and pulled out a folded piece of paper. The edges were slightly worn, and his name was written on the front in her usual neat handwriting. "This is for you."

"What is it?"

"A letter. Don't read it now. Read it when you're leaving Misty Peak, on the plane or something."

He slipped the note from her fingers, every part of him wanting to open it and read it there and then.

"I'm going to go back to the party." She squeezed his leg before rising and moving away.

Just like every other time she left him, his legs twitched to go after her, even if it was just to be near her.

He didn't. His gaze shifted down to the piece of paper in his hand. Though small, it felt heavy and important.

Screw it.

He unfolded the paper, and the second he did, he let her words weave into his soul. Words about how proud she was of him, dedicating his life to saving others. Of how much she'd miss him, but that she understood he needed to go.

It was the last line, though, that had him pausing. Had him reading again and again.

You're too loved to lose.

Loved. The word almost hurt to read.

Because he didn't feel worthy of her love. Not yet.

CHAPTER 1

Present Day

Elle couldn't move. Her hand literally wouldn't reach for the car door handle. Because there, sitting in the very bakery she'd planned to go to, was Jace Walker.

She should be braver than this, right? So she'd loved the guy fifteen years ago. Fifteen years was a long time. She was older now. More mature. She looked completely different. Felt completely different. Basically, she wasn't the chubby, insecure teenager anymore, so she had no reason to hide from him.

Then why was she sitting in her car like a hostage, seriously considering going back home?

Was he still cute? Sure. Okay, maybe not cute. Freaking gorgeous, with the widest shoulders she'd ever seen and dimples that cut the breath right out of her.

But she was an adult. A freaking adult. And she *did not* love Jace Walker anymore.

With an emphatic nod, she climbed out of her car and walked toward the bakery.

The windows allowed her to see everyone inside, exactly how she knew he was in there, but she didn't look at him through the glass, and she certainly didn't look at him as she stepped inside. Maybe it was immature of her, or just weak, but she was very careful to keep her eyes away from the spot where he sat with one of his brothers.

Mrs. Sandler stepped up to the counter opposite her. "Hi, Elle, how are you?"

"Oh, you know, just trying to enjoy a rare day off work." She usually loved what she did. She ran a small café at the visitors center in the mountains, and she was good at it. Her customers loved her. She made a killer coffee. But lately she'd just been feeling like she needed time off.

Mrs. Sandler offered an understanding smile. "We all need a break sometimes. What can I get you?"

"A caramel latte would be wonderful."

"Won't be long."

Mrs. Sandler walked to the coffee machine and Elle turned, only to gasp at the huge chest blocking her vision.

Holy crack on a cracker. Jace. He was there. Right freaking there, dimples and everything.

Not affected, Elle, remember?

She straightened her spine. "Hi, Jace."

Good. That was good. Cool, calm and kind of collected.

That damn grin of his widened, looking too damn sexy. "Hey, Tink." His gravelly tone as he used the nickname he'd given her when they were kids slipped under her skin, heating her limbs. "Wasn't sure if you were gonna say hello, so thought I'd come over here."

"Oh, I didn't see you."

Lie. Big, fat lie. And the look on his face told her he knew it. Shit. When would she learn not to lie to this man? He saw right through her like a human lie detector.

He tilted his head toward his table. "Come have a coffee with me and Kay."

"No." Dammit. Too fast. She'd said that too freaking fast. "I have somewhere to be."

Another lie. They were just rolling off her tongue now. Unless you called deep cleaning her apartment "somewhere to be."

"Come on," he urged. "Your best friend comes back to town after over fifteen years away. Surely I'm worth breaking some plans?"

Ex-best friend. Something he conveniently left out.

"Besides"—his grin widened—"I've been trying to catch up with you since I got back, but so far haven't had any luck. It almost feels like you're avoiding me."

Avoiding her devastatingly gorgeous ex-best friend, whom she'd spent most of her life pining over? No. Why would she do that? Because he could break her heart? Rip it right out of her chest and leave her hollow?

"You know how crazy that sounds, right?" she started, forcing her voice to come across relaxed, when relaxed was the last thing she felt. "What woman in her right mind would avoid the great Jace Walker?"

"I can only think of one."

Exactly.

Her phone vibrated, and she looked down to see it was one of those dating apps she'd signed up for. Damn waste of time they were. The guys were more disappointing than unsalted pretzels.

"Boyfriend?"

Her gaze shifted back up at Jace's question. "No."

"Caramel latte's ready, Elle."

Thank the heavens above. She turned to take the cup. "Thank you." She sucked in a quick breath before looking back at Jace, and yes, he was just as annoyingly gorgeous as a second earlier. Although now, he was lifting a brow at her, humor in his gaze.

She frowned. "What?"

"A caramel latte? Really? We used to make fun of the caramel latte kids in high school."

"High school was a long time ago."

"Doesn't feel that way. In fact, I think you're lucky I'm home, so I can steer you back on track."

She rolled her eyes as she moved toward the door. "The only track I need steering toward is the one away from you." Shit, had those words really left her mouth?

"See, now *that's* the Elle I remember. Not afraid to hurt my fragile ego."

She scoffed and turned back toward him. "Fragile? Jace, Tori Pilone once called you a walking penis, and you thanked her."

He lifted a shoulder. "It was the first compliment I'd gotten that day."

Jesus Christ. "You're something else."

"Something charming? Something handsome? Wait, I know, something ridiculously cute with blue eyes you could fall into."

Um, all of the above, but he did not need her to fluff his ego. "I'm going now."

"Where did we land on the catch-up thing?"

She rolled her eyes again. "I'll see you around, Jace."

She turned and was just stepping out when he called, "You can't avoid me forever, Tink."

She kept her breaths even and her spine straight right until she dropped into her car. Then she let it all out in one big puff of air as she bent over the wheel.

Why? Why did Jace Walker have to return to Misty Peak looking and sounding even more gorgeous than when he'd left? To torture her? To pull her back into her harrowing teenage years of pining for something she couldn't have while feeling insecure as hell?

At least she knew he wouldn't be here for long. He had a restless personality. Always looking for the next adventure. And there was nothing in this town to tie him down. So she just had to protect her heart and *not* fall for him until he left again.

* * *

FOR A MOMENT, Jace didn't move. He just watched Elle through the glass until she drove away from the bakery.

She was different. More distant. A new cautious look in her eyes. But she also wasn't. Her smile was the same. Her gray eyes still darkened when she got mad.

Fuck, he'd missed her.

He scrubbed a hand over his stubble before moving back to his brother.

"Everything okay?" Kayden asked.

"No. She's avoiding me."

"Why?"

"Don't know. I wasn't expecting to come back to town and for us to be best friends again, but I thought she'd at *least* want to hang out every so often." At Kayden's silence, Jace looked up to see his brother watching him closely. "What?"

"What happened between you two? You were attached at the hip when you were younger."

He blew out a breath. "Nothing happened. I left, we kept in contact for a while, then we stopped."

His older brother lifted a brow. "Then you stopped? Did you ever see her when you came home on leave?"

"Not really." That was his fault. He never reached out to her because he knew if he did, he wouldn't want to leave again. That probably made him weak.

His gaze returned to the window, even though she wasn't there.

"Well, if you're wanting her back in your life, just give her one of those dazzling smiles of yours. Most women can rarely say no to those."

Ah, but Elle wasn't most women.

He looked back at his brother, one side of his mouth lifting.

"You're so different from how you were. What happened to my big angry, broody brother?"

"Guess he's happy now that he's found love, so he doesn't have to be angry and brooding anymore."

Love. Kayden, the brother he'd *least* expected to use that word, had actually just admitted to being in love. "Good for you. You deserve to be happy."

"Thanks. Appreciate it. So do you."

For a moment, something deep inside Jace's chest pulled so fucking tight, he could barely breathe. Happy. Had he ever felt happy? True, unfiltered happiness?

He forced himself to smile. "Come on. We need to get back to work before they fire our asses."

They rose and thanked Mrs. Sandler before heading outside and climbing into Kayden's truck.

"How's it feel being back?" Kayden asked.

"Strange, because I guess I didn't know if I'd be back at all." Yet here he was.

He'd wanted to leave this town and see the entire world, and his job as a Combat Controller in the Air Force had allowed him to do that. He'd also wanted to get away from the loss of his mother. The loss of his friend.

Instead, loss had followed him.

"Your team must miss you," his brother said quietly.

Jace fisted his hands, Kayden's words bringing back a memory he'd rather leave in the past. "Yeah, they didn't want me to leave, but it was time."

He felt Kayden's eyes on him before he saw them.

When he remained quiet, Jace finally asked, "What?"

"You're okay though, right?"

He laughed, hoping it didn't sound as forced as it felt. "I'm better than okay. I'm working at a skywalk in my hometown. I'm back with my brothers. Now get your eyes on the road before you kill us both."

Kayden looked back at the road, and Jace filled the silence with a story about a teammate getting patted down at the airport by a good-looking security agent, getting a few laughs out of Kayden.

When they pulled into the parking lot outside the visitors center and climbed out of the truck, the air finally slipped into his lungs with a bit more ease. But that had nothing to do with the building. It was the mountains beyond.

Fuck, they were radiant. *This* is when he felt like he was home.

"You coming into the center?" Kayden asked.

"So I can see you and Tilly make out like teenagers? No, thanks."

Kayden shoved his hands into his pockets. "Your loss."

His brother went into the building, while he rounded the truck toward the skywalk. It wasn't far from the visitors center, just a couple minutes' walk. The air brushed over his skin, the sharp sound of birds echoing in the trees.

But none of that held his attention because all he could think about was Elle.

His hand itched to pull his phone out and text her. But for some goddamn reason, she didn't want to catch up with him, not even for a coffee.

Why? Because so much time had passed? He just wanted to see her. Spend time with her. It felt wrong being back in Misty Peak and not talking to her every day. Because they *had* talked every day when they were younger. And seen each other. Texted each other. If a day had ever passed where he hadn't made contact with the woman, it almost felt like a part of him had been missing.

He stepped onto the skywalk. He'd been working here for a week, and that week had been busy with people wanting to come and check out the newest attraction in town. Tourists making trips just to see the Smoky Mountains from up high.

His job was to make sure everyone was safe. To give tours to those who wanted them. And even to run some rappelling sessions from the center point of the skywalk, where a large tree sat.

He loved it, especially the rappelling. Anything that got his heart pumping was good for him.

He was striding along the skywalk when a rustling noise sounded from behind. He turned to see a woman standing at the skywalk's starting point. She had long red hair and looked at the walkway with an anxious frown on her face.

He turned back and moved toward her, smiling. "Hey. Can I help you?"

Her eyes widened. "Oh. Hey. Do you work here?"

"I sure do. I'm Jace Walker. I run the skywalk tours and rappelling sessions."

Another small frown tugged her brows together before her expression cleared. "Okay. Great. I'm here on vacation. How would I book a tour with you?"

He pointed back the way she'd come. "You would have passed a building next to the parking lot. That's the visitors center. The lady at the desk should be able to slot you into a tour group."

"Thanks, Jace."

"You're welcome."

He watched her walk away, his mind involuntarily going back to Elle. On the way no other woman seemed to capture his attention more than her.

He wanted her back in his life. He just had to figure out how to make *her* want that too.

CHAPTER 2

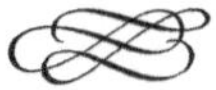

Thirteen minutes. Thirteen minutes until it was midday, and she was dreading every one of them. Like full-sweats, clammy-hands, would-rather-be-anywhere-but-here kind of dread. Because at midday, Elle was supposed to go on a tour of the skywalk.

Tilly, the center manager, wanted everyone who worked here to be familiar with the skywalk in case tourists asked about it. And most people—normal people—wouldn't have a problem with that request. In fact, she was sure most people would be excited about it.

But she hated heights. Pounding heart, dripping sweat, could barely breathe. *That* kind of hate.

And sure, she probably could have talked to Tilly about her fear and the woman no doubt would have told her to sit it out... but she hadn't. She hated people knowing about her fear of heights.

The milk she was heating splattered onto her hand, causing her to flinch. Goddammit, she was so nervous she couldn't even make a cup of coffee.

Quickly, she wiped the milk off her arm, finished the drink, and took it over to the lady sitting in the corner. On her way back to the counter, her gaze flicked to the time again.

Nine minutes.

Jesus Christ, her hands were shaking. Literally shaking. She should have just bitten the bullet and told Tilly she couldn't do it. That's what a normal, sane person with a phobia of heights would do.

The staff of the visitors center were doing the tour in two groups, so the front desk and café could continue running. Molly, the other worker here at the café, was in the first group and would be back any second…then it would be her turn.

Maybe she wasn't scared of heights anymore. She hadn't actually tested herself in years. Was that possible? Could someone just *outgrow* a phobia?

The door opened, and the second Elle saw Molly's long blond hair, her stomach did a little twist.

Nope. The phobia hadn't gone anywhere. She didn't need to be up high to know that.

Molly's smile was wide as she came around the counter. "That. Was. Awesome!" The girl was significantly younger than her, having only just graduated high school a few years ago. Sometimes the age gap didn't feel like much; other times, it felt huge.

Elle raised a brow. "You're a fan of the skywalk?"

"Oh, the skywalk was fine. It was the *tour guide* I liked. Jace Walker is *hot*! And when I say hot, I mean capital HOT. That man will star in my dreams tonight." She grabbed an apron. "You were friends with him, right?"

"Uh, yeah. But that was a long time ago."

"Pfft. A man like that probably came out of the womb looking like a heartthrob. And that velvet voice of his!" She fanned herself before looking back at Elle. "Do you know if he's single?"

Single? Jace Walker? Depended on whether he was still a chronic dater. And this was not a conversation she needed to have minutes from a mental breakdown. "I'm not sure, but I'm running late so I should get out there."

She started to step around the counter, but Molly grabbed her arm. "Do yourself a favor—touch his biceps." She giggled and leaned forward, lowering her voice. "They're *magnificent*."

Yeah, she knew they were magnificent. Every inch of Jace was magnificent, like a perfectly sculptured piece of art.

"I'll see you when I get back."

The skywalk wasn't far from the café, and right now, it felt *too* close. Despite that, she was running late. Just a few minutes, but who knew, maybe they'd already left without her?

Ha, then she'd probably have to do a one-on-one tour with Jace. No, thank you.

When the start of the skywalk came into view, she saw two of the guys on the search and rescue team, Jake and Hendrix, and Nikita, the new girl who worked at the front desk of the visitors center. Oh, and Jace. Of course, he was the first to look up. He didn't smile though. In fact, he almost looked angry. What the heck?

He marched toward her, looking so damn big and fierce, she almost stepped back.

"What are you doing here?" he growled as he stopped in front of her.

Her brows shot up. "Excuse me?"

"You're not doing the skywalk."

This time, she did step back. "I certainly am."

"Really? So you've cured your fear of heights, have you?"

Of course he remembered. He remembered everything. "I'll be fine."

"That's not an answer. You're not doing the skywalk." He turned and started walking back to the group.

Where the hell did he get off, telling her what to do? Now she wanted to do it just to spite him. She raced after him. "You can't just make that call."

"I can, and I am."

"Uh, *no*, you're not. Tilly wants everyone who works here to go through the entire skywalk at least once, and I work here, so that includes me."

He spun so quickly that she almost bumped straight into him. "Remember ninth grade when we did that tree climb excursion? You got to the top and freaked out. It took an hour for you to let go of the tree."

Oh, she remembered like it was yesterday. "That was a long time ago."

He raised a brow. "Has anything changed?"

"Yes, I'm older."

He crossed his arms. "Why do you want to do this?"

She squirmed. "Because I do."

"Not an answer." He started to turn, but she grabbed his arm.

"Jace, I have to. I don't like being scared of anything, and I don't want to be seen as weak."

A muscle ticked in his jaw. "Is this because of Casper and his friends?"

Her heart thudded against her ribs, the memory sending her spine ramrod straight. "No. Why would this be about them?"

"Because after the tree climb, they never let you forget it. They were assholes about it for a long time."

Not a long time...forever. Or at least until Casper moved away and she didn't have to see his face again. He used to grab trees and scream to make fun of her. Even threaten to push her over anytime she got near any kind of railing.

Okay, maybe that *had* affected her a tiny bit. "I'll be fine, Jace."

He blew out a breath, his head dropping back and his eyes staring into the forest around them before his gaze returned to her. "Fine. But if you're not okay, you tell me."

"If I'm not okay, I tell you."

He looked at her like he didn't believe her, which was fair; she didn't know if it was true herself.

With a clench of his jaw, he turned and walked back to the group, and she hurried to catch up.

"Are we ready to go?" Jace asked.

"Let's do this," Jake said, clapping his hands together.

Jace walked onto the path first, followed by Jake, Hendrix and Nikita.

Elle tried to step on, only to stop when her belly did a little turn. It almost felt like it dropped into her pelvis.

You can do this, Elle. It's just a skywalk. You're safe.

She touched the railing, letting the cool of the metal seep into her skin. When she glanced up, it was to see everyone in the group still moving forward...except Jace. He'd stopped and let everyone pass him. Now he just seemed to be waiting for her. A part of her almost expected him to come back and tell her again she wasn't doing it. He didn't. He just...waited.

And that's when she realized that looking at him took an edge of the fear away. Maybe he was a distraction, or perhaps a comfort. Or hell, maybe both.

It didn't matter. She let her eyes bore into his ocean-blue ones, and she took a step forward. Then another. Her heart still beat too fast, and her breathing still felt too shallow, but she was doing it.

When she reached Jace, something flashed in his eyes. Pride, maybe? "Good job, Tink. You proved me wrong. That doesn't happen very often."

Despite everything, she scoffed. "I'm sure it happens more than you care to admit."

He threw his head back and laughed. "Glad you've kept your sense of humor. Come on." The second he fell into step beside her, and she couldn't look into those blue eyes anymore, the fear tried to choke her. But then his hand went to the small of her back, the heat of his skin seeping through her clothes.

His head lowered, his voice almost a whisper. "We both

already know this, but in case you've forgotten, Casper was a jerk."

Oh, there was no forgetting that. "He was worse than a jerk, and I didn't feel sorry for him when he couldn't find a job here in Misty Peak."

He'd moved to New York but still came back to visit every so often because he had friends and family here. Anytime she saw him in town, she pretended she didn't, because she had nothing to say to him. Well, nothing nice anyway.

In a moment of weakness, her gaze lowered, and she saw just how high they were—really freaking high.

Oh God, oh God, oh God!

She wasn't sure if her breathing changed or her steps slowed, but somehow Jace knew she was internally freaking out, because he leaned down, letting his breath brush her cheek as he whispered, "Hey. I've got you."

She glanced up at him, letting the gravel of his voice fight off that fear again. Let his side touching hers chase away the chill.

He was still looking down at her, and her gaze was hopelessly chained to his when Jake called out.

"Yo, Jace, I need to ask you a question."

He didn't look up. His gaze didn't so much as flit away.

"Go," she said quietly. "I'm okay." Or at least, she wanted to be okay. She didn't want to *need* him.

"You sure?"

"Absolutely." To prove her point, she stepped out of his touch. The panic tried to take hold once again, but she breathed through it.

There was a flicker of his brows before he moved forward, his steps a heck of a lot faster than anything she'd attempt. But she'd been telling the truth. She *was* okay. She was actually on a freaking skywalk and she wasn't a blubbering mess.

Keeping her eyes up, she walked forward with slow,

purposeful steps. Nikita and Hendrix walked together, and behind them, Jake and Jace.

She'd never liked Hendrix. He and another member of the SAR team, Theo, had always been dicks. Jake, on the other hand, was friendly enough.

They were about ten minutes in, and she was so focused on her breathing and remaining calm that she barely recognized that they'd stepped out onto a lookout.

She paused. This felt different. There was a slight wobble to the lookout, probably due to the fact it had a type of support structure designed to let it move with the wind. There was also a sign at the end that read "no rocking."

It was fine. She was safe.

She took a few more steps, only to suddenly stop when the walkway beneath her feet rocked harder, more aggressively. It was a full body rock, and there was no way it was just wind.

She grabbed the railing, her heart jumping into her throat.

Someone laughed up ahead, maybe Hendrix, then Jace shouted at him to stop rocking the walk. But she couldn't focus on them because the floor beneath her was still moving.

She looked down to the ground beneath the walk, immediately realizing her mistake. Her huge, gigantic mistake.

She was too high, the skywalk too unstable.

Her vision began to haze, a light-headedness coming over her. Her heartbeat sped up so fast she could hear it in her ears. Heavy thumps accompanied by the rushing of blood. She lowered to her knees, her fingers wrapping tightly around the railing in a death grip—and she knew there was nothing and no one that could get her to let go.

* * *

"How long does it take to do a full circuit of the skywalk?"

Jace only half listened to Jake's question. He itched to turn around and go back to Elle.

She hated heights. She'd *always* hated heights.

Dammit, she was stubborn.

"Anywhere from half an hour to an hour, depending on how fast you walk," Jace finally answered. "But I've had a few tours that've taken longer. Usually people who like to stop and take a lot of photos on the way."

"Has it been busy?"

"Yeah, really busy. I've had a few teenagers who I've had to yell at for being idiots and doing things like hanging over the railing or rocking the walk." Of course, it was only the lookouts, like the one they were coming up to, that could be rocked.

Jake scoffed as they stepped onto the lookout path. "I bet you scared them enough that they don't do it again."

Hell yeah, he did. Safety was important and part of his job here. No one would be getting hurt or killed on his watch.

He glanced up at Hendrix to see him lightly pushing Nikita.

"Feel good being back?" Jake asked.

"It's different. I haven't been back much since high school, and while I feel completely changed from the person I was the day I left, this town feels the same."

Jake laughed. "Must be a small-town thing."

Jace just opened his mouth to respond when Hendrix grabbed both sides of the railing and started shaking it from side to side.

For fuck's sake.

"Hendrix! Stop rocking it!" When the asshole didn't listen, Jace stormed forward. "Stop. *Now!*"

Finally, Hendrix turned, a shit-eating grin on his face. "Come on, I was just playing around."

Nikita joined them, frowning as she looked behind Jace. "Is Elle okay?"

He turned—and his chest pulled too fucking tight at the sight of Elle crouched low, knuckles white as she held the railing with her eyes scrunched closed.

And the fucking lookout was still swaying.

"No one move," Jace growled as he walked over to her. He kept his steps slow so he didn't shake the skywalk anymore. When he was close enough, he lowered beside her. "Hey, Tink, you okay?"

She didn't move and her eyelids didn't so much as flicker open. All he could hear were her panting breaths.

She couldn't hear him. She was having a panic attack.

Shit.

He inched closer and gently touched the small of her back, then placed his mouth so that his lips just touched her ear. "Tink, you're safe. I'm here."

For a moment, her chest stopped moving. The air stopped rushing between her lips. There was a second of silence before she whispered, "Jace?"

"Yeah, Tink, I'm here. You're safe," he repeated, in case she hadn't heard him the first time. Or in case she just needed it repeated.

"Safe?"

"Yes. I'd never let anything happen to you."

It took a few heartbeats, and finally she glanced up. Her eyes were slightly glazed over, but they seared into him, so open and vulnerable. "Maybe you were right. I shouldn't have come."

He shifted a lock of hair from her face behind her ear. Damn, her skin was so smooth. "Nah, I wasn't right. You did it. You walked the skywalk. But then, I knew your stubborn ass wouldn't allow anyone to tell you that you couldn't."

Despite everything, she laughed, only to quickly sober. "I don't know if I can move."

"I could carry you?"

She rolled her eyes. "That would be weird."

"Weird isn't a bad thing." In fact, having her pressed against his chest sounded pretty damn good.

She sucked in a deep breath. "Can you…get my hands? I don't think I can physically move them myself."

He reached up and slipped his hands under her wrists. Slowly, she untangled her fingers from the railing and grabbed his hands, holding him tightly.

"I won't let go," he whispered.

"I know you won't." She swallowed. "I just have to remember not to look down."

"Why would you look down when you have someone as handsome as me to look at?"

Her lips twitched. "Thank you."

"I've *always* got your back, Tink."

CHAPTER 3

"*D*arling, I just don't understand that fear of heights you have. I thought you were past it."

Elle bit the inside of her mouth, her hands tightening around the glass in front of her. Of *course* her aunt didn't understand her fear of heights. Her aunt was her complete opposite in every way. She loved the woman, but man, was it hard relating when they were so different.

She looked around the busy bar, not sure how to respond. In the end, she didn't need to.

"I mean, if it was me," Jewel continued, "I would have rocked the skywalk right along with Hendrix. He sounds fun!"

"Of course he does."

Her aunt leaned forward, her currently pink hair falling into her face. "I'm not saying that to brag. Just to remind you that the skywalk was built by professionals. I doubt a little bit of rocking could bring it down. And sometimes we need to live a little."

"The rational part of me knew that. The part of me that's never liked heights turned into a blubbering mess."

Jewel grinned as she lifted the beer to her mouth. "Well, at least Jace was there to save you."

"He didn't *save* me." Okay, he kind of did. And she was pretty sure his deep, gravelly voice was the only one that could have pulled her out of her panic attack. But she *was not,* under any circumstances, going to admit that to her nosy aunt.

A wistful look came into Jewel's eyes. "I always thought you two would marry. You sure spent enough time together growing up."

Yeah, and her aunt had definitely helped facilitate that. While everyone else her age had a strict "no sleepovers with boys" rule, her aunt had encouraged it. But then, that was Jewel for you, never one to set many boundaries.

Most kids would have loved it, but as a teenager, Elle craved the guardrails that she'd never had. Her mother had left Elle when she was five, and her father had then left her with Jewel when she was eight.

"So," Jewel continued, "he came over to you and whispered in your ear that you were safe like one of those romance story heartthrobs. What happened next? Did he carry you in his arms to safety? Did you nuzzle into his big chest?"

Despite everything, she laughed. Was it funny that he'd actually offered to carry her? And she was sure, had she said yes, he would have followed through.

"You read too many romance novels." She fiddled with the edge of a napkin. "No, he didn't carry me back, but he stuck close." Hand firmly on the small of her back, something she swore she could still feel.

"Did he yell at Hendrix? He has that growly, alpha-protector thing going on. Or at least he did the last time I saw him."

"I have no idea."

"I bet he did." Her aunt studied her for a moment. "You're going to lock this down, right?"

"Lock *what* down?"

"This thing between you. Make a move on him, kid. What's

stopping you? You're both home and single. Plus, you have a history."

"A history as *friends*. Jace and I will not be dating."

Her aunt wrinkled her brow. "Why not?"

"The man had our entire high school career to date me. He never did. In fact, he dated everyone *except* me, because he wasn't interested." Not only did he not date her, he'd also only kept in contact for the first couple of years. Two pretty big tells, if you asked her.

Jewel shook her head. "You're both older now. He's matured; you're at a childbearing age."

Elle scrunched her nose, not really sure how to respond to that, when her phone vibrated on the table. She looked down at the text.

Sadie: He sounds like he likes you. Why did you never date?

Jesus, now she was explaining herself to her aunt *and* Sadie.

"Who's that?" Jewel asked, trying to peer at the phone from across the table.

"It's Sadie. I texted her about what happened today and she's on Team Jewel, asking why Jace and I never dated."

"Oh…I'll answer that."

Jewel reached for the cell, but Elle swiped out of the text and lifted the phone so it was out of her aunt's reach. "Absolutely not."

She pouted. "Why not?"

"I can reply to my friends, thank you."

Jewel rolled her eyes, making Elle grin. Her aunt was only twenty years older than her, but she'd always acted younger than her age.

She set her phone back down just as Harper arrived beside their table.

The other woman smiled. "Hey. Sorry I haven't had a chance to come over and say hi. We've been slammed tonight." Harper was fairly new to Misty Peak. She'd stepped into this bar on her first night in town and had been here ever since. Of course, that had everything to do with Cody, Jace's brother and the owner of the bar. The two were inseparable.

"That's okay," Elle said. "We're fine. I'm glad the place is busy."

Harper laughed. "Yeah, a lot of locals but also a few tourists. Don't get me wrong, I love it, but I also like slower nights when I can slip out back for a sneaky kiss with Cody."

Right on cue, Cody came up behind Harper, his hands sliding around her waist. "Did I hear my name and kiss in the same sentence?"

Harper blinked innocently. "No."

"Liar," Cody growled.

"Never." Harper smiled down at Elle and her aunt again. "Shout out if you need anything."

"We will." When they'd left the table, Elle turned back to her aunt—only to see *her* phone in Jewel's grasp. "Hey!" She tried to grab it, but Jewel whisked it out of reach.

"Calm down. I'm explaining to your friend why you never dated."

This should be good. If she was texting anyone other than Sadie, she would have snatched her cell straight back, but Sadie was a good friend who knew Aunt Jewel, so it didn't really matter what she wrote. "At least tell me what you're writing before you hit send."

Her aunt's fingers moved quickly on the phone. "I'm telling her that you never dated Jace because he was too tall. His dimples were too distracting. And he had far too many ab packs."

She frowned. What on earth were ab packs?

"But," Jewel continued, "now that he's home, he might be able to tempt you into a long night of hot shower sex."

Elle snorted. There was no way Sadie would think this was from her. Maybe *drunk* her, but even then, it was a stretch.

"And...send." Jewel grinned—but that expression only lasted a second before it changed to confusion, then shock. "*Shit.*"

"What?"

Jewel looked up, nervousness widening her eyes.

Oh God, what happened? Her aunt *never* looked nervous.

"Um…well, I may have accidentally sent the text to the wrong person?"

Elle's heart began to beat faster. "Who?"

Jewel scratched the back of her neck. "Well, I was thinking of him when I searched for the number, and I just…"

Her jaw dropped. "You didn't."

"I did."

* * *

"I'm glad you bought this place," Kayden said as he leaned back in a deck chair.

Jace and Eastern both nodded.

It was good to be home. A bit strange to be sleeping in his parents' old bedroom, but he'd get used to it. The house was on a huge block of land, surrounded by forest. It was the home he'd grown up in. The home they'd all grown up in. His father had sold it to their neighbor, but just before coming home, Jace had been approached by that neighbor about buying it back, and he'd taken it.

"I keep expecting Dad to walk into a room and catch me drinking beer or sneaking out," Jace said, a grin on his face.

Eastern chuckled. "Yeah, you aged that man."

Not intentionally. But he and his father had been opposites in many ways. "He didn't really understand me. Probably because he was most like you, Eastern."

Eastern scoffed. "No. Cody was his clone. It's why that bar's still so successful."

True. Cody was good with people, just like their father was, and Eastern was a man of the law. Jace was… Hell, he didn't even *know* what he was.

"We all have part of him in us," Kayden said quietly, gaze moving over the trees surrounding the house.

Kayden was the oldest, and he'd taken their father's death the hardest.

Eastern looked at Jace. "I heard there was a run-in at the visitors center today between you and Hendrix."

Jace scowled. "The guy's an ass. He rocked the skywalk when there's a clear fucking sign saying 'do not rock.'"

"And that warranted you grabbing his shirt and yelling in his face?" Kayden asked. "I thought you were gonna hit him."

"If you hadn't pulled me off, I probably would have." He drank some of his beer. "Elle was with us on the walk, and she has a fear of heights. She had a panic attack." Just thinking about her crouching in fear made him want to go out, find Hendrix, and remind him just how stupid what he'd done was.

Understanding crossed his brothers' faces.

"Still," Eastern started, "Hendrix wouldn't have known that."

His fingers tightened around his beer. He didn't give a fuck if the guy knew or not. He shouldn't have done it.

Eastern's phone vibrated and when he pulled it out, a huge grin spread across his face.

"Let me guess. Sadie?" Jace asked.

Eastern turned the phone around to show a photo of Sadie and his daughter, Avery, kneading dough, chocolate on Avery's cheeks. "I better get home before Avery's full of sugar."

Kayden frowned. "It's not cooked yet."

"That's never stopped them."

Kayden laughed. "I should get back to Tilly too."

They rose from the deck chairs and walked through the house to the front door.

"Thanks for having us over," Kayden said, scanning the wooden staircase behind him, then the living room to the right. "Every time I step foot in here, I feel them—Mom and Dad."

Jace felt them too. It was both a comfort and a reminder of how much he'd lost.

After a goodbye to his brothers, he closed the door and moved to his bedroom. He was about to jump in the shower when he noticed a message on his phone.

Elle: I never dated Jace because he was too tall. His dimples were too distracting. And he had far too many ab packs. But now that he's home, he might just be able to tempt me into a long night of hot shower sex.

Jace's lips stretched into a grin. There was *no way* Elle wrote this. No way in hell. Her Aunt Jewel, though? Yeah, this could definitely be her. But he'd play along.

Jace: Just one night?

The three dots immediately popped up, then her text.

Elle: I didn't write that.

Jace: And if you could break down exactly how I should tempt you, that would be great. Chocolates? Flowers? Allowing you access to my ab packs?

Elle: Ab packs are not a thing.

Jace: Your text suggests otherwise.

Elle: I told you, I didn't write that. I'm going to dig my head into a hole and die now.

Jace: If you do that, you'll never know what gift I got to tempt you.

Elle: You don't have a gift for me.

Jace: I do. I would never joke about a gift, especially not one this good.

Elle: Why would you buy me a gift?

Jace: Because I'm a nice guy with a great many ab packs.

Elle: Stop saying ab packs.

Jace: Can we go back to the shower sex then?

Elle: No.

Jace: Doesn't give us much to talk about, Tink. What about my height? I didn't realize it was an issue. I could hunch?

Elle: I'm going to stop texting now.

Jace: Fine, but can I say one more thing before you go?

Elle: What?

Jace: One night with you would never be enough.

Fuck, he probably shouldn't have written that. They'd never crossed that friendship line. But things felt different now…and he didn't care so much about crossing lines anymore.

Because what he said was true.

The three dots appeared, then disappeared. In the end, it was Jace who sent the next text.

Jace: Good night, Tink. Have sweet dreams about my ab packs and dimples.

CHAPTER 4

*E*lle's gaze flashed to the clock, then back to the coffee machine. Fifteen minutes. Almost finished with her shift. And she'd spent the entire thing watching the door, hoping for Jace to walk in. Craving just one glimpse of the man.

One night with you would never be enough.

Argh. The words had been playing in her head all day. Not to mention, they'd kept her up last night. It was all she'd been able to think about.

Why? Why had he written it? He'd never said anything like that to her before; it was like he'd always been ridiculously careful to keep everything in the friend zone. Sure, they'd been much younger when they were best friends, kids really, but that didn't change anything. He'd still never shown even a hint of romantic interest, back then or in the years since.

She sucked in a breath as she fitted the lid onto a coffee cup and turned toward her customer. "Here's your cappuccino."

The older man dipped his head. "Thank you."

Her phone vibrated, and she pulled it out to see a message from a guy on the dating app. Man, she needed to hurry up and delete the thing. She wasn't sure why she hadn't already. Laziness? Or maybe it was something else. Maybe she still needed confirmation that there was *someone* out there who wanted to date her. The problem was, since Jace had returned to town, *she* didn't want to date anyone.

Jeez Louise, she was losing it.

"Ohh, who's that?" Molly asked, peering over her shoulder. "Another potential suitor? Is he cute? Is he a lawyer? Oh, maybe a doctor?"

"I don't know." She locked her phone and pushed it into the back pocket of her jeans, turning to lean her hip against the counter. "And it doesn't matter. I'm not dating at the moment."

Molly pouted. "Come on, you had a couple of average dates so you're ready to give up?"

"A couple? Molly, the last guy asked me if I'd be open to a polyandrous marriage?"

Molly cringed. "Yeah, okay, he kind of sucked, but one bad apple shouldn't shade the whole tree."

"You know there's been more than one bad apple. I'm done."

"Done with what?"

Elle gasped and spun around.

Jace. How in the world had he entered the café and walked to the counter without her so much as noticing?

"Dating." Molly gave Jace a flirty smile as she leaned over the counter. "Will you tell Elle that she's beautiful, and by *not* dating, she's denying some poor guy all of that beauty?"

Jace's eyes bore into hers. "You *are* beautiful."

Heat crept into her cheeks.

"See!" Molly threw her arms up. "She thinks a couple of bad dates and she's done."

Jace lifted a brow. "You had a couple bad dates?"

She opened her mouth, but Molly got in first.

"She did. They were *terrible*, but sometimes you just need to get back on the horse." Her smile widened. "So, Jace, are *you* dating anyone?"

Jace watched Elle for another second before looking at Molly. "No, I'm not."

"Interesting. Maybe we could do something sometime."

Oh, God. Elle *could not* stand here and listen to Molly hit on Jace, because there was no way he'd ever turn down someone like her. She had the perfect body. The perfect long, thick blond hair and butt chin…yeah, she was calling it a butt chin.

She grabbed a tray and moved around the counter to the tables, forcing herself to block out any conversation between the two of them.

Over the years, she'd lost her baby weight. She still had curves, she just looked…different now. And she'd *thought* losing the weight would change things. It hadn't, not really. Because when she looked at herself in the mirror, she still saw the same thing…plain, boring Elle. The girl no one had dated in high school. The girl whose smile *didn't* light up a room and whose personality didn't pull people in.

But self-love was a journey…a journey she was still on.

When she returned behind the counter, it was to find Jace and Molly still talking, her coworker smiling way too widely.

Elle cleared her throat. "Molly, you can go now if you want."

The other woman turned, brows raised. "Really? We still need to clean the coffee machine and mop the floors."

"I'll do it." In fact, she was more than eager to be alone because she didn't want to be witness to whatever they were planning.

"Okay, great, thanks!" Molly grabbed her bag from behind the counter. "I'll see you both tomorrow."

She winked at Jace as she passed him, and Elle gritted her teeth to stop the scowl.

She started on the coffee machine, scrubbing the thing with a bit more force than necessary. She shouldn't be angry. She had absolutely zero right to be angry. Both of them were single, consenting adults. If they wanted to date and flirt, they were allowed.

So why did she feel an irrational need to simultaneously be sick *and* kick Jace in the balls?

She scrubbed the machine with more force.

"Going a little hard at the coffee machine, aren't you, Tink?"

Shit. She forced her actions to gentle. "You didn't want to walk her out?"

"Nope. I want to walk *you* out."

She paused. "Really?"

"Yeah, really. I have your present in the car."

She frowned. "You actually have a present for me?"

"I told you, that's not something I'd joke about. I remember how much you like presents."

She *did* like presents, but mostly presents from Jace. Every year on birthdays and Christmases, the thing she'd been most excited about was seeing what he'd gotten for her.

All that had stopped, of course, when he'd stopped contacting her.

"I still have a lot to—"

"I can help," he interrupted her.

"No."

"Let me help, Tink."

She wet her lips. Fine, if he wanted to help… "You can put the chairs on the tables if you want."

"You got it."

For the next ten minutes, the two of them worked together in silence as they closed the shop. It was only when they were outside in the parking lot, walking toward his car, that the silence began to feel *too* quiet.

She told herself to shut up. To not ask the damn question. But her mouth betrayed her.

"So…are you going to go out with Molly?" *Shut. Up. Elle!*

One side of his mouth lifted as he glanced at her. "*Should* I go out with Molly?"

"That's not my decision."

A strange expression crossed his face before he focused back in front of him. "No, I'm not. She's not my type."

Elle laughed. "Blond, beautiful and funny isn't your type? It used to be."

He lifted a shoulder. "I used to be a lot of things that I'm not anymore."

What did that mean? She opened her mouth to ask when a blur of movement in the trees on the other side of the parking lot caused her to stop.

Jace stopped with her. "What is it?" He followed her gaze, but whatever she'd seen was gone.

She shook her head. "Nothing, I guess."

He gave that spot one more look before unlocking his car and pulling out a large bag from the trunk. "Your gift. It's not wrapped or anything, but hopefully the gift itself makes up for that."

For some reason, she didn't want to take the bag from his hold. Maybe because of a deep gut feeling that whatever it was might change things. Make her feel something she didn't want to feel.

She forced herself to reach out and slip it from his fingers.

At first peek inside, she wasn't sure what she was looking at. Bags. Many of them. Some white paper. Some black. A couple transparent. She pulled out one of the clear packets to see candy. But not just any candy...

"Swedish candy. My favorite." She glanced up. "They closed the candy shop here in Misty Peak years ago." Right around the time they'd graduated high school. But before that, she'd been a frequent visitor, and Jace had usually been right by her side.

Jace shoved his hands into his pockets. "I know. I picked these up for you while I was away. From every country I visited that sold Swedish candy, which is quite a few. Every time I saw a store, I looked to see if they had any. Some of it's pretty old, but does candy even have an expiration date?"

For a moment, she didn't know what to say. To anyone else, it was just candy, but to her it was so much more. It was a sign that he'd thought of her in every country he'd gone to. It was proof he hadn't forgotten her, like she'd thought he had.

Without thinking, she threw her arms around his waist. "Thank you."

* * *

For a moment, Jace didn't move. He couldn't. Because she surrounded him. Her dark hair. Her fresh scent. He felt fifteen years younger and a shitload stupider.

Hug her, you idiot!

The voice in his head pushed him to wrap his arms around her. To tug her closer. And God, it was everything.

She smelled exactly the same. A mix of sweet and floral. And the softness of her skin made him want to run his hands over her every curve.

When she started to pull away, it was too soon. He didn't want to let go. He wanted to pause this moment, get so fucking lost in it that he forgot the day, the time, and where he stood. Forgot everything but her.

But she stepped back, and he had no choice but to let her.

She shook her head. "I feel silly being so happy about candy, but I can't help it."

"Don't feel silly—I like seeing you smile. I've been starved of it for fifteen long years."

The smile slipped, and for a moment she looked like she wanted to say something, but then she shook her head.

"Say it, Tink."

She frowned. "What?"

"Something's on your mind. Say it."

She lifted a shoulder. "I just thought…you *could* have seen it on the few occasions you returned to Misty Peak over the years. My smile, that is."

She was right, he could have. Why hadn't he?

Because he'd been afraid that if he'd gone to her, heard her voice, he might not have had the will to leave again? Because he was afraid to want her?

"I'm sorry." He wasn't sure if he was apologizing for losing contact or not visiting her more often. Maybe everything.

"You don't need to say sorry. You were off saving the world. You were exactly where you were meant to be."

Really? Because right now, standing in this parking lot with Elle, he wondered if that was ever true.

She sucked in a quick breath. "Well, I should get going." She lifted the bag. "Thank you again."

"Anything for you, Tink."

Another flicker of her brows, then she dipped her head and moved around him. She'd only taken a couple of steps when she stopped and turned. "Can I ask you something?"

"Anything."

"Did you do it?"

"What?"

"That night we were in the mountains, at the party. You told me you wanted to get out of Misty Peak so that you could make something of yourself like your brothers. Did you do it?"

Did he? Sometimes he thought he had. But now? "You want the truth?"

"Always."

"I don't think I ever knew what I was trying to achieve. Not really." One side of his mouth lifted. "But I'm glad I'm back."

He got a small smile from her for that. "I'm glad too, Jace."

And the second she got in her car and drove away, he felt that same thing he always felt. Like a part of himself had just left with her. Gone. And he had no idea what to do without it.

CHAPTER 5

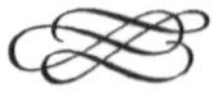

$\mathcal{J}$ace sipped his beer as he sat at the end of his brother's bar, watching the people around him.

You could tell a lot about a person if you paid enough attention. Little things gave them away. Like how a person dressed. How they smiled or the volume at which they spoke.

The guy in the corner, for example, wanted people to think he had money. He was hitting on a redhead and kept flashing his watch. A Rolex that was likely as fake as the knockoff Oxfords on his feet.

People with money didn't try so hard. They didn't have to. And they certainly didn't wave their watch around, desperate for the person they were hitting on to see.

Jace switched his attention to the other side of the bar, where a group of guys were getting loud and rowdy. The loudest one had been pulling most of the attention in the group with his remarks and little skits. He wanted people to think he was confident. Self-assured. When really, his actions reeked of someone who was desperate for validation.

"Never seen you so quiet for so long, brother."

Jace looked up at Cody. "There a problem with being quiet?"

"If you were Kay, I'd say no. But I've never seen *you* quiet for more than five minutes before."

Jace lifted a shoulder. "Maybe I'm not the kid I used to be."

Cody frowned before leaning over the bar. "What's going on in your head?"

"Not a whole lot." A damn lie. A hell of a lot had been going through his head since returning to Misty Peak.

"I don't believe that for a second."

"Fine. Right now, I'm watching people and thinking about what a fucking lie it all is."

Cody swung a rag onto his shoulder as he straightened. "What are you talking about?"

"People put on a show to make others think they're one way, when they're really not. Rich. Confident." His gaze flicked to the redhead's fake smile. "Interested."

"How many beers have you had?"

Too many. He already felt them going to his head.

"If we're gonna talk about honesty," Cody started slowly, "I have a question for you."

Why did Jace suddenly not want to hear it? He took a swig of his beer. "Shoot."

"Why are you home? You were only in the Air Force for fifteen years. You had plenty of years left to give and gave up your retirement benefits."

He shook his head, gaze lowering to his beer. "Nope. I had none. Zero. I was done and I needed to get out."

"Why?"

His brows pulled together as a memory flashed in his head. One he tried to chase away every damn day, but it returned. "I lost someone." Something he seemed to be pretty damn good at.

For a moment, his brother was quiet. "A teammate?"

"Yeah. He was young. The newest member of our team. Had

his whole life ahead of him." And Jace could have saved him. He hadn't.

"Shit. I'm sorry, Jace. But he knew what he was signing up for. It's special operations. It's dangerous."

Yeah, but he also expected his team to have his back.

Jace tightened his fingers around his beer and threw back the last of it before pushing the empty bottle across the bar. "Don't forget, you left early too."

Cody took the empty bottle and replaced it with a new one. "You know why I left. Dad was sick and Nylah needed help."

Yeah, their father. Another fucking loss. They seemed to follow him everywhere.

Jace's gaze shifted back to the guy with the fake watch. He stood a bit closer to the redhead now, and when he smiled, his teeth were so white they had to be veneers.

"You spent much time with Elle since coming home?" Cody asked, drawing his attention back to him.

He'd seen her every day, and every day, he felt the same thing. A kick in the gut at the sight of those gray eyes. Tightness in his chest at the sound of her voice.

"She's so fucking beautiful." The words slipped from his mouth, and he was completely incapable of pulling them back. It had to be the beer. "Her eyes, her hair. The way her brows pinch together when she's angry."

A grin curved Cody's lips. "You should tell *her* that."

He took another swig of his beer. "I hugged her last week and it just messed with me. *She* messes with me."

"Tell me again why you never dated?"

So many fucking reasons, none of which he could properly vocalize. "Because she's Elle Marshal. She's the woman who could light up a fucking stadium, and she doesn't even realize it. She's the heart and the calm and the reason you take a second look."

"Yeah, and you're Jace Walker. You're pretty badass yourself."

Jace scoffed.

"You don't give yourself enough credit, brother."

The loud drunk cheered, pulling Jace's attention. "I was so sure some lucky son of a bitch would have snapped her up by now." And that thought had terrified him. Had that contributed to him coming home? Because he knew if he stayed away any longer, she'd be taken?

"Maybe she was waiting for someone."

Jace shook his head. "No. That's not it. It's been hard enough to get the woman to talk to me. *You've* probably talked more to her since I got back than I have."

"I've seen her a bit, but that's because she lives around the corner from the bar."

Jace frowned. "She does?"

"Yeah, on East Avenue in that big apartment building."

Jace's gaze slid to the door, his feet suddenly itching to go to her, even though he knew that would be fucking reckless.

* * *

ELLE SAT ON HER COUCH, laptop open on her lap as she flicked through old photos. She wasn't sure why she was doing this. Every second photo was of her and Jace.

She traced the ample curves of her hips with her eyes. Curves that had caused her so much angst as a young girl. She wished she'd just been able to love herself. But then...even now, looking so different, she still didn't love herself. Not completely. Why exactly, she wasn't sure. Maybe because the people who'd called her beautiful in her life were few and far between.

Maybe because the man she'd loved for years had always dated women who looked so different than her.

She paused on a photo of her and Jace during a school camping trip. They were both drenched in water after he'd fallen into the river and asked for her help getting out. But when she'd extended her hand, he'd just pulled her in with him.

She could still remember the chill of the water on her skin. The shock and anger that had coursed through her body. But one look at Jace's head thrown back in laughter, and she'd laughed along with him.

With a sigh, she closed her laptop and set it on the coffee table before going into the kitchen to make a hot cocoa. The large window over her sink felt too exposed, and she flicked the curtain closed. She lived on the fifth floor of an apartment building, and there was a keypad downstairs to get in. She was very safe up here, but for some reason over the last week, she kept getting this feeling like she was being watched. Not so much while she was in her apartment, but when she was at work, or while running errands around town. A chill would sweep down her spine, or sometimes she'd go as far as swearing she could hear a rustle of movement around her. Sometimes behind. Sometimes in front. It was strange.

She shook her head and took the milk out of the fridge. The candy from Jace toyed with her. She'd poured it into a large glass container, sat it on her kitchen counter, and so far, she hadn't eaten a single piece. Which was nothing like her. She loved candy, to the point that when the candy store here in town had closed, she'd cried real tears. Her aunt had thought she was insane.

Her gaze caught on the cola skulls. They'd always been her favorite. Jace had joked that they didn't last two seconds in her company.

But she couldn't bring herself to eat them. Because every time she so much as looked at them, they reminded her that she hadn't been completely forgotten by Jace. That she'd been on his mind, even when he'd been doing God knows what in God knows where.

Dragging her gaze from the jar, she poured milk into a

saucepan. She'd just taken out a mug when her apartment buzzer dinged.

What the hell? What was the time? Ten? It was ten o'clock. Who on earth could it be? Her neighbors minded their own business, to the point she didn't even know their names.

Cautiously, she moved toward the door. She was almost there when a voice sounded through the intercom.

"Tink? You there?"

She stopped, jaw dropping.

Jace?

"Please tell me you are," he continued. "Because this is the twentieth apartment I've rung, and I'm pretty sure some old lady called the sheriff. Don't think my brother would arrest me, but you never know. He can be a dick when he wants."

She closed the distance to the door and pressed the talk button. "Jace…what are you doing here?"

"Thank fuck! Can you buzz me up?"

She opened and closed her mouth, so many questions rattling around inside her head, but first she needed to get him in here, because there *would* be unhappy residents if he'd already buzzed that many apartments.

She hit the button. "Door's unlocked. Come up."

She stepped away from the door, her mind swirling.

Jace was here. He was going to step into her apartment. She scanned the small space, and everything she'd thought of as cute and comfortable suddenly appeared cluttered and messy.

She ran around, cleaning up quickly. She was just grabbing a few items she'd left lying on the kitchen counter when the knock came at the door. Suddenly her heart was racing, even though she had no idea why. This was Jace. Her longtime friend Jace. She didn't need to be nervous.

Just breathe, Elle.

Slowly, she made her way to the door and tugged it open.

Jace towered over her, his eyes slightly glassy, his smile easy. "Hey, Tink. Can I come in?"

Wait, she knew that look. "Are you drunk?" She probably should have known from his rambling over the intercom, but she'd been so shocked she hadn't connected the dots.

"I may have had a little bit of beer."

Her lips twitched. "Liar. This is not 'a little bit' of beer, Jace." She shifted back, and when he entered the apartment, his steps weren't quite as steady as usual. She'd just closed the door when he stumbled, and she grabbed his arm, even though he was twice, maybe three times her size. "Let's get you sitting down."

When they reached the couch, he dropped, his head lolling back and his eyes closing. "Thanks. I knew I could count on you." He reached into his pocket and tugged out his phone before throwing it onto the coffee table. "Damn thing keeps ringing."

She lifted it to see Cody's name flashing on the screen. "It's your brother."

"Asshole took my car keys. Told me I had to wait for him to drive me home."

This time, she chuckled. "And what? You gave him the slip?"

"Fuck yeah, I did. I don't need a babysitter."

Hm, kind of looked like he did. "Why are you here, Jace?"

He turned his head to look at her, his beautiful blue eyes boring into hers. "Because *you're* here."

CHAPTER 6

*E*lle's heart gave a funny little twist. Jace had been coming into the café at the visitors center every day, and every day she had to fight a million emotions inside her. But now, with him sitting on the couch, saying sweet things like that…how was she supposed to remain immune to him?

The phone stopped ringing only to immediately start again. She sighed and leaned over to answer it. "Hello?"

There was a short pause before Cody spoke. "Elle?"

"Yeah, it's me. Jace is here."

"I'm gonna kill that guy. He just ran out on me. Want me to come get him?"

"Tell him to leave me alone," Jace groaned, head falling back onto the couch once more.

Elle's lips twitched. "I'll look after him."

"You sure?"

"Yeah."

"Thanks, Elle. I'll call off Eastern."

The phone wasn't on speaker, but Jace clearly heard, because he scoffed. "I woulda given him the slip too."

Cody chuckled. "Okay, call if you need anything."

"I will."

She hung up and moved into the kitchen to pour some coconut water into a glass. When she gave it to Jace, his fingers brushed hers, causing a tingle to run up her arm.

"Thanks." He took a sip and made a face. "What the hell kinda water is this?"

"It's coconut water, and it's hydrating, something you need right now." She cocked her head. "Why are you drunk, Jace?"

He gave her a lopsided grin. "Because drunk looks good on me."

"Don't do that. Don't use humor to conceal the truth. Not with me. You never get drunk. Not since Lawson died."

Lawson had been Jace's high school best friend. He'd been killed by a drunk driver running a red light while Jace had been in the car, and it had affected Jace on a deep level.

The smile slipped from his face.

She leaned forward. "You can talk to me. Why are you drunk?"

"Because sometimes it hurts to breathe, and tonight I got this delusion that alcohol would help."

The air halted in her chest. He'd never revealed anything so heavy to her before. "Why does it hurt to breathe?"

"Because I lose people. It's what I do. Sometimes I feel like poison."

This time the air didn't just halt. It cut off completely, refusing to let another breath in.

She shifted closer, setting a hand on his leg. "Stop talking like that. You don't lose people, and you're definitely not poison."

"I lost my mom. Then I lost Lawson."

"Your mom had cancer, and some drunken idiot ran a red light. Neither of those are things you could have changed."

"Then my dad died. I knew he was dying, and I barely came back to say goodbye."

She swallowed. "He was sick for months and you were in the

military. Your job wasn't like most. You couldn't just take time off to be with him for months on end."

"And then there was Dean."

She frowned. "Who's Dean?"

"He had his whole fucking life ahead of him."

She tightened her fingers around his leg. "Jace. Who's Dean?"

"He was the newest member of our team. He was so damn excited to be there. And he looked up to the rest of us, me especially. No fucking idea why. He started to feel like a little brother. We should have protected him. *I* should have protected him."

A sick feeling began to churn in her belly. "What happened?"

He ran a finger over the back of her hand. "It was a sneak attack we didn't see coming. We weren't prepared."

When he paused, Elle's skin chilled, knowing what was coming.

"He was right next to me," Jace said, a frown etched deeply into his brow. "I took my eyes off him for a second to engage with someone coming at me from the other direction. A single fucking second, and someone took him out."

Her heart fractured. Not just at his words, but at the pain in his tone. The way the pain was a part of him, leaching into his expression…his voice.

Leaning forward, she whispered, "That doesn't sound like it was your fault. You and the rest of your team were fighting for your lives."

"He trusted me to have his back. To look after him. Instead, I watched him die."

"Don't." She shook her head. "Don't take on that blame."

He leaned his head back, eyes closing again. "I couldn't even go to the funeral. I couldn't face his family. It hurt too much. I wrote a letter and gave it to a teammate to pass on like a fucking coward."

"What did the letter say?"

"Everything. That I was sorry. That I wanted to do more. That

I *should have* done more." Again, he turned to look at her, the pain in his eyes almost cutting straight through her heart. "He had a big family. A family who loved him. A brother and sister. Nieces and nephews. He talked about wanting kids…and about his cute fucking chihuahua he'd left with his parents."

She turned her hand over and slipped her fingers through his. "That was a tragedy, Jace, and I'm so sorry you were a part of it. That you lost someone you cared about. But he didn't die because of you. None of the people you've lost have been *because* of you."

"You were."

Her heart slammed into her ribs. "What?"

"I lost you because I stopped calling. I stopped telling you when I was in town. I just…stopped. And out of all my losses, you hurt the most."

Her lungs seized as every word suddenly died on her lips.

"Did it hit you as hard as it hit me?" he asked.

Emotions welled in her chest. Emotions she had no idea how to handle. A part of her wanted to lie. To tell him that his absence hadn't shaded every part of her life. But she couldn't. Not to him. So she said nothing.

He leaned forward. "If I left again, would you miss me?"

"Jace, I've spent years missing you. The pain has just become a part of me."

His eyes darkened, and when he cupped her cheek, she knew she should pull away. He was drunk, and as the sober person, she needed to put space between them. But she just…couldn't.

He leaned forward, and she remained so perfectly still that her lungs didn't even fill with air. For a moment, she thought he might kiss her, and she had no idea what she'd do if he tried. But then his temple touched hers, he closed his eyes, and he just seemed to breathe her in.

"Sometimes I can almost forget the time we've spent apart…almost."

She closed her eyes and for a few seconds just let the touch of his temple, the feel of his hand on her cheek, seep into her. But she had to get up. She couldn't take advantage of his drunken state, no matter how good his skin felt against hers.

"I'll get you a blanket."

He shook his head. "No. Lie with me. Just for a few minutes. Please?"

She should say no. She knew she should. But then he was rearranging them, tugging her down onto the couch so that her back was pressed to his front, and he slipped an arm around her waist, and suddenly she couldn't move.

She couldn't do anything but close her eyes and let herself imagine, just for a moment, that she was his.

* * *

A SWEET FLORAL scent filled the air around Jace, causing his nose to twitch. It was a familiar scent. A scent he'd dreamed about for far too long. *Her* scent.

His eyes flicked open to see a living room. Beige and pale pink shades—definitely not *his* living room. The lights were still on, but one glance at the wall clock told him it was three in the morning.

His night came back to him. The bar. The beers. Showing up at Elle's apartment.

Fuck, he'd fallen asleep. Not a huge surprise. He shouldn't have drunk so much.

Stupid. So stupid. And the things he'd said to Elle, the things he'd revealed…he wanted to hit his damn head against a wall. She didn't need to know about Dean. About the guilt that plagued him day in, day out.

But at the same time, telling her felt good. Like a weight lifted from his chest.

Elle's soft breaths whispered through the quiet. It reminded him of the times she'd slept over at his place when they were younger, usually because she'd needed a break from her eccentric aunt.

His arm was tucked around her waist as she lay on her side. It was the way he'd tugged her down before falling asleep, and it looked like neither of them had moved an inch.

He hadn't slept this deeply since… Well, in a long time.

He wanted to stay. Keep her wrapped in his arms and allow them both to fall back to sleep.

He didn't. Instead, he crept out from behind her. A gentle hum sounded from her lips, and it was almost his undoing. But he forced the ache in his chest to dull as he stood. Then, bending down, he slipped his arms under her back and legs and lifted her slowly.

Another moan released from her lips before she nuzzled into his chest. His heart beat so fast that for a moment, he didn't move. He just held her. Felt her. Let all that was Elle, all he'd been missing, put the fractured parts of him back together.

Why did she have to be so…everything?

I've spent years missing you. The pain's just become a part of me.

Her words killed him. But wasn't that the same for him? And wasn't that a huge reason he was home?

With gritted teeth, he forced himself to step around the coffee table and into the first room off the hall. Her bedroom. He didn't need her confirmation to know. The pale pink sheets gave her away.

He crossed the space between the door and her bed and laid her down. She wore yoga pants and a T-shirt, which would be comfortable enough to sleep in. He'd just pulled the sheet and blanket over her when five whispered words released from her lips.

"Jace…don't leave me again."

Her words gutted him. Tore the insides right out of his stomach.

Unable to stop himself, he lowered his head and touched a

light kiss to her temple. "I already left you once, and it was the hardest thing I ever did. I don't have the strength to do it again."

Another sweet moan from her, and she snuggled into her bedding. For a second, he felt rooted to the spot. Unable to leave her. Unable to shift closer. He was just...stuck.

Without thinking, he reached under his shirt and traced the tattoo. Traced her handwriting. Her words. He didn't need to look at it to know exactly where every letter sat; he'd looked at it every day for the last ten years, since he'd had it inked onto his skin.

A few more minutes passed, and he finally forced himself to turn toward the door and walk out of the room. He grabbed his phone before stepping into the hallway. He waited until he was halfway down the hall to call Cody.

Even though he was sure his brother was asleep, Cody answered on the second ring. "Jace? You okay?"

"Yeah, can you come get me and drive me home?" Even if Cody didn't have his keys, there was no way he'd drive himself when there was a chance the alcohol was still in his system. He didn't do reckless shit like that.

"Of course. You still at Elle's apartment building?"

"Yeah, but I'll walk back to the bar. See you in ten." He hung up before his brother could respond, because he knew Cody would offer to pick him up from Elle's. He didn't want that. He needed the ten minutes of fresh air to get his head on straight.

He'd told himself he'd come back to Misty Peak because this was home. But every day that passed made that glaring lie more obvious. He'd come back for *her*. Only her. And now he needed to figure out what he was going to do about it.

CHAPTER 7

"Jace, sweetie, this is gorgeous. And just what the visitors center needed."

Jace smiled at Ali Stapler. She was a local who owned rental cabins here in town. "Thanks, Ali. It's been great so far."

"And you," she said, touching his arm, "are the perfect person to work the skywalk. Charming. Friendly. You'll draw in the tourists."

"I think the mountains do that all on their own."

He glanced back at the rest of his group. There were five other people. A mother and father, their young son, an older man, and the redhead he'd met a couple weeks ago who'd asked him about the skywalk. The woman had said she was from out of town, so he'd assumed she'd have left already. Had Misty Peak drawn her in and gotten her to extend her trip like it did so many others?

Ali leaned closer. "She's pretty."

Jace frowned, turning back to the path in front of them. "What?"

"Her name's Stephanie and she's on vacation from Charlotte. Nursing student. Loves dogs."

"You got all that from one conversation?"

Ali lifted a shoulder. "Must be my Southern charm."

Yeah, it probably was.

They stepped off the end of the skywalk and he turned to face his group as they came to a stop. "That brings us to the end of this tour. Thank you for coming. There's a café off the deck that serves great coffee if anyone wants to head there next. And if anyone's interested in booking a rappelling session, stop into the visitors center and Nikita can help you with that. Any questions?"

The boy lifted his hand.

"Ask away," Jace said.

"Does the café here have ice cream?"

His lips twitched. "I believe they do. Tell Elle I told you about the secret stash, and she might just serve you some."

The boy's eyes lit up. There were a couple more questions, then the entire group made their way to the café.

Ali spoke to the other woman before they both slowed to walk beside him.

Ali touched his arm. "Jace, dear, I was just telling Stephanie about your time in the Air Force."

"It sounds exciting," she said quietly.

He shook his head. "Not really. I was only in for fifteen years."

"Pfft." Ali smiled at Stephanie. "He downplays himself. He was special forces."

Her brows lifted. "Very impressive."

He gave a tight smile. Ali continued to talk him up as they neared the café, but a lot of what she said became white noise for Jace because he was about to see Elle. What would she say after he'd snuck out of her apartment last night? Would she call him out on it? Or would she pretend it never happened?

Probably the latter.

When they finally stepped inside, his gaze went straight to her. She was making coffee while Molly served. His group joined the line to order, but he hung back, unable to take his eyes off her. It had always been like that. Even when he was a twelve-year-old kid, she'd demanded all of his attention. He'd fought it, *fuck*, he'd fought it, but now…he was just about out of fight.

Once everyone had been served, he watched as she took a coffee to a corner table. Was she intentionally avoiding him?

He waited until she was on her way back to the counter to step in front of her. "Hey."

There was a small flare of her eyes. Then she blinked and it was gone. "Jace."

"Have a coffee with me."

The shake of her head came before he'd finished speaking. "I'm too busy."

She stepped to the side, but he mirrored her move, blocking her again. "Come on. One drink."

"I really—"

"Tink. Please. Take pity on a man desperate for your company." Then, as if to prove his point, he reached out and grazed the back of her hand.

Her chest rose as she sucked in a sharp breath. "I'm due to have a break in five."

He grinned at her. "I'll order and wait for you."

She rolled her eyes. "I know your order. I'll join you in a few minutes."

Fuck, he loved her sass. He walked over to a table by the window and watched her work behind the counter. He didn't have to wait long. She helped Molly make the drinks, then joined him at his table with a coffee in each hand, setting one in front of him.

"Extra-hot cappuccino."

He grinned at her. "No sweetened mocha?"

She scrunched her nose. "Absolutely not. I felt sick just

watching you drink that last time."

It had been their go-to drink as teenagers. It had also been his order the first time he'd stepped into this café after getting back to town. It tasted like shit, but he'd stubbornly drunk it.

"It wasn't that bad," he lied.

"I tasted it after you. It was awful." She set her phone on the table and sipped her own coffee. "So, why do you want to have coffee with me?"

"Because I like talking to you." He liked every crumb of time she gave to him.

"Really?"

"Yeah, Tink. And I'm sorry about last night."

Her lips parted, like she was surprised he'd bring it up.

"I dumped all my shit on you, and that wasn't fair." He never spoke about that mission. Hell, he kept that part of himself as locked away from others as possible, but last night, he'd told Cody *and* Elle.

"I'm glad you told me," she said quietly. "The more you talk about it, the easier it will be."

A part of him knew that, but the other part, the part that was scared shitless of reliving that day over and over again, preferred to bury his head in the sand and make the people around him believe he didn't have a care in the world.

She leaned forward and lowered her voice. "Talk to me about it whenever you want, as often as you want."

He stared at her, his chest feeling unbearably tight before he nodded. "Thanks, Tink." One corner of his mouth lifted. "Still a heavy sleeper, I see."

Her cheeks tinged pink. "I can't believe you got me to bed without me waking up."

He scoffed. "You once fell asleep at a house party where the music was so loud it could be heard on the next block."

"Hey, I was tired. I'd spent the entire week cramming for tests."

"That was not an isolated event."

She sighed and was just opening her mouth to say something when Molly called to her from behind the counter.

"Elle, could you give me a hand with the register? It's sticking again."

Elle's brows rose. "Sure."

She'd just left the table when the screen of her phone lit up with a text. He glanced at it, about to look away…when he saw it was a message from a guy.

Art. What the fuck kind of name was Art? And why was the word "date" in the text?

He should leave it. A voice in his head shouted at him to mind his own fucking business. But hadn't Molly mentioned that Elle was doing some online dating?

His fingers tapped the table, and he looked away…but at the image of Elle on a date with another guy, he snapped.

Fuck it.

He reached across and unlocked her phone. It wasn't hard. She'd had the same number password since she was a kid.

Art: Did you really just say maybe to a date with me? How can I turn that into a yes?

Hell no.

Jace ground his back teeth together. Not caring that it was immature or stupid or an invasion of her privacy, he lost what was left of his mind and responded as if he were Elle.

You can't. I was just being nice. It's not gonna happen. You're not my type. Don't message again.

* * *

AN ENTIRE FREAKING hour had passed since Jace had walked in here, made her smile and laugh a dozen times, and she still couldn't get the guy out of her head. And that was after spending the entire morning thinking about how she'd fallen asleep against him last night.

Oh God, last night. It was the entire reason she'd told the guy from the dating app that she might be interested in a date. What was his name? Art?

Her feelings for Jace had resurfaced with force, and they scared the hell out of her. She couldn't go back to being the same person she was in high school. The girl who pined after a boy—now a man—who only wanted her friendship. A man who made her feel everything and yearn for even more, when in reality, all they were ever going to be was friends.

And, okay, maybe things felt different now. They were both adults; they'd both changed and grown...but he'd always been a serial dater and an adventure junkie. Did she really think that even if he was interested in her as more than a friend that he could settle down in Misty Peak long term? The idea felt insane.

"Someone looks deep in their own head."

She turned to glance at Molly, who was wiping down the counter. "I'm..."

"Thinking about Art?"

She lifted her brows. She'd mentioned the lawyer earlier, even said she might go on a date with him...lies. All lies.

Molly held out her hand. "Give me your phone. I want to see those dreamy brown eyes again."

Dreamy? Yeah right, the only dreamy eyes in her head were ridiculously blue.

She unlocked her phone and clicked into Art's profile before handing the cell to Molly, who proceeded to swoon. "He's cute. And a lawyer, so he's got to be smart and have his life together. And it says he's six foot."

"If it says he's six foot, he's five ten. Guys always lie about their height on that thing." It was something she'd learned early on. And she shouldn't care, right? She shouldn't obsess over the fact that none of them were six four...like Jace.

Stop thinking about him, Elle!

"I think you should go out with him."

Elle shook her head. "No."

"What? Why? He's perfect on paper. And he's been sweet and patient in messages."

Maybe that was it; she didn't want sweet and patient. She wanted fun and playful. Someone with some attitude. "I'm just a bit over dating these random guys." Sure, she'd only been on a handful of dates, but when they were all as terrible as hers had been, it felt like more.

Molly frowned. "Because you like someone else?"

"What?" Shit. That came out way too quickly and high pitched.

"I mean, you and Jace seemed quite close at the table earlier today, and—"

"No." She shook her head so vigorously, it probably looked like she was having uncontrollable chills. "We're friends. We've been friends for a million years, and it's never surpassed that. I don't think it ever will."

Why did her heart ache when she said that?

Molly watched her closely. "Are you sure? Because I was thinking I might..."

Elle's heart dropped. It shouldn't. She knew Molly was interested in Jace. Hell, she'd basically asked him out already; this shouldn't come as a surprise.

"You should. Ask him out again, I mean." She swallowed the lump in her throat. The words hurt, but there was no way she was going to tell another person *not* to make a move. She had no right over him. At the end of the day, it would be Jace's choice whether he said yes or not.

Molly frowned at her. "Really? Because if you tell me you like him in that way, I won't. I'll stay away."

"Molly, you're gorgeous, he's gorgeous, and you've got nothing to lose."

She handed back the phone. "Okay. If you're sure. You'll have to tell me more about him so I know what to talk to him about and he won't get bored."

"A man getting bored of you? I can't see that happening."

"Pfft. I'm not that great. And what about you? You gonna date the lawyer?"

She sighed. "It doesn't look like he's—"

At that moment, a text came through from Art…but it wasn't the text she'd been expecting.

What the heck?

Molly peered over her shoulder. "What is it?"

"He asked if he did something wrong."

"What? Why? Didn't you just tell him you might be interested in a date?"

"Yeah, I…" She clicked into the text messages—and gasped at the sight of her last text to the man.

You can't. I was just being nice. It's not gonna happen. You're not my type. Don't message again.

Who the heck had—

Suddenly, it hit her. *Jace.* She'd left her cell at the table with him when she went to fix the register. She couldn't *believe* he'd do this! But…hadn't he done this very thing in high school time and again? Scared guys off so she'd ended up dateless, while *he'd* dated every girl in their grade?

But God, they were adults now. Was he really still doing this?

Molly sucked in a sharp breath as she read the text. "Elle. That was a bit harsh."

She locked her phone and looked at Molly. "I need to take a quick break. Will you be okay here?"

"Sure, but—"

"Call if you need anything."

Then she stormed out onto the deck, ready to give that no-good jerk a piece of her mind.

CHAPTER 8

"What's this I hear about you getting plastered last night?"

Jace internally cursed Cody for telling Kayden. "I wasn't plastered, just had a few more than usual."

"So many that our brother had to take your keys so you wouldn't drive yourself home?"

He rolled his eyes. "You know I'd never drink and drive."

"So you admit you'd had too many to drive?"

Jace's gaze ran over the mountains as they neared the end of the skywalk. He'd just finished packing up after a rappelling session that Kayden had helped him run. "Yeah, but I was a happy drunk."

"So happy you waddled on over to Elle's house."

"Did Cody give you my whole life story?"

"Just the *CliffsNotes*." Kayden squeezed his shoulder as they stepped off the skywalk. "Hey. I know you're usually the easygoing, adventurous brother, but if everything's not okay—"

"It's fine, Kay. I'm fine. Just like I told Cody I was fine." He crossed his arms, not wanting to talk about his shit anymore. Not here, not now. "You heard from Lock lately?"

Their last remaining out-of-town brother was on a Ghost Ops team. They never knew where he was or what he was doing, and he rarely checked in.

Kayden sighed but let the change of subject go. "Nope. Haven't heard from him in a while. For all I know, he's on the other side of the world doing God knows what."

One side of Jace's mouth lifted. "And loving every second of it."

Kayden opened his mouth to respond, only to stop and frown at something over Jace's shoulder. Jace turned and followed his gaze to see a very angry-looking Elle storming toward them.

"Shit, she looks mad," Jace said, more to himself than his brother.

"What did you do?"

Jace glanced back at Kayden. "Why do you assume I did something?"

"Because that is the face of a woman who's about to unleash hell on you." He clenched Jace's shoulder again. "Good luck. Looks like you're gonna need it."

"You're just gonna leave me?"

Kayden was already walking away. "Yep."

Chickenshit.

Elle stopped in front of him, slamming her fists onto her hips. "Why? *Why* did you do it?"

"Give me a hint of what we're talking about here, Tink." Acting innocent felt safe right now.

"Don't play dumb with me." She jabbed a finger into his chest. "You texted Art from my phone, telling him I wasn't interested!"

"You're not."

Her jaw dropped, and if possible, the red of her cheeks darkened further. Damn, she was gorgeous when she was mad.

"You son of a bitch," she gasped. "You don't get to tell me who I am and am not interested in. Who I date is *none* of your business. It wasn't fifteen years ago, and it isn't now!"

"But that's where I disagree. You have always and *will* always be my business. And when I say you deserve better than some guy named *Art*, I'm serious."

Anger darkened her eyes. "You infuriate me! You know that? You're a…a…"

"Charmer? Comedian? God-given gift to women?"

"A jerk! You're a *jerk*. It was bad enough that you scared off any guy who tried to date me in high school. Now you're an adult and *still* doing it. Do not *ever* meddle in my dating life again." She spun around and started back toward the visitors center.

He caught up to her in a few strides. "Come on, don't be mad."

"I'm not mad."

He almost laughed, or maybe he did, because he got an angry glare pointed his way. "Really? Because you look mad."

"No. I just don't like you."

"Yes, you do."

"No, I don't."

"Tink—"

"And don't call me that. My name is Elle—use it."

"You've always been Tink to me. And I think you like it."

"No, I don't."

"You do."

She stopped and spun. "Stop it! Stop presuming to know me so well."

"I *do* know you."

"You *used* to. Not anymore."

"Really?" He stepped closer, catching the sharp intake of her breath. "So a ring of black doesn't surround your irises when you get angry? Cola skulls aren't your favorite candy, and you haven't watched every episode of *The Office* at least twenty times?"

Her mouth opened and closed. "They're just facts. They're not who I am."

"I *know* who you are." His hand twitched to touch her. Cup

her cheek. Grip her hip and tug her closer. "And you deserve better than Art."

She swallowed. "Who then? Who *do* I deserve?"

One word came to mind. A word with two letters that crawled up his throat, threatening to break free, but he didn't let it.

As the silence lengthened, something akin to disappointment crossed her face. It came and went so quickly he almost thought he'd made it up in his head. Then the anger returned.

"We're done. Do not show up at my house again. Do not message me. Just let me live my life in peace."

Every word felt like a kick in the gut. It was only when she turned away from him that he knew he couldn't let those be the last words she said to him.

He jogged to catch up with her again. "I can't do that."

"You don't have a choice."

"Look, I'm sorry I texted him. That was wrong. I just feel protective of you."

"I don't need protecting."

Yeah, he knew that. Elle was strong; but *he* felt so fucking weak these days. "What can I do to make it up to you?"

"Nothing. And it doesn't matter anyway. We're not friends, Jace. We haven't been friends for a long time."

He lifted a brow, almost finding that funny. "*I* consider *you* a friend."

"Stop it."

"Why can't we be friends?"

"Go away."

"Not until you answer my question."

"No."

He grabbed her arm to stop her. "Tink—"

"Because I *loved* you, you idiot!"

* * *

ELLE WANTED to slam her hand over her mouth. Either that or dig herself a hole so deep that she'd never get out.

Shit. Shit, shit, shit.

Had those words really just released into the world? Had she *really* just told Jace Walker that she'd *loved* him?

No. She had to be dreaming. Stuck in some dark nightmare she couldn't find her way out of.

Jace frowned, and for a moment he was silent. "Loved? Past tense?"

Really? That was all he had to say about her earth-shattering, world-changing confession? And why the heck was she so disappointed? She hadn't actually expected him to say he'd loved her too, had she? Because she always knew he hadn't. Not in the way she'd loved him, at least.

Holy crap, she needed to get out of here.

She pulled her arm back and moved faster toward the café.

"Tink, stop. Let's talk about this."

"There's nothing to talk about. Forget what I said. I just came down here to tell you to stay away from me. And I'm going on a date with him."

"The fuck you are!"

"I am."

"You really want to go on a date with a guy named *Art*?"

"*Stop* saying his name like that."

"Like what?"

"Like there's something wrong with him."

Again, he grabbed her arm and tugged her to a stop. It took her two entire seconds to gain the courage to look up at him, and when she did, it felt just as gut-clenching as usual.

"You loved me?" Jace asked.

"As a friend." Big. Fat. Lie. "Let me go, Jace."

His brows flickered. "I just want you to be happy."

"I'm trying." She'd been trying since the day he'd left town. Hell, since before that.

Again, he inched closer. "I'm sorry. I crossed a line today."

Her heart sped up in her chest. When he stood this close, she couldn't breathe. She couldn't speak. She could barely think.

She needed to go. Get away from him in case more stupid words about loving him slipped out. "I need to go."

She didn't wait for him to respond, just turned away again, almost running back to the café. When she realized he wasn't following her, she felt relieved, but there was also this other part of her, a part she hated, that was disappointed.

That was stupid, though. Disappointed that he'd done exactly as she asked? Disappointed that he hadn't chased her down for a third time?

She crossed the deck and pushed into the café, almost running straight into Molly.

The other woman gasped. "Elle! Are you okay?"

No, she wasn't. She was a stone's throw away from falling apart. "Do you mind if I leave early? I'm not feeling great."

"Oh no. Are you all right?"

"Yeah, just a headache."

Molly nodded. "Of course. Go. Rest. I've got the shop."

"Are you sure?"

"Absolutely."

"Thank you." She grabbed her bag and rushed out to the parking lot. The entire time, she expected to see Jace again. To see him running out after her.

She'd told him she *loved* him. Love! God, what was wrong with her?

She slid behind the wheel and for a moment, just scrunched her eyes closed. Because a part of her had wanted him to say it back. And wasn't that the most pathetic part about all of this? That a big part of her, even after all these years, still hoped he cared about her in the same way she cared about him?

But he didn't say it, because he didn't love her. He never had. What he felt for her was friendship. It had always been friendship. He'd proven that time and again by dating girl after girl right in front of her. Gorgeous girls. So beautiful that she just faded into the background in comparison. And for years, she'd stood and watched, her heart breaking.

And now he was back in Misty Peak, and she was falling for him all over again.

Her fingers trembled as she lifted her phone and sent a text to Art.

Elle: I'm sorry, my friend took my phone and sent that last message. They thought it was funny or something. How about Saturday for our first date?

CHAPTER 9

"Uncle Jace, can I ask you a question?"

He smiled down at his eight-year-old niece. He'd spent his Saturday night crashing Eastern, Sadie and Avery's dinner at the local Italian restaurant, and he didn't feel bad about it at all. Of course, he'd pushed for ice cream for dessert, and Avery had been in full support.

"Shoot."

"Do you think you'll have kids one day?"

Whatever he'd thought she'd ask, it wasn't that. But then, maybe it should have been. She'd already asked if he planned to get married, how many girlfriends he'd had, and whether he had one right now.

"I don't know, kid. Maybe, if the right woman should be so lucky." He grinned at her, not missing the eye roll from Eastern.

A little girl with gray eyes and dark hair flashed in his mind.

He shook his head, needing to get that image out of his head because it would drive him crazy.

Avery nodded. "Good. Because I want cousins like my friend Quinn at school, but Daddy said I might be waiting a while."

Jace shot a look at Eastern, who simply lifted a shoulder. He was holding Sadie's hand and the two of them looked too damn cute. "I'm putting my money on Kay and Tilly being the first."

Sadie shook her head. "No, I think Cody and Harper."

Avery jumped up and down. "I know! They can have babies at the same time and grow up like sisters."

"Or brothers," Eastern cut in.

Avery wrinkled her nose. "I want girl cousins."

They'd just reached the ice cream shop when Jace's phone rang. His muscles tensed when he saw who it was. AJ, a member of his former team. For a moment, he just stared at the cell, memories he preferred to keep buried crawling to the surface. It was only Eastern grabbing his shoulder that pulled him out of it.

His brother frowned at him. "Hey. You coming in?"

He looked at the ice cream shop. "You go. I'll take this call real quick."

"I'll choose Uncle Jace's flavor," Avery said, already tugging her father toward the door. "I'm good at choosing flavors."

"Pick me a good one," Jace called.

Avery's grin widened, and Eastern gave him one last look before stepping into the shop with Sadie.

Jace took a breath before answering the call. "AJ, hey. How are you doing?"

"Good, brother. Just got home from a trip. I wanted to check in. None of us have heard from you for a while."

Jace ran his fingers through his hair, knowing he should have reached out at least once by now, since leaving the Air Force. "Sorry. I've been busy getting settled back into my hometown."

"So you're *not* avoiding us because of what happened to Dean?"

Looked like Avery wasn't the only straight shooter tonight.

A part of him wanted to lie. To tell AJ he was fine and that the mission was behind him. But he'd never lied to a teammate before and he didn't plan to start now.

"I'm angry," he said quietly.

AJ's voice lowered. "Me too, J. We're all angry. But what happened to him wasn't your fault. He knew the risks of the mission."

"I should have had his back."

"We all did everything we could to stay alive that day." AJ paused. "The kid worshipped you, but that didn't make him your responsibility."

He scrubbed a hand over his face. Hearing his friend's assurance didn't make it any easier. "Have you spoken to his family since the funeral?"

It was AJ who'd passed on the note to Dean's family for him. And he was grateful to his teammate for doing so. Because even though he hadn't been able to bring himself to attend, the family deserved to know what had happened from his perspective. They deserved his apology.

"I've checked in on his mom and dad a couple times. They're doing as well as can be expected. I haven't made contact with the brother or sister."

Jace nodded as Sadie stepped out of the ice cream store, cone in hand. "I've got to go. I'll talk again soon."

"Don't be a stranger, man. I mean it. You may have taken off the uniform, but we'll always be family."

His chest clenched. It was true. He might have five siblings by blood, but he had several more brothers from his time in the service. "You too."

He hung up and turned to face Sadie. "Hey. Avery and Eastern still choosing?"

"Oh yeah. Avery is taking her job as flavor chooser very seriously. I think she's taste-testing every one they have." She tilted her head. "You okay?"

"Yeah, just excited to see what I get." He pushed his phone into his pocket. He should keep his damn mouth shut, but the question was out before he could stop it. "You're friends with Elle, right?"

Her brows rose. "Elle?" Her gaze flicked down the street. "Um, yeah, we're friends."

He frowned and followed her gaze, checking out the few businesses farther down the street. The only one open was the Thai restaurant. When he looked back at Sadie, her features were completely blank.

"Did she tell you about our fight the other day?" he asked, again knowing he shouldn't ask. But Elle had been avoiding him since that day, and it was killing him.

Sadie's mouth opened and closed. "Yes…no…I mean, she mentioned it. Briefly. Something about a fight about a guy from an online dating app." Again, Sadie's gaze flickered to the restaurant before hitting the ground.

Why did she keep looking over there?

Suddenly, a sick feeling began to churn in his gut as suspicion made him step closer. "Sadie, tell me she's not in that restaurant, on a date with Art."

Her head shot up, her eyes widening. She was silent for a full five seconds. It told him everything he needed to know.

"They are," he growled under his breath. Suddenly he was angry, even though he had no damn right to be angry. But the thought of her eating dinner with some guy she didn't even know, that man walking her home, touching her…

Hell no.

He stepped back. "Can you apologize to the others for me?"

"Wait, Jace—where are you going?"

"I'll see you next time, Sadie."

She continued to call out to him as he strode down the street, but he was past stopping or slowing or, hell, thinking the least bit rationally. Elle was in his head. In his *skin*. All he could think about was the fact that she was on a date, *a fucking date*, with someone who wasn't *him*—and how he wanted her to be as far from the guy as possible.

* * *

ELLE PINCHED her left thigh under the table to stop herself from falling asleep. Yes, literally falling asleep. That's how boring Art was. Like, never stopped talking about himself, or his life goals, or his job, or anything and everything Art-related—*that* kind of boring.

How could a person talk about himself for so freaking long?

She could count on one hand the number of questions he'd asked about *her*, and even then, he'd interrupted every one of her answers, directing the conversation straight back to himself.

She lifted her glass and took a big gulp of wine. It was her second glass, but there'd probably be a third. And good God, where was the food? It felt like they'd ordered hours ago.

Art had arrived in a suit—probably the only man she'd ever seen wear a suit to a Thai restaurant. And his black hair was packed with so much shiny gel, it looked plastic. She'd told herself not to judge a book by its cover, but it looked like she should have done some judging.

"So, yeah, that's where I hope to be in my career in ten years. Of course, I'll have to get out of Misty Peak to do that. This small town doesn't offer much in the way of career progression. Have you thought about leaving?"

Her brows rose. He was asking her a question? Would she get a full answer out before he cut her off this time? "No, not really. I like it here. I like the mountains and my job."

"You said you work in a café making coffee?"

Why did he say it like that? Like working in a café was something to be ashamed of? "Yeah, I work in the café connected to the visitors center. I'm good with people, and I'm good at making coffee, so it makes sense."

He seemed to think about that for a second before leaning forward. "You know, I could probably get you a job at the firm if you want?"

Okay, he was definitely throwing shade on her profession. "No, thank you. Like I said, I enjoy what I do."

His nose scrunched. "Really?"

Jesus, where was the food?

She took another gulp of wine as the waitress finally stopped at their table.

"One seafood pad Thai, and one green chicken curry with steamed rice."

Thank the Lord. She breathed in her pad Thai as it was placed in front of her. At least the food looked good. "Thank you."

She'd suggested they share a few dishes, but Art had said something about food sharing being unhygienic. Apparently, sharing was a *boundary* of his. He'd actually used the word boundary.

The server left, and Art wrinkled his nose for the second time. "Argh, I hate it when they use shredded chicken instead of whole thighs."

"Isn't it still the same?"

"Not even close. Next time, I'll choose where we eat."

Oh, there would not be a next time. But she'd let Art know that at the end of the meal…if she made it that far.

Honestly, she probably should have left by now. Why hadn't she? Just because she wanted to prove Jace wrong?

Damn her stupid stubborn streak.

She looked longingly at the door. How quickly could she down this pad Thai and get home to her comfy bed and pajamas? Ten minutes? Fifteen?

She was still mentally calculating her escape when the door to the restaurant opened and Jace walked in.

Her back straightened, the air catching in her throat.

What in the ever-loving hell was he doing here? He scanned the room and when his gaze collided with hers, it felt like a kick to her midsection. But…he didn't look surprised. Had he known she was going to be here?

When he started toward her, she almost felt like she was in a dream. One of those nightmares you wanted to wake up from but couldn't.

Jace stopped at the table. "Elle. Fancy seeing you here."

"What are you—"

"Funny you should ask. I was just down the street getting ice cream when Sadie let it slip that you were here, on a *date*."

Her jaw dropped. Sadie told him? And his immediate reaction had been to come and *crash* her date?

Jace looked to the other side of her table, his smile so wide she wanted to slug him. "You must be Art. I'm Jace."

Art frowned. "Uh, hey. You know Elle?"

"Really well, actually. We're best friends."

"*Ex*-best friends," she cut in, but no one seemed to hear.

"Do you mind if I join you?" Jace asked. "I'm starved."

"Yes." Elle gasped. "We mind."

But again, no one freaking listened. Jace reached behind and pulled a chair over to the table. He frowned at the plates. "You're not sharing? Isn't that a rite of passage at a Thai restaurant?"

Art cleared his throat. "I don't share."

The humor in Jace's eyes made Elle's blood boil. He turned toward her. "That must have made you sad, Tink. You love sharing. What did you used to say? Sharing food is a love language?"

Art lifted his brows. "Tink?"

Jace lifted her fork and swirled some of her noodles onto the tines. "She used to wear this Tinker Bell chain on her bag at school. It was cute, and she kind of looked like a fairy, so she became Tink. To me, at least."

Elle huffed. "We're on a *date*, Jace."

"Ah, yes, and how's it going?" he asked, a frown between his brows as he ate her food.

Art pulled at the top of his collared shirt and opened his mouth, but Elle got in first.

"It's going great. And I'd like you to leave." A lie…well, the first part. And why the hell would Sadie have told him she was here?

"Great? Really? That's awesome." Jace lifted her glass of wine and took a sip before looking at Art. "What do you do, Art? Accountant? Broker? Lawyer?"

She ground her back teeth together.

"Lawyer," Art said. He still hadn't touched his food.

"Man, I'm good at picking these things. Like your job?"

Art's mouth opened and closed. "Love it. I'm working my way up to a senior position."

"I thought you looked ambitious. How are you going to get there, exactly?"

Elle wasn't sure what she expected. Art had already let her down on every other front for this date. But for him to start eating his food as he told Jace about his work goals, repeating everything he'd just said to her, *still* surprised her.

Un-freaking-believable.

She snatched her wine from Jace's hold and gulped down the rest. She was definitely going to need a third. Maybe a fourth, depending on how long this three-way date lasted.

CHAPTER 10

"Thanks for a great night. We should do it again some time," Art said to Elle before turning to Jace. "Feel free to join. We could all go out for a beer."

Jace grinned at the guy. "I'll get your number from Elle."

Elle rolled her eyes before giving Art a tight smile that didn't come close to reaching her eyes. She was mad, but then, Jace had known she would be.

"I'll message you," she said through gritted teeth.

Art stepped forward and leaned down, only to have Elle turn her head so that his kiss landed on her cheek. Even that was almost more than Jace could stomach.

Then Art turned to him and held out his hand. "Thanks for joining us. It was great to chat."

Jace shook his hand. "You too, man."

Art turned and walked down the street. Jace didn't even get a chance to look at Elle before she swung around in the opposite direction and started marching away from him. He caught up easily, shoving his hands into his pockets.

"Come on, Tink, you're not really mad about me joining your date, are you? That guy was a self-absorbed snoozefest."

She shot him a glare. "Really? Because you two seemed to get along *super* well."

"Well, ask a guy like that a few questions about himself and it's like Christmas for him."

She stopped and faced him. "How could you do that? After you saw how angry I was after you *texted* him, how could you crash our date?"

He probably should feel guilty about that. He didn't. Not even a little bit. "I didn't like you going on a date with a guy named Art."

She lifted a brow. "You're saying this would have turned out differently if his name was Josh? Or Matt? Or Jeremy?"

"Well, I've never met a Jeremy I've liked. And Joshes and Matts are usually assholes."

"Argh. You're impossible!" She started marching down the street again, and again, he matched her step for step.

"Tell me the truth—did you like him?"

"No. But that's not the point. You did something you knew I'd be angry about. You crossed a line you had no right crossing...*again*."

He ran his fingers through his hair. "Would you forgive me if I said I was sorry?"

"No. Because sorry only means something if you regret what you did."

True. "I regret that you're upset."

She scoffed.

"Come on, the guy didn't even offer to walk you home."

"I would have said no."

"He doesn't know that."

"Maybe he thought *you* were walking me home, you know, because we're *best friends* and all."

"I *am* walking you home."

"No, you're not."

"I am. I was raised to be a gentleman, and gentlemen walk women home, especially at night."

She cocked her head. "Really? And do *gentlemen* also show up to dates they're not invited to?"

"If their goal is to protect their best friend, then yes."

"*Ex*-best friend."

"You know, I really wish you'd stop saying that. I'm starting to get offended."

"I'm not talking to you anymore."

"Fine with me. I like quiet evening walks with my best friend."

Elle mumbled something under her breath that sounded like it had a curse and the word "ass" in it.

The corners of his lips twitched.

During the walk, he noticed her gaze roaming the street, as if she was looking for someone. He frowned. "Everything okay?"

"It's fine." Her answer came quickly. Too quickly?

"Don't lie to me."

Her arms wrapped around her waist.

"Elle—"

"It's nothing, just...for the last week or so, I've had this strange feeling that someone's watching me."

Something hard twisted in his gut as he scanned the streets around them. He didn't see anything, but that didn't put him at ease. "Why do you think that?"

"I don't know. I just...I feel it. It's stupid and I'm sure it's nothing. I haven't actually seen anyone. I just hear rustling sounds around me sometimes. I hear occasional footsteps during my walks." She shook her head. "It's probably nothing."

"But it feels like something to you. Why did you walk to dinner by yourself then?"

"Because there's not actually anyone following me. I'm just being ridiculous. And besides, maybe Art would have offered to drive me home if you hadn't come along."

He grabbed her arm and tugged her to a stop. "You're joking, right? You'd have actually let a man you met on a first date drive you home?"

Her lips twitched. She was screwing with him. And he deserved it.

"You know me better than that, Jace."

Yeah, he did.

She continued forward, and when they reached her apartment building, she put in the code and opened the door. He slid in after her.

"You don't need to come up."

He sure as hell did. "I'm seeing you to your apartment door."

She shook her head. "Jace—"

"Gentleman, remember?"

She rolled her eyes before stepping toward the elevator.

Fuck, he loved those eye rolls.

They went up the elevator together, and when they reached her door, he thought she'd say goodbye to him there, but instead, she unlocked it and stepped inside, leaving it open for him. Because she was sick of fighting with him? Or because, despite what she said, she liked his company?

He grinned and stepped inside, closing the door after him.

She dropped her bag onto a side table and turned. "There. You crashed my date and walked me home. You got everything you wanted. Your job is done."

Everything he wanted? That wasn't even close to being accurate.

He stepped toward her. "I can't leave until you say you forgive me."

"Not gonna happen."

She started to turn, but he gently gripped her arm and tugged her back. "Tink, I don't like you being mad at me."

Something flickered in her eyes. Some kind of heat...maybe even desire? But then, maybe that was in his head.

Her voice was low when she spoke again. "I don't like you crashing my dates."

"Liar." The word was barely a whisper. His thumb caressed the soft skin of her arm, and her eyes flared. He should turn around and go home, leave her the hell alone, but right now, he felt rooted to the spot. Stuck.

He inched closer.

Her eyes flared again. "What are you doing?"

"I have no fucking idea. But I know I don't want to leave you." He didn't just know it; he *felt* it. *Breathed* it. His need for her was in his blood, and he had no clue how to chase it away.

ELLE'S PULSE picked up speed. Jace stood too close, his ocean-blue eyes boring into her as he spoke words about not wanting to leave her. *Her.* Boring, plain Elle. It felt like a dream she'd had a million times before. A dream she'd believed would never become reality.

She shook her head. "We're friends."

A ghost of a smile stretched his lips. "You're finally admitting it."

When his thumb grazed her a second time, her skin burned from her shoulder right down to her fingertips. "You don't date women like me."

This time, he pulled back, a frown bunching his brow. "Women like you?"

"Is it because I've lost weight?" The words were out before she could stop them, and she immediately wanted to tug them back.

"*What?*" He almost sounded angry.

She squirmed. "The reason you see me now. The reason you almost seem to…want me. That's the only thing that's changed."

"You thought I didn't see you in high school?"

She bit her bottom lip, her gaze falling to her feet. She wished the floor would open up and swallow her. She did *not* want to have this conversation, yet she was the one who'd initiated it.

"Tink."

She glanced up at the softness in his voice.

"Answer my question."

"You didn't see me the way you saw the girls you dated. You dated the most gorgeous girls, and I…"

His eyes narrowed. "You what?"

She lifted a shoulder. "I *wasn't* gorgeous." Her gaze lowered again.

He placed a finger on her chin, tilting her head up, waiting until her gaze met his. "Tink, you have always been, and will always be, the most beautiful woman in every room. You are *all* I see."

Time seemed to slow, and her knees suddenly felt weak.

A part of her struggled to believe his words. But the way he looked at her, like she was every bit as important to him as he was to her, made her *want* to believe it.

"I want to kiss you so badly right now that it's like a physical ache in my chest," he whispered. "*Not* kissing you hurts."

Her lips parted and her heart thumped so fast that she could hear it as much as she could feel it. Because *she* was the one who'd always dreamed of kissing *him*. *She* was the one who'd been hopelessly consumed by this man for years.

He inched another step forward, until his front touched hers. Until she felt heat radiate from his body. The rise and fall of his chest.

When his head began to lower, her breath stuttered, and a part of her almost felt scared at the prospect of finally kissing him. So scared that she wanted to run. But her feet refused to move.

Then his lips touched hers. Soft lips. Lips that just grazed against hers.

He cupped the back of her head, and a soft hum slipped from her lips. She grabbed his shirt, nearly afraid that if she didn't, her knees would cave.

When the hand on her arm slipped around her waist, nudging her closer, she gasped, and his tongue slipped inside her mouth. Then she was tasting him. And God, he tasted exactly how she'd dreamed he would. Of wine and spices and something else. Something infinitely Jace.

Another moan escaped her throat, and he growled and turned them, pressing her to the hallway wall before grinding against her. It was both ecstasy and torment, igniting this deep need inside her for more. More of Jace. Of his kisses and touches. Of the way he made her skin tingle and her heart beat out of her chest.

His hands were everywhere, his tongue tasting hers, when something buzzed. His phone. She probably could have ignored it, but Jace didn't. He pulled his mouth away and cursed, touching his forehead to hers.

"I need to be careful with you," he pushed, his breath brushing her face. "You could make me lose myself."

She'd already lost herself the second his lips touched hers. Her chest heaved just inches from his, and she could barely catch her breath. "We've never done that before."

He chuckled. "No, we haven't. But it felt good." He lowered his head and pressed one more kiss to her mouth. She wanted to sink into it, beg for more, but he was already pulling his head away. "I should go while I still can. But this won't be the last time we do this."

Her breath stuttered. "It won't?"

Another grin. "No, Tink, it won't. I'll see you on Monday."

He caressed her neck with his thumb before finally stepping away and opening the door.

"Lock up after me."

They were his last words before he stepped into the hall and pulled the door closed after him, leaving her wondering what the hell had just happened.

CHAPTER 11

The ringing of Elle's apartment buzzer cut into her sleep, making her groan and roll onto her belly.

Go away.

She was exhausted. It had taken far too long to get to sleep last night, thoughts of Jace, of that damn kiss, rattling around in her head and making her stomach do all these wild somersaults. She'd tossed around in bed for so long she'd wondered if she'd *ever* fall asleep.

The buzzer sounded again, this time followed by her intercom.

"Elle Marshal! Wake up! I brought breakfast and I'm starving."

Oh, Jesus…it was Jewel. Anyone else, and she'd have a chance of them leaving if she ignored them long enough. Not her aunt. The woman had once camped out at the entrance of the building for hours because she was worried when Elle didn't answer, but she hadn't even been home.

With a sigh, she rolled onto her side and pushed out of bed. Her gaze flicked to the clock.

Six a.m.? *Really?* Good God, could the woman not have waited until a decent hour to harass her? Because it *was* harassment when you made a person get out of bed before the sun had even risen.

"Elle, I know you're there. Let me up or I'll start singing the theme song to *Happy Days*."

Despite the hour, Elle laughed, because her aunt absolutely *would* do that and *had* done it before, knowing perfectly well that Elle despised that show. She reached the door and pressed the intercom. "I'm going to kill you. You know that, right?"

"Well, you'd need to let me up to do that."

Not true. She knew where the woman lived—that was all she needed.

"Come in." She pressed the button to let her up and flipped her lock before retreating to the kitchen. She opened her fridge, only to groan when she realized she had no milk. None. Not even a drop. Heck, she didn't even have juice to give her a morning hit of sugar.

Goddammit.

She filled a glass with water and sipped. It did nothing to wake her up.

The door to her apartment opened. "Good morning!" her aunt sang.

Elle wrinkled her nose. "It should be illegal to be so cheery at this hour."

Jewel crossed her apartment and set a paper bag on the counter. "Oh, don't be so dramatic. Plenty of people are up and about at this time."

Yeah, plenty of *crazy* people. She opened her mouth to tell her aunt just that when the woman pulled out two Styrofoam cups.

Elle groaned and grabbed one. "Oh my gosh, yes. I need coffee in an IV."

"It's not—"

She sipped the warm liquid, only to almost spit it right back out. *Not* coffee. Not even close to coffee. "What in the ever-living hell is this?"

"Herbal tea. It's good for you."

"It's not good for my mood. Or my taste buds. And it's definitely not good for my exhaustion."

Her aunt tapped her arm. "It's hibiscus tea. I read that it helps lower blood pressure, and by the look of you, you could use it."

Oh, Jesus, she was not rested enough for this. "Please tell me you have a bagel with egg and bacon in there."

"Better." She pulled out two containers. "Gluten-free granola and coconut yogurt topped with blueberries...the perfect way to start your morning."

She should have stayed in bed. Maybe she could "accidentally" break the intercom and bell, turn off her phone, and this would never happen again. "I need to sit down." Or just die on the couch.

In the living room, she lowered to the sofa, taking another sip of the herbal tea. Christ, it got worse with every sip. It wasn't that she disliked tea, just that the liquid was in a cup typically reserved for coffee. It was like a cruel mind game.

Jewel crossed the space between them and settled on the couch beside her, handing her one of the containers of granola. "Did you have a good evening last night?"

Elle frowned. She hadn't told her aunt about her date with Art because she knew she'd get a million questions, but right now, the woman was looking at her like she already knew. "Yeah, I had a good night. Why?"

"Funny you should ask. I received a call from Marie Alvaro last night."

Oh jeez. Marie was a single mother whose entire life seemed to revolve around small-town gossip.

"And," Jewel continued, "she mentioned she saw you."

"She saw me?"

"Mm-hmm. She was eating at Thida Thai with her daughter and said you were in the same restaurant."

So that was the reason for the early-morning wakeup. Lord grant her patience.

Carefully, Elle set the herbal tea on the coffee table before opening the container of granola. "And what exactly did she say, Jewel?"

"That you seemed to be on a date with a very nice-looking man. Then Jace Walker *joined* you on the date."

"It's true." She scooped some granola and yogurt onto the spoon and placed it in her mouth. Interesting. It wasn't terrible. In fact, it was actually quite good. It just wasn't bacon or coffee.

At her aunt's silence, she looked up to see her staring with a lifted brow.

"And?" Jewel pushed.

"And what?"

"Elle Marshal. You know what I'm waiting for. I want the story behind what happened last night. You're like a daughter to me."

Guilt hit her in the chest. She was right. Jewel had raised Elle since she was eight; she was as close to a mother as Elle had. "There's not much to tell. I was on a date with a guy I met online. Jace saw us together and decided to join." It was the semi-truth. Or at least it sounded better than what actually happened. Better for Jace anyway.

A small smile played at her aunt's lips. "He was jealous, wasn't he?"

"What?"

"Jace. He saw you on a date with another guy and decided he couldn't leave you alone with him."

She pushed the granola around the container. "He's ridiculous."

"Ridiculously into you."

Memories of their kiss last night slipped into her mind, and her cheeks heated. For so long, she'd dreamed about the prospect of getting close to him like that. Touching him. Kissing him. And that kiss had lived up to every one of her fantasies. Hell, it had been better.

Her aunt straightened. "What's that?"

"What's what?"

"You're blushing. Something happened, didn't it?"

Shit. "Jewel—"

"If something happened, you tell me right now!"

She wanted to lie, but she'd never lied to her aunt, and she didn't plan to start now. "We kissed."

Jewel's eyes widened. "Who? You and online dating guy, or you and Jace?"

"Me and Jace."

Her aunt's scream was so loud, Elle almost jumped off the sofa. "Jewel! Shh, my neighbors are still sleeping!"

"You kissed? You *finally* kissed?"

"Yes. Or he kissed me."

Suddenly, Jewel flew across the sofa and threw her arms around Elle. She barely had time to swing the granola to the side.

"I am so freaking happy for you, baby," Jewel cried, sounding overly emotional.

"It was just a kiss."

The older woman pulled away, visible tears in her eyes. "With a boy you've known since you were a kid, it's never *just* a kiss." She sat back opposite Elle. "Where were you when you kissed?"

Elle glanced at the wall beside the door.

Jewel followed her gaze. "Here? In your apartment?"

"Yeah, he walked me home." And touched her and called her beautiful and set off a million butterflies in her belly.

She shoved more granola into her mouth.

"I'm so happy for you," Jewel gasped. "And I *knew* it would happen. I always knew you two would end up together."

Elle pushed a blueberry around in the yogurt. "I'm scared." Crap, maybe she shouldn't have admitted that out loud.

"Why are you scared?"

"Because this isn't some random guy. This is *Jace*. The boy I spent basically my entire childhood in love with. The boy I forced myself to accept I would *never* have."

"And now you're scared he'll hurt you."

"No, I'm terrified he'll break my heart." Because if she let herself believe that she could have him, and he left...it would destroy her. "He was never with the same girl for long."

Jewel lifted a shoulder. "Maybe you're both different people now."

Old insecurities crawled up her throat. About not being pretty enough. Outgoing enough. She didn't voice a single one of them.

"You know what motto I like to live by?" her aunt asked.

Elle's lips twitched. There were many mottos her aunt lived by, not many of which aligned with Elle's. "What?"

"If you risk nothing, you gain nothing." Jewel leaned forward. "Besides, I've always had this reckless faith in you two. I think you should go for it."

* * *

JACE PUMPED his arms as he jogged through the mountains, the cool morning air gliding over his face. Fuck, it felt good to move his body. He liked to get outside for a workout every day, sometimes twice a day. He was used to pushing his body to the limit as a Tactical Controller. To having a team pushing themselves beside him.

His gaze shifted toward the mountains. Even after fifteen years away, the familiarity remained. Like this forest had weaved itself inside him, becoming a part of him. How often had he gotten lost out here as a kid? Hidden in the trees and run around with his brothers?

Every damn day.

But today, it almost felt like he was running away from something. The taste of Elle on his tongue. The feel of her skin on his fingertips.

Her skin had been so damn soft and warm. And the way she'd reacted to him, her soft groans and hums…they'd replayed in his dreams over and over again last night.

Was he done running from his feelings for her? Was he finally ready to accept that he couldn't stay away from the woman?

With a growl, he sped up his jog. Being back, being around her, made him feel weak. Made him want to take something he'd never allowed himself before.

Her.

And kissing her, holding her in his arms, had just intensified his lifelong need for Elle. It felt like he'd finally been exactly where he was meant to be.

He pushed his body so hard that his chest began to tighten and his limbs ached, but he didn't stop or slow. He liked the burn. The pain. It reminded him that he was alive. That he was home.

When he finally reached the house, sweat ran down his forehead as he unlocked the front door and stepped inside. The eerie quiet surrounded him. The house had never been quiet growing up. With six kids, the home had been loud and warm and busy. He had a hundred memories in every room. A hundred sounds from past moments that rang through his ears.

He stepped into the master bedroom off the hall. There were five bedrooms upstairs, but the master and his old childhood bedroom were the only ones on the first floor. It had made it easy for Elle to sneak inside when she came over.

He smiled at the memory. The lock on his window had broken when he was fifteen, but he'd never told his parents, because a part of him had liked that Elle had had access to his room whenever she liked. Was it still broken or had the previous owners fixed it? He hadn't checked yet.

He pulled his shirt over his head as his phone vibrated in his pocket. He tugged it out to see a text from his brother.

Eastern: Please tell me Sadie misinterpreted last night and you didn't crash Elle's date.

Jace: I didn't crash Elle's date. I prefer to see it as being a welcome guest at the table.

Eastern: Jace...what the hell were you thinking?

Jace: That I didn't like her dating another guy.

Eastern: She's allowed to date whoever she wants. Unless you're going to date her?

Jace scrubbed a hand over his face.

Eastern: If you came back for her, tell her. Otherwise, don't go crashing her dates.

His gaze caught on the tattoo on his hip bone, in the mirror. *You're too loved to lose.* Her words, in her handwriting. And every time he read them, he heard her voice in his head. It had given him hope during his deadliest missions. It had allowed him to breathe when sometimes breathing got too hard.

Jace: Thanks for the advice, big brother. And thanks for letting me crash your family night.

Eastern: You know you're always welcome. Just be careful with Elle. You could both get hurt if you're not.

Didn't he know that? Wasn't that the exact reason he'd denied himself for so long?

Jace: When am I not careful?

He dropped his phone onto the bathroom counter and gave the tattoo one more glance before stripping off the rest of his clothes and stepping into the shower. The warm water beat down on his shoulders, and the second he closed his eyes, memories came back to him. Of missions that had been so difficult and dangerous, he'd wondered if he'd make it out alive.

Throughout it all, his team had kept him sane. His team had kept him alive...but he hadn't done the same. Not for everyone.

He squeezed his eyes closed as memories of that day flashed in his head. Of the whisper of steps from behind. The flash of movement before gunfire sounded.

Jace flattened his hands against the cool tiled wall, breathing through the guilt that tore at his chest. The pain at the memory of turning away from the enemy to see Dean drop to the ground.

He'd been right there…right beside him. And he hadn't been able to save him.

Fuck.

When breathing became too hard, Jace turned off the water and stepped out of the shower, suddenly needing something, anything, to calm him. He grabbed a towel and wrapped it around his waist before lifting his phone. He had to text her; the one person he knew could help get air into his lungs.

Jace: Come out with me tonight. Meridian. Let me buy you a drink.

When Elle didn't immediately reply, he sent another text.

Jace: Please. Eight o'clock. I'll be there. And I hope you will too.

His gaze remained on the screen for another beat, and even though she didn't write back, his heart still started to slow and his skin felt less clammy…just at that small connection with her. *That's* what she did for him.

He'd just dried off and thrown on some jeans and a T-shirt when his phone vibrated. He lifted it, expecting to see a text from Elle. It wasn't. The text in front of him was from an unknown number—and it made every muscle in his body lock.

You didn't protect him. You're the reason he's dead. And I hope that knowledge plagues you for the rest of your worthless life.

CHAPTER 12

Jace wrapped his fingers tightly around the bottle of beer. It had been a shit day. Elle never texted back about meeting him here tonight, and he'd been so damn busy at the skywalk, he hadn't been able to visit her at the café. And all the while, that text from the unknown number had tortured him, playing over and over in his head like a bad fucking dream.

You didn't protect him. You're the reason he's dead. And I hope that knowledge plagues you for the rest of your worthless life.

Who the hell had sent it? Someone in Dean's family? It had to be. It couldn't be one of his teammates, and they were the only other people who knew.

He threw back his head as he downed a third of the beer in one go. He'd read that text over and over throughout the day, almost not believing it was really there. A part of him wanted to believe he'd conjured it up. Because it was exactly what every angry, ugly thought in his head had told him every damn day since his teammate's death.

He checked the door for the hundredth time. Even though he

was sure Elle wasn't coming, there was still a bit of hope inside him. Had his kiss scared her off? He'd been so sure she felt the same way he had, but maybe that was just in his head. Maybe he wanted her so badly he'd felt something from her that hadn't been there.

She'd told him that she loved him in high school. Loved. Past tense. He couldn't really blame her for not loving him anymore. He'd been gone so long. Fifteen years, and over the years he'd lost contact. Even when he'd returned to town for his father's funeral, he'd barely spoken to her. Barely spoken to anyone.

He lifted the beer again, taking another sip just as the soft booth seat beside him dipped. He looked up, hopeful it would be Elle. It wasn't. It was Molly from the café.

She grinned. "Hey. I saw you sitting over here by yourself. Thought you could use some company."

"I'm not in the best mood for company, Molly." Understatement of the fucking century.

"But that's where you're wrong. You see, we get into these funks where we assume we're best off on our own, but then we let someone else in, and we're like, shit, I *do* feel better with company." She leaned in close, and he could smell the vodka on her breath. "I get into funks a lot, so I would know."

He scrubbed a hand over his face, not even sure why he was still at the bar. He'd come hoping that even though Elle hadn't texted back, she might still show up. But it was eight thirty, and if there was anything he knew about Elle, she was always punctual.

"I'm actually heading home now."

She shook her head. "I'm afraid I can't let you do that, Jace. Not until I know I've cheered you up."

"That's not gonna happen tonight."

"How about one dance? I guarantee it'll turn your whole night around."

The idea of dancing with any woman who wasn't Elle made

his gut churn. "Molly. I'd like to get out of the booth now." He was trying not to get angry—the woman had clearly had a few to drink—but fuck if it wasn't hard when all he wanted to do was get home.

She pouted, but after a few seconds of him not wavering, she sighed. "Fine." She eased out of the booth.

He stood, just as she took a step away and stumbled. He grabbed her and tugged her up, and she turned and grinned at him. "Sorry. I guess alcohol and heels aren't a good combination."

"Probably not. Good night, Molly."

He tried to go around her, but she stepped in front of him. "Come on, one dance. I did hear correctly that you're the fun brother, right? Plus, you're single, I'm single..." She inched closer. "I promise you won't hate it."

He opened his mouth to tell her he was going home when his phone buzzed with a text. He held his breath, needing it to be Elle.

Unknown number: Nothing to say?

The air hissed through his teeth as he replied.

Jace: Who the fuck is this?

Distracted by the text, he almost didn't feel Molly slip her hand around his neck. But then she was pulling his head down. Her lips didn't touch his, but they came close, her breath brushing over the skin beside his mouth as she whispered, "One dance..."

He cursed as he grabbed her wrists and gently broke her hold. "No." Stepping away, he opened his mouth to say more, but a quick motion at the door distracted him. A woman who'd already turned and was walking away, almost running out.

Elle.

* * *

Elle hurried out of her car and toward Meridian. She was late. Actually, was she? She hadn't replied to Jace, so technically she couldn't be late if she'd never confirmed she was coming, right?

She should have replied. The only problem was, she'd gone back and forth all night on whether she was going to come. One minute she'd typed out, "sounds great, see you then," and the next, "sorry I'm busy."

She hadn't been able to send either.

Coming here tonight had ended up being a spur-of-the-moment decision. One she'd made while feeling utterly pathetic, standing alone in her living room, eating three-day-old Chinese takeout from the container.

Her aunt's words flashed in her head as she jogged to the door of the bar.

If you risk nothing, you gain nothing.

Well, Aunt Jewel, this was her taking a risk.

She pushed inside and scanned the room, nerves tickling her spine. *Why* she was nervous, she wasn't sure. Maybe because she hadn't seen Jace all day and had no idea how to act around him after their kiss last night.

She frowned as she moved farther inside. There were people everywhere. Maybe he'd already left?

She was about to take out her phone and text him when she suddenly spotted him. His head was down, and a woman in a short, tight blue dress was blocking most of Elle's view of Jace. She stood close...so close it looked intimate.

Were they—

She didn't have a chance to finish her thought before the woman slipped her hand around his neck and tugged his head down for a kiss.

Elle's heart thumped, and every insecurity, every thought of not being enough—pretty enough, outgoing enough—gushed through her system, making her want to not be here, to not *exist* in this moment.

His fingers wrapped around her arms, but Elle couldn't watch any longer. She swung around and beelined for the door. Her eyes stung with the threat of tears. She blinked them away, refusing to let herself cry over this.

It shouldn't hurt so much. She'd seen Jace kiss a hundred girls before. But after last night? God, it hurt so much that it felt like someone had punched a hole into her chest, right where her heart used to be.

She rushed toward her car, and when she heard Jace's deep voice calling her from behind, her steps turned into a jog. She didn't want to speak to him right now. She didn't even want to look at him. The pain was too much, weaving itself into her veins, causing every part of her to hurt.

She'd just reached her car and was about to tug the door open when strong fingers wrapped around her arm and swung her around.

"It wasn't what it looked like," he rushed out.

She shook her head, feeling the threat of tears in her eyes once again. "I need to go."

"Did you hear me? I was looking at my phone, Molly was drunk, and she pulled my head down."

Molly...of course it was Molly.

"I can't do this." The words were out before she could stop them.

"Do what?"

Her heart pounded in her chest, so hard and loud, it was all she heard and felt.

Just like last night, Jace touched her chin and lifted her head until their eyes met. "Tink. Do what?"

"I waited for you to see me, Jace." The words were barely a whisper. "I waited so long that parts of me started to ache that I didn't even know existed. And the *entire time*, I had to watch you date these other women...these beautiful, perfect women who looked nothing like me. And every time you chose one of them over me, I felt a part of myself slip away. And the parts that were left started to believe the whispers in my head, that I wasn't enough for you."

Pain flickered across his face. "That's not true. Elle, I—"

"Don't. Don't tell me you choose me now. Even if you weren't kissing Molly, it doesn't change anything. This isn't just about what I saw in there. It's about the fear that I felt just walking into that bar. The fear I've felt since you got back to town. Fear that I'll spend my entire life chasing something that will never truly be mine." *Him. He* would never truly be hers. "I can't hear you say you choose me, after *not* choosing me for decades, because it will make me want something I can't possibly allow myself to want."

"Why won't you allow yourself to want me?"

"Because you walked away from me, and you never even bothered to see if I was still here waiting for you." But she had been. God, she'd waited so long she'd started to forget time and space. She'd waited until waiting just hurt too much.

"I walked away because I had to," he whispered.

"But that's the thing…you *didn't* have to. People leave, but they keep in contact. You stopped. Stopped replying to my messages. Stopped calling."

A muscle in his jaw clicked, and he shook his head. "I'm sorry. I'm so damn sorry."

"I don't need you to be sorry. I need you to be separate from me." Even though the words were from her own lips, they almost killed her to say aloud.

He shook his head. "You can't tell me all that and just expect me to walk away."

"I will *always* care about you, Jace, but it needs to be from afar. Because otherwise there might not be anything left of me."

"So what are you saying? What do you want from me?"

What did she want? She wanted to feel valued and important and secure. She wanted to walk into a bar and be sure that the man she was meeting, the man she loved, loved her back just as much.

"I want you to let me go," she whispered, pain weaving into her words.

"I can't do that."

"You don't have a choice."

CHAPTER 13

"The texts came from a burner phone."

Jace scowled as he leaned toward his brother. "You're serious?" They were sitting in Eastern's office at the sheriff's station, and his brother had just traced the unknown number that was texting him. "You're saying someone purchased a fucking burner just so they could send me these texts?"

"Looks like it. I'm sorry, man." Eastern frowned, quiet for a beat, before he said, "You didn't tell me you lost someone."

He knew asking for Eastern's help would lead to him having to share what had happened to Dean. He'd done it anyway. Probably because he was so pissed after what had happened at the bar last night, and he needed something in his life to make sense.

"His name was Dean. He was the newest member of our team. Young but enthusiastic. He died during a mission. The rest of my team survived, but Dean was shot in the back of the neck."

At what point did that story get easier to tell? Or did the pain just remain a permanent part of him?

Eastern's features remained completely clear, but Jace knew that didn't mean he didn't feel anything. Eastern had been a Navy SEAL—he knew how much losing a team member hurt.

"And why is this person saying it's your fault?" Eastern asked.

"Because I was closest to him. Because he looked up to me. Because I took my eyes off him."

"None of those things make his death your fault."

That's what people kept telling him. But it didn't feel true. Not to him.

When Jace didn't answer, Eastern leaned forward. "Who knows about what happened?"

"Just my team and his family."

"So, it's one of them."

"My team wouldn't do this."

Eastern frowned. "Give me Dean's details and I'll look into his family."

Jace clenched his teeth. He didn't want to think it could be any of them, either, but then, he didn't know them. "Thanks."

When Eastern continued to study him too closely, Jace bit back a curse. He knew what was coming.

"Are the texts all that are bothering you or is there more?" he finally asked.

Jace scrubbed a hand over his face.

"What happened?" Eastern asked when he didn't respond.

"Elle walked into the bar last night and thought she saw Molly kiss me."

Eastern raised a brow. "Did she?"

"No. *Hell* no. I wouldn't have let that happen. I was distracted by the text, and she tugged my head down, but we didn't kiss."

"Did you tell Elle that?"

He could have laughed even though there was nothing remotely funny about this. "Of course I told her. She said it didn't matter if another woman kissed me or not. She reminded me that I cut contact with her. And that before that, I dated other people over her." A pulse beat in his temple at the memory of her words. At the pain in her eyes. The way she'd barely been able to look at him. "She said she'll always care about me, but it has to be from afar."

What the fuck did that even mean? They lived in the same small town. Worked at the same damn place.

Eastern frowned. "I'm sorry, but I have to ask, why *did* you lose contact with her?"

"Because I wanted *more* for her." The words were out before he could stop them, like little explosions of truth detonating between him and his brother.

"Why didn't you think you could give her more?"

So many fucking reasons. "I'm not like you, Eastern."

"What does that mean?"

"I messed up a lot as a kid. I gave Dad hell. I wasn't good at school. And people around me had a tendency to get hurt. So I stuck to relationships I knew wouldn't last and had a plan to get out of here and make something of myself, like you and the rest of our family."

"Jace. Dad was just as proud of you as he was of the rest of us. We were *all* proud of you."

He shook his head. "It didn't feel that way. I felt like a fuckup. While Elle was…God, I don't even know how to describe her. She was kind and generous and funny, even though she'd experienced both her parents walking away from her. I didn't even feel like I deserved her as a friend some days."

Eastern frowned. "And now?"

"Now, I still don't feel deserving. But I also don't feel capable of staying away. But I might have fucked it up too much to finally have her anyway. A part of me wouldn't be surprised if I lost her completely. I seem to be really good at losing people. Mom. Dad. Lawson in high school, now Dean."

"Hey. Stop talking about yourself like there's something wrong with you. There isn't, and Elle knows that. She just needs some faith that you're in it for the long haul. *Show* her."

He ran his fingers through his hair. "It might be too late."

"When the hell does Jace Walker say something's too late and not pursue what he wants?" Eastern lifted a brow. "Go to her. Make it right. Make her see that you're in this."

* * *

"Oh my gosh, Elle, that sounds intense."

Elle's fingers tightened around her iced coffee at Sadie's words. They were sitting in Sugar and Spice, and Sadie was taking a break while the shop was quiet and her grandmother was behind the counter.

Elle gave her friend a small nod. "It *was* intense, and I'm not sure I handled it very well. I just…panicked. I saw them together, and I felt like an insecure sixteen-year-old again."

Unwanted. Undeserving.

"But he said he wasn't kissing her?" Sadie asked.

"He did, but by that point I was too far gone. It just hurt so much, and it hit me…what am I doing? He could have chosen me so many times, but he didn't. Time and time again he chose other girls over me, and now…what? I'm just going to trust that he finally sees me? Trust that if I fall in love with him all over again, he won't break my heart?"

"You really think he'd break your heart?"

"As far as I'm aware, he's never been in a long-term relationship, and I don't know if it's a risk my heart can take." That much was true. If she let herself believe that she could have Jace, that he was hers, she might not survive the aftermath if it turned out to be untrue.

Tears she couldn't control pressed at her eyes, but she blinked them back.

Sadie reached across and set her hand on top of Elle's. "You can cry with me. God knows I came to you enough about Eastern."

She shook her head. "No, I can't. Six months after he cut

contact with me, I cried for him. It wasn't the first time, but I promised myself it would be the last. So I don't want to cry."

"Then don't. Let's curse and yell instead."

Despite everything, she laughed. "*That* I can get onboard with."

Sadie frowned. "You said something before. You said he would date these beautiful women."

"Oh my gosh, they were *gorgeous*."

"So are you."

She ran her finger up and down the straw in her cup. "I used to look a bit different, and that affected my self-esteem. Of course, now I look back and my heart hurts for the teenage version of myself, because she *was* beautiful, she just didn't know it. And even after I lost the weight, nothing changed immediately. It took me a long time to realize that my body is the only home I'll ever get, and it's *my* job to look after it and love it, not someone else's." She lifted a shoulder. "I still struggle a lot of the time, but self-love is something I'll forever be working on."

Sadie's eyes softened. "I think we all have days where we struggle with self-love. I'm glad you feel better about yourself now though. You *are* beautiful, inside and out."

"Thank you."

"Sadie?"

They both looked up at her grandmother, Mrs. Sandler, who had three people in front of the counter. "Sorry, dear, but would you be able to take the cookies out of the oven in the back?"

"Sure."

Elle stood with Sadie. "I need to get going anyway. Thank you for the chat. I really needed it."

"Of course." Sadie tugged her into a hug. "Thanks for coming by. Let's catch up again soon. Ooh, let's try that new yoga and Pilates studio that just opened up in town."

Elle frowned. "There's a new yoga and Pilates studio?"

"Sure is. It's only a street over from here."

"Sounds good. Text me the time and place." Not that she'd done much yoga or Pilates in her life. Quite the opposite.

Elle waved to Mrs. Sandler before stepping outside.

Today was a rare day off, which she was grateful for. She'd woken up feeling like crap after what she'd said to Jace last night, and a quick catch-up with Sadie was exactly what she'd needed.

The midmorning sun hit her skin as she headed down the street. One thing she loved about where she lived was that she could walk to so many places from her apartment. But thank God she'd driven to the bar last night. If she'd walked, she was sure Jace would have walked her home, and with her being on the verge of a mental and emotional breakdown, that would not have been a good idea.

Was she being ridiculous? Was she letting fear rule her life?

She had no idea. All she knew was that she was scared because Jace had the power to hurt her like no one else.

She passed Meridian, her gaze lingering on the spot where she'd parked last night. The place where she'd word-vomited to Jace every fear that lived inside her. Every pain and heartache. A part of her had been wondering if he'd text or call today. So far he hadn't, and she wasn't sure if she was happy or disappointed by that.

When a car drove past, she frowned, only noticing it because it drove so slowly. Her gaze caught on the man behind the wheel. He was bald with a sleeve of tattoos down both arms, as well as what looked like a snake tattoo on the side of his head—and he was looking directly at her.

She dragged her gaze away, ignoring the uncomfortable pit in her belly.

She'd taken a few more steps when the car pulled over to the side of the road a block ahead.

Her steps slowed as the man opened the door. She wasn't generally a scared person, but right now, there were alarm bells going off inside her head. Because he looked a bit rough? Or because of the way he'd been looking at her? She wasn't sure, but an inner voice *yelled* at her to turn and run.

He rose from his car and shut the door, his gaze flashing to hers again, only for a second, before he shoved his hands into his pockets and started directly toward her.

Screw it. She spun around and moved, almost running toward Meridian before pushing against the door handle.

Shit. It was locked.

She pounded her fists against the wood, probably looking like a psychopath to anyone who saw her but not caring. The panic was alive inside her as every second brought the man closer.

"Cody? Harper? Hello? Is anyone there?"

They might not be. They didn't live above the bar anymore, and the place was closed on Mondays.

The man was only a few yards away, a couple more steps and—

The door opened and she all but fell into Cody's arms, just as the guy passed the bar. Just strolled on past without even looking at her.

He wasn't after her. He didn't even care about her.

Cody frowned. "Hey. Are you okay?"

She blew out a long breath. Insane. She was totally and completely insane. "No. I don't think I am."

CHAPTER 14

$\mathcal{J}$ace rose to his feet, Eastern doing the same from the other side of the desk. He'd stayed at the station to have a coffee with his brother. It tasted like shit, but the company helped him feel semi-okay, which was a far cry from when he'd stepped into the station.

"You heard from Lock lately?" Eastern asked as they walked toward the door.

"Nope. Why? Have you?" Kayden had asked the same thing not too long ago.

Eastern rubbed his chin. "Nah, I haven't heard from him either. I know he doesn't check in a lot, but this feels like the longest he's gone radio silent."

"You worried about him?"

"A bit. But then I remind myself the guy knows fifty ways to kill someone with his pinkie, so he should be okay."

Jace laughed. There was never a truer statement than that one. But then, they all had special ops backgrounds, so defending themselves was second nature. The problem was, the toughest soldiers went into the most dangerous terrain, and they didn't always make it out unscathed.

Jace stopped at the door and was about to say goodbye when Eastern's cell rang.

He tugged it out, frowning before pressing it to his ear. "Cody. What's going on?" A second passed and Eastern's eyes narrowed, his gaze moving to Jace. "Is she okay?"

Who was he talking about? Harper?

"No. I'm glad you called. It's better to be safe than sorry, especially if she's shaken up. I'll come down and talk to her."

Jace gave him a chin lift as Eastern hung up. "Is everything okay?"

"It's fine."

He was lying. Jace didn't need to be a lie detector to know that. "Tell me."

His brother ran his fingers through his hair. "I probably shouldn't…"

Unease coiled in Jace's gut. "*What*, Eastern?"

"It's Elle. She thought some guy was following her so ran into the bar. She's pretty upset."

"What the *fuck*? Did he follow her in?"

"No. But Cody stepped out and said he didn't recognize him. He also said Elle was shaking. I'm going down to get a description so I can keep an eye out for him."

"I'm coming."

Eastern sighed. "Of course you are. Come on."

Jace climbed into his own car and followed his brother to the bar. The entire way, his gaze kept flicking to his phone and back to the road. She hadn't contacted him. It shouldn't surprise him after last night, but fuck, it still hurt. If she was scared, he wanted to be the person she called. He wanted to be the person she turned to for protection.

The drive was only a couple of minutes, but it felt far longer. He climbed out of his car and was about to step inside when Eastern grabbed him.

"You need to stay calm in there."

Jace frowned. "What the hell are you talking about?"

"You already look like you're gonna kill someone, and nothing's even happened."

"Someone scared her."

"But she's okay. So just…keep your head on, okay?"

His brother was right, dammit. He needed to remain calm.

It was only after Jace nodded that Eastern pushed inside.

The second Jace stepped in after him, his gaze went to Elle. She was seated at the bar, glass of water in front of her and Harper by her side. Cody stood on the other side of the bar, arms folded.

Elle glanced up, her lips parting when she saw Eastern, like she was about to say something. She stopped when her gaze hit him. "Jace…"

Eastern scrubbed his chin. "Sorry. He was with me at the station when Cody called."

Jace walked straight over and loosely wrapped an arm around her, touching her hip. "Are you okay?"

"I'm fine." Her eyes held his for an entire beat before she swallowed and turned to Eastern. "Really, I'm okay."

"Tell me what happened," Eastern said, so calm—it was the complete opposite of everything Jace felt.

Elle wet her lips. "I was walking to my apartment from Sugar and Spice and a car drove past."

"Make? Model?"

Her nose scrunched. "Maybe a Volkswagen? Black. I don't know the license plate, sorry."

Cody pushed a piece of paper across the bar. "I had a look when I stepped outside and wrote it down for you."

Eastern slipped the piece of paper into his pocket. "Great." He turned back to Elle. "What did he look like?"

"Bald with sleeves of tattoos, and he had this snake tattoo on the side of his head."

Jace grazed her side with his thumb. Thankfully, she didn't pull away.

Cody cleared his throat. "I caught a glimpse of him from behind, and he looked to be about six feet tall and well-built."

"I'm being paranoid, right?" Elle rose to her feet. "I'm unfairly judging this random guy who pulls over and walks down the street, because of his tattoos and the way he looks. He walked straight past me."

"You were scared," Jace said softly. "And that wouldn't be just because of his looks. Why?"

She lifted a shoulder. "I guess because he was looking at me as he drove past really slowly, then he pulled over. He wasn't looking at me as he got out, but he walked in my direction. Cody opened the door just before he reached me, and he walked right past without even glancing my way again."

Jace's muscles tensed. It was possible the guy hadn't been heading toward her. But it was also possible he *had* been, and the sight of Cody had deterred him. "You said you feel like someone's been watching you lately."

"Is that true?" Eastern asked sharply.

Elle's mouth opened and closed. "Well, yeah…but again, it's just a feeling. I've never actually seen anyone."

"The feeling was strong enough for you to mention to Jace though," Eastern said. "How long have you had this feeling?"

She lifted a shoulder. "A couple of weeks maybe."

Eastern nodded. "Okay. I'm going to run these plates and look into this guy. Until I find out more, I don't want you walking around town by yourself."

Elle shook her head. "Eastern—"

"He's right, Tink," Jace cut in. "We need you safe." *He* needed her safe.

She met his gaze, her brows pinching. For a moment, he was sure she'd argue with him. But finally she nodded. "Okay. I'll drive around town instead of walking."

Thank fuck. "I'll drive you home." She opened her mouth, looking like she was going to say no, but he got in first. "Tink, I'm taking you home. This is about your safety." And it wasn't up for negotiation.

* * *

ELLE SNUCK a peek at Jace beside her. Neither of them had spoken the entire way to her apartment. Not that it was a long drive, but it was still probably the longest she'd ever been in his company without speaking.

A part of her wanted to be mad at him for coming down to the bar with Eastern and demanding to take her home after she'd told him she needed distance from him. But she just couldn't be. Not with the way he was constantly scanning their surroundings like he was searching for a threat.

Because regardless of everything happening between them, she'd always felt safest in his company.

Not that she needed a protector. The guy had walked straight past her, for God's sake.

Man, she'd overreacted. Big time. What was wrong with her? It was so unlike her to make a big deal out of nothing. That, combined with this feeling of being watched...it was *all* so unlike her.

He pulled over in her apartment parking lot, and without a word, they both got out. When they reached the door, she unlocked it and opened her mouth to thank Jace for walking her home, but he was already stepping inside.

Okay, looked like he was walking her up to her apartment again.

She followed him to the elevator. There was something about standing in an elevator in silence with someone that was so much more awkward than driving or walking in silence. She snuck another peek at him, and yep, he still looked tense as hell. The muscles in his arms were bunched, and he had a frown between his brows that wasn't common for Jace. Usually, there was a permanent grin on his face.

The doors opened and she stepped out. When they reached her door, she unlocked it and stepped inside. She probably should have been annoyed that he followed her in, but again, she wasn't angry. She was tired.

She opened her mouth to thank him for bringing her home, but he spoke first.

"I want to be the person you call when you need help."

Her mouth snapped shut, and a million different emotions rolled through her head.

He stepped closer. "I heard you last night. I heard everything you said. I *still* want to be the person you call when you're scared. I want to be the first person you think of. The first person you *need*."

He moved closer again, his hands going to her hips, and suddenly her breathing became choppy. She shook her head. "Jace. I don't…we can't."

"I know." He dipped his head, his temple touching hers. "I know you want to be…separate." He said that word like it pained him. Like it took too much energy just to get it out into the world. "But I've never felt separate from you, and I never will. Even when I was away, you were a part of me, even if you didn't know it."

She closed her eyes, heavy emotion clogging her throat. She should step away. The fear of getting hurt was still there in her chest. It was alive and clawing at her. Nothing had changed, and their past together could never change. But when he touched her, putting space between them felt like the hardest thing in the world. Like it was the equivalent of lifting a million pounds.

He cupped her cheek, the heat of his palm seeping into her skin, and suddenly she was turning her head, leaning into him. Because this was all she'd ever wanted. No matter how much it scared her. No matter how much she'd fought it. His touch was everything.

He lowered his head, his breath brushing her cheek. "I've tried to stay away. I can't. Not with you being so close."

The fine hairs on her arms stood on end, and she turned her head to look into his ocean-blue eyes. So beautiful. Always so beautiful. And his lips… God, they were so close to hers, all she had to do was shift that bit closer.

Like her body had a mind of its own, she leaned forward, and then her lips touched his.

The kiss was everything their first was—an explosion of sensations. A deep dive into the unknown.

His lips moved over hers as his hand shifted into her hair, slipping through her locks. She wrapped her fingers around his neck, tugging him closer, as an almost desperate need to have him took hold of her.

Suddenly, she was lifted off her feet. She gasped, wrapping her legs around him as he pressed her to the wall, her core pushing hard against his stomach. Then his tongue was in her mouth.

She groaned at the taste of him. At the rough texture of his palm as it slipped beneath her shirt and up her side. Her heart beat hard as he neared her chest, an almost light-headed ecstasy taking over.

He cupped her breast, palming her and making her whimper deep in her throat.

"Fuck, I love those sounds," Jace growled.

He found her nipple and rolled it with his thumb. Her breaths were short, the beats of her heart stumbling over one another—

Her phone rang.

At first, she barely heard it, but as it continued, it began to prick at the bubble surrounding her and Jace, allowing reality to slip back in.

What was she doing? She'd just given him this big speech last night about needing to be separate from him, and now she was allowing him to kiss her? To press her to the wall and touch her?

Jesus. She pushed at his shoulder. "Jace, put me down."

His hand paused on her chest, his head rising. "What's wrong?"

"I...we can't do this."

Pain skittered across his face, pain that he didn't even try to hide. He straightened her top slowly before letting her slide down his body. But he didn't step back. Instead, his intense blue gaze bored into her. "I just need to say one thing."

A part of her was almost scared of what she might hear. "Okay."

"What if I didn't miss my chance? What if...I was just waiting for it?"

She swallowed. "Why would you do that?"

"Because you were... Fuck, Elle. You were *everything*. Beautiful and kind and resilient, and I was none of those things. In my head, I was nowhere near good enough for you. I had to prove that I could be enough for you, before I made my move. I needed to be everything you deserved."

Blood roared between her ears, almost deafening the world around her. "Jace..."

"I chose them over you, not because *I* wanted more, but because I wanted *you* to have more. Because even at that young age, I knew that people close to me just got hurt."

Pain for this beautiful man rippled in her chest. "You honestly believe that?"

"Yes, I believe it. I *live* it. And I'd die if I ever truly hurt you. But I'm weak...too weak to stay away from you."

She cupped his cheek. "Jace, you are the strongest man I know."

He kissed her palm. "Don't push me away, Tink. Please. I need you."

Need...not want. She closed her eyes, letting those words sit inside her for a moment. It wasn't a one-way thing. She needed him too. She'd just been trying to convince herself she could live without him.

Her eyes opened, and she sucked in a long breath. "Can we just try to be friends for a bit first?"

One side of his mouth lifted. "We can try."

She bit her bottom lip as her phone vibrated with a text. "That's all I ask."

CHAPTER 15

$\mathcal{E}$lle heated up some milk for a customer's coffee. It had been a busy morning in the café, but thankfully the rush was dying down. Usually, she didn't mind being busy. She loved people and enjoyed her job, plus the influx of visitors made time speed by.

Today, she did mind.

How many mistakes had she made? So many she'd lost count. She'd dropped and broken a plate, undercharged one customer, then overcharged another, and burned two croissants. Why? Because she was distracted. *Really* freaking distracted—and that distraction came in the form of one man. Or, more specifically, a kiss from one man, which had taken place days ago, but she still couldn't get it out of her head.

God, she couldn't believe she'd kissed him *again*. Actually, that wasn't true. She *could* believe she'd kissed him after what he'd said to her. *Most* women would've probably thrown themselves at him.

Memories of being lifted in his arms and pressed against the wall made her cheeks heat. Of the way he'd palmed her breast.

Too. Freaking. Addictive. That's what his kisses were.

"What has you blushing?"

She jumped at Molly's voice beside her, some of the milk splashing out and burning her hand.

"Crap." Elle lowered the milk and ran her hand under some cool water in the sink, feeling Molly's stare on her.

"Hey, are you okay?"

"Yeah, just distracted." It was becoming a common theme for her. She looked up at the other woman. "Everything okay?"

"Actually, now that we're quieter, I can finally tell you about my disastrous night at the bar last weekend."

Her muscles tensed. Molly hadn't mentioned the bar incident, and Elle hadn't asked. She was pretty sure Molly had no idea that she'd even made an appearance that night.

"Disastrous night at the bar?" Elle poured the milk into the to-go cup before popping on the lid.

"I drank *so* much." Molly groaned. "And proceeded to absolutely humiliate myself."

Elle turned and smiled at the customer as she pushed the coffee across the counter. "Here you go." She grabbed a wet cloth and started cleaning the machine.

"I did something really stupid," Molly said quietly.

Elle raised her brows. "What did you do?"

"I hit on Jace. Well, drunk Molly did, and she did *not* take the hint that he wasn't interested. But once I'd sobered up, I remembered everything, including his not-so-subtle hints that he wanted nothing to do with me."

She scrubbed the machine harder, not taking her eyes off it. "Really?"

"Yep. It may go down as one of my most embarrassing evenings in history. I apologized to him the next time I saw him, but I still don't want to show my face in front of the guy."

Elle paused, looking at the younger woman. "You apologized?"

"Oh yeah, and he was so good about it. Told me it was already forgotten." Molly sighed. "The entire time, his big, burly muscles were pushing against the fabric of his shirt, and all I could think was, he's going to make some woman a very happy lady."

Elle's heart rattled. "I'm sorry he wasn't interested."

"Eh. These things happen. I regret throwing myself at him, but not that I expressed my interest. Sometimes you need to put yourself out there, otherwise you'll never know what could be."

Elle tilted her head.

"Speaking of guys," Molly continued, "have you been on any more dates since Art?"

"Nope. I deleted the app." She started heating more milk. "Do you want a coffee?"

Molly frowned. "No, thanks. And let's back up a step. You deleted the app? Why? You've only been on a few dates."

"Five. I've been on five dates, and I am done." Done with a capital D.

"Elle, you're so hot. Get out there and let the world *see* that hotness!"

A laugh bubbled from her chest. "Let the world see my hotness?"

"Hell yeah! Maybe you and I should go out together."

Ha. That was a big fat no. She was too old for Molly's kind of evenings out. She was pretty sure the other woman's nights didn't finish until midmorning, at which point Elle would probably be asleep in the booth.

"Maybe." That was as committal as she planned to get. "Do you mind if I go for a walk for my break? I could use the fresh air."

"Go for it. Plus, it will give you time to think about where we could go for our night out." Molly winked before stepping up to the counter to serve the next customer.

Elle shook her head as she walked out onto the deck. The second she breathed in the fresh mountain air, she was hit by that familiar sense of peace. Man, she loved this place. Everything about it just put her at ease, even on her hardest days. How often had she gotten lost out here after Jace left town, needing to be alone with her thoughts?

So many times.

She stepped off the deck and onto the path. A couple minutes into her walk, Kayden came around a bend up ahead, a small group behind him.

He dipped his head. "Hey, Elle."

She smiled and said a quick hey. It must be nice for him to get to spend all day, every day, out here. She'd only been out for a few minutes, and already she felt like a new person. Since promising Eastern she'd drive everywhere, she hadn't been getting nearly enough fresh air or exercise. The feeling of being cooped up was driving her crazy.

Her mind flickered to the missed call and text that had interrupted her kiss with Jace the other day. Both were from Eastern, telling her that the tattooed guy's car was stolen. That meant they didn't know his identity. They didn't know *anything* about him… except that he was a thief. Probably a criminal.

A shudder coursed down her spine.

She sipped her coffee, passing a couple more groups of people before hearing a small crack in the leaves somewhere in the woods beyond the path. She paused and frowned, glancing around her.

There was no one there. No one that she could see anyway.

She had to be going mad. Because this kept happening. These little sounds. This feeling of being watched. But there was never anyone around. So, what on earth was it?

Swallowing, she continued forward. She'd taken several steps when she heard it again, but this time behind her. She turned— only to yelp at the sight of a big chest. Jace's big chest.

The air rushed out of her, and she put a hand over her heart. "Jace! You scared the crap out of me."

He frowned. "Sorry, I thought you heard me coming. Everything okay?"

"Yeah, I'm just a jumpy mess."

His gaze moved over the trees around her. "It's probably not a good idea for you to be out here by yourself."

"I can't stay cooped up inside all the time."

A corner of his mouth lifted. "Well, lucky for you, you have a big strong best friend."

"Where?"

His grin widened. "Ha ha."

With a chuckle, she turned and started walking again. "Did you know I was out here or is this a random coincidence?"

"I may have gone to the café looking for you. Molly told me you'd gone for a walk, then I ran into Kayden, who told me which direction you'd gone."

"Wow, you're like a detective."

"Well, I barely saw you yesterday. I'm getting Elle withdrawals."

"That must be tough. I don't know how you're managing."

"Me either, Tink."

While she'd been joking, he had a ring of truth in his voice that felt…intense.

She gulped down another mouthful of coffee, the hot liquid burning her throat. "Being away from a friend can be difficult."

"Friend. Right."

"We shouldn't have kissed, Jace. That was a mistake." The words fell from her mouth, and the second they did, they felt wrong.

"I will never call a kiss with you a mistake. Way overdue? Sure. Hot? Hell yeah. But not a mistake."

She blew out a breath. "Jace, we've been through this, and you agreed we'd be friends. We were always friends. We were good at friends. We should stick to what we know."

"I said we'd be friends *first*."

She frowned, opening her mouth to respond when he got in first.

"April twenty-sixth, fourth grade."

She stopped. "What?"

"You walked into class. You were wearing your backpack with the Tinker Bell key chain dangling from a zipper. Your hair was in a braid over your left shoulder. Casper was being an asshole to Bianca. He told her she looked like shit in her overalls."

Why was he—

"You walked straight up to him and told him that if he ever spoke to your friend like that again, you'd kick him between the legs and make sure he didn't get back up."

She *had* said that. She'd been new to the school, and Misty Peak, and Bianca had been her first friend. Her only friend for a while.

"You came up to me after and said you wanted a friend like me." Her voice was soft, almost a whisper. She hadn't known Jace before that, but one look into his ocean-blue eyes and there'd been no saying no.

* * *

"And you said yes." He inched closer.

"Why are you telling me this?"

"Because that was the day I knew I needed you in my life. Not for a moment. Not for a few years. Forever." He'd just forgotten for a while.

"That was the first day we met."

"Yeah, it was." And he remembered it like it was yesterday, because it was the day his world changed. He lifted a lock of hair from her cheek. "I want to give you what you're asking for and be your friend again. But when I'm close to you, it becomes impossible to *not* touch you."

"You used to do just fine," she whispered.

He shook his head. "Not true. Even when I was sixteen years old, not touching you was torture."

She sucked in a full breath before responding. "That's not true."

"It is. I ran from it for a long while. For years, actually. I'm done running. You don't even realize how easy you are to fall for, Elle." He lowered his head, and the need to kiss her was so strong that it pulsed through his veins. But she didn't want that right now, and goddammit, he had to respect that. Instead, he grazed her cheek with his lips, moving across to her ear. "So. Damn. Easy."

"Jace." She pressed her hand to his chest, and he expected her to push him away. She didn't. It was almost like she was as torn as he was. They couldn't kiss because of the boundaries she'd put in place. He couldn't back away because her pull was undeniable. So here they remained, frozen in this in-between.

"Come to my family dinner next Monday night," he asked, finally breaking the silence.

"What?"

He lifted his head, only a fraction, then immediately slipped a hand around her waist, needing the contact. "We do family dinners most Monday nights. I'm hosting the next one."

One side of her mouth lifted. "You mean I get to return to our old hangout spot? The Walker family home?"

So many memories lived in that house. Of evenings when she'd come over for dinner. Afternoons together after school. Nights when they'd been a bit older, and she'd had her license and driven over to see him.

"Yeah, come to the Walker family home and have dinner with me." He stroked her hip with his thumb. "It'll be like old times."

Her bottom lip disappeared between her teeth before she nodded. "Okay."

Why did he have a sudden need to punch a fist into the air in victory? He grinned at her. "Good."

"As friends."

"As friends." *For now.* The quiet, unspoken words whispered in his head. "And as a friend, I feel it's my duty to walk you back to the café."

"How can I say no to that?"

He slipped his hand into hers and led her toward the visitors center, and damn, even that felt amazing.

They were just nearing the building when his cell rang. He frowned when he pulled it out and saw it was an unknown number. The burner phone? They'd never called before.

Elle looked up at him, questions in her eyes.

He answered the call. "Hello?"

For a moment, there was silence. Not even the sound of a breeze over the line. He was about to hang up when heavy breathing sounded. It was so fucking creepy, he stopped in his tracks.

Elle stopped with him and touched his arm. "Hey." She inched closer. "Everything okay?"

Another few seconds of breathing and he hung up. "Yeah, it's fine."

"Jace—"

"Hey. It's okay. Come on, let's get back before someone at the café sends out a search party."

It *wasn't* fine. Someone was fucking with him—and he needed to figure out who the hell it was.

CHAPTER 16

"And all you heard was breathing?"

Jace's muscles tightened at Kayden's question. "Yeah, just breathing. It was fucking creepy."

His three brothers here in Misty Peak now knew all the details about his last mission with Dean. The conversation wasn't easy, but they'd all done their time in the military. They knew the significance of losing a teammate, regardless of how it happened.

For what felt like the twentieth time that evening, his gaze shifted across the yard to Elle. She sat with the women and Avery, glass of wine in hand as they talked. She was smiling. Laughing. And she fit so fucking well into his family.

"I've done a check on his parents," Eastern said quietly. "They're still in Alabama and, as far as I can tell, haven't left. But there's no way to confirm if the messages are from them. I've also looked into the brother and sister. The brother's a police officer in Georgia. Again, doesn't look like he's left. The sister's in Charlotte. She's a teacher, but when I dug a bit, I found that she's taken leave. I'm going to keep looking into her and see what she's doing with her leave."

"How'd you get all that?" Cody asked.

Eastern lifted a shoulder. "I knew where to look."

Jace frowned. That tourist he'd met on the skywalk had said she was from Charlotte. "Can you pull up her driver's license so we have a photo?"

"Yeah, I can do that."

Jace nodded, a frown etched on his brow.

"They still contacting you?" Kayden asked.

"Not since I blocked the number."

Cody frowned. "I don't like that you don't know who this person is."

"Me either, but I'm also not going to let them affect me." That was exactly what they wanted.

"I'm sorry about Dean," Kayden said quietly, gripping his shoulder.

Jace dipped his head. "Thanks. Me too."

"You doing okay with it?" Cody asked.

"I wasn't…" His gaze returned to Elle. "But every day becomes easier. Being here, living a different life… I'm starting to feel normal again."

He watched as she laughed at something Tilly said. Damn, she was beautiful. How it was possible for one woman to be so gorgeous, he had no idea.

"What's going on with you two?" Eastern asked.

That was a good question. He looked back at his brothers. "She wants to be friends. And when I first got back to town, so did I."

"But something's changed," Kayden said when Jace didn't continue.

"Me. I've changed. I fought my feelings for so long, and I'm done fighting. I get why she's struggling to have faith in me. I cut off contact with her. I wouldn't trust me either. I just have to convince her I'm a safe bet."

"She'll come around," Eastern said quietly.

Cody grinned. "Yeah, just be your normal charming self and

how could she resist?"

Jace scoffed, because the charm wasn't exactly working right now.

Eastern's phone rang, and he tugged it out. "Look who it is." He answered the call and pressed a button. "Lock. I've got you on speaker with Kay, Eastern and Jace."

Lock's deep voice sounded over the line. "Hey, everyone."

"Where have you been?" Kayden asked. "Haven't heard from you in months."

Wind whistled through the speaker. "Sorry. Been deep underground for a while. The team only just got back to base."

Wherever the hell base was for Lock.

"You doing okay?" Jace asked.

"Yeah, it's been a busy year. Missing you guys and Nylah and Avery. How's everyone doing?"

Jace grinned. "Well, our three brothers are well and truly coupled up."

Cody scoffed. "And Jace isn't far behind with Elle."

Lock blew out a long breath. "Whoa. Seems I've missed a lot."

"Maybe it's time to come home," Kayden said soberly.

"Yeah. Maybe it is."

They talked a few more minutes before their brother had to go, then finished grilling and took the food to the table. Jace made up a plate for himself and another for Elle before heading over to where she sat on a log around the backyard fire pit.

He held out the plate as he lowered beside her. "I got you a bit of everything."

"A bit of everything is my kind of meal." She slipped the plate from his hand, their fingers grazing. "Thank you."

"Just trying to be a good *friend.*"

The corners of her lips lifted, and she playfully nudged his shoulder.

God, that smile in combination with the way she bumped

him…he felt fifteen again, crushing on the same girl, only this time he wasn't fighting it.

The group chatted and laughed around them, Avery even giving them a little glimpse of her school dance. He could barely concentrate on anything but Elle. Every curve of her lips. Every laugh that bubbled from her chest. He wanted to memorize all of it. Either that or pause this moment and stretch it.

Once he'd finished eating, he set his plate aside and slipped an arm around her waist. A part of him thought she might pull away, and yeah, that would gut him. She didn't. She leaned into him like she needed the contact as much as he needed to be in contact with her.

It was half an hour later when she rose.

He frowned. "Hey, where do you think you're going?"

"To the bathroom." She raised a brow, a hint of a smile on her lips. "Is that okay?"

"You remember where it is?"

"I know this house better than I know my aunt's."

Right. Because this was where she'd grown up. With him. "Don't take long."

One more smile from her before she headed into the house, and the second she was out of view, he wanted her back.

* * *

WHEN ELLE STEPPED INSIDE, the breath caught in her throat. This house, the memories within it…they were everywhere. Of Jace's dad in the kitchen, cooking and laughing with Nylah. Of the guys in the living room, playing video games or wrestling or just being loud.

She walked through the rooms, running her fingers over surfaces and letting every memory slip through her. Some of the furniture was even still the same. The same brown leather couch. The same coffee table.

The memories felt good. Warm. Because when she'd come to this house as a kid, she'd felt at home. More at home than she had in her aunt's house. But maybe that was because Jewel's home was so quiet, while this place had been busy and loud…and Jace had been here.

With a sigh, she crossed the living room toward the bathroom off the hall. When she was done, she was about to head back outside when her gaze caught on a closed door.

Jace's old bedroom.

For a moment, time stood still as her feet itched to go to the room where she'd spent so much of her time. It was silly, wasn't it? It was just four walls.

She took two steps forward, only to stop again.

One look. She'd have one look inside the bedroom and go back outside.

She moved toward the door and wrapped her fingers around the knob. With a deep breath, she pushed inside.

It looked the same. Sure, there were no sheets on the mattress and no TV on the wall, but the bed was pushed up against the wall, beneath the wide window, just like it had been in high school. The built-in closet still had the floor-to-ceiling mirror, and Jace's old oak dresser sat beside the bed like always. A bed that she'd lain on beside Jace so many times. A bed she'd laughed on. Eaten on. A bed she'd snuck into, sleeping beside him…just as friends, of course. Always friends.

How was the furniture the same? Jace's father had sold this house before Jace bought it back. Even the wallpaper was still there—the moon and stars. She stepped forward, tracing one of the stars, remembering how, in an attempt to not stare at Jace, she'd traced the stars with her eyes. Counted them.

"Flint kept a lot of the stuff in the house."

She gasped and spun at the sound of Jace's voice. Jesus, she hadn't even heard him come in. "What?"

His attention shifted to the bed, then the wallpaper. "Flint

Matthews, the farmer next door who bought this property. He really just wanted the land, so the house remained untouched. And my father moved into the apartment over the bar, so he didn't have room for a lot of the furniture. When I first stepped in here, I couldn't figure out if I was happy or disappointed that my room was still the same."

"Why would you be disappointed?"

He lifted a shoulder, slowly crossing the space between them. "I guess it made me feel like a teenager again. A kid who needed to prove his worth in a family full of heroes."

She frowned. "You never needed to prove anything, Jace."

"With you, I'll always want to be better." He stopped in front of her and slipped a finger into the waist of her jeans, tugging her toward him. "With you, I want to prove that I'm worthy."

She gaped at him. "Jace, you've *always* been worthy."

One side of his mouth lifted, but she was certain he didn't believe her. "I haven't checked, but I bet the lock on that window's still broken. I should really make sure it isn't...you know, safety and all. I just haven't been able to bring myself to do it, because there's a comfort in you having access to my home."

Her lungs stuttered, and she had no idea why.

"Do you know how often I wanted to kiss you in this very spot? Do you know how hard it was to resist you every time you were in here with me?" His head lowered, his breath brushing her ear as he whispered. "It was torture."

She shook her head. "No. It was *me* who had to distract myself with the stars on your wall to stop myself from kissing *you*."

His lips grazed her cheek. "How did I resist you for so long? How did we not fall together as easily as I want to now?"

"I was different back then."

"Kind of. But you were also the same. The same beauty. The same sweetness." His head lowered to her neck. "The same soft skin that haunts my dreams."

A shudder rolled down her spine. "What are you doing?"

"I have no idea. With you, I never know what I'm doing, Tink. But every day I'm around you, and I can't touch you, I lose a little more of my sanity." The hand on her jeans moved below her shirt to touch bare skin.

"You said friends." The words were a whisper from her lips, but dammit, she could barely speak.

"I'm trying. God, I'm trying so hard..." His hand slipped farther under her shirt and moved up to her waist. "But I'm not as strong as I was when I was a kid, and you're impossible to resist."

His lips pressed to her neck. Then her jaw.

A voice in her head told her to push him away. But no matter how loud it got, the voice that said she needed Jace always seemed louder.

* * *

A PART of Jace knew he needed to step away. Respect her boundaries. He'd told her he'd be her friend for a while. And friends didn't kiss. They didn't touch each other the way Jace needed to touch Elle.

But he *couldn't* step away. He couldn't handle even the smallest of spaces between them. And when her hands slipped below his shirt, running over his skin, he almost lost it then and there. He cupped her cheek, letting her heat run into his veins like lava.

When one of her hands moved around to his neck, the air got stuck in his lungs, and he couldn't move. Every part of him needed to know what she was about to do.

He didn't have to wait long. One second, then she lifted to her toes and kissed him.

It cut off every thought in his head. Every feeling except the one of her against him. And it awakened something deep within. Something hot and primal and territorial. Something that screamed *his.*

She was *his.*

He hauled her against him so there was no space between them and slipped his tongue inside her mouth. And there it was again. That spicy sweetness that was Elle. The perfect combination of candy and wine.

He ran his tongue over hers, his lips sliding and grazing.

When that wasn't enough, he lifted her against him, and her legs immediately wrapped around his waist. They fit so damn well together, like two puzzle pieces that were always meant to find their way back together.

He kicked the door closed and twisted the lock before walking over to his childhood mattress and easing her down so she was lying on her back, covering her body with his, pressing into her.

"Jace." She groaned his name and it rippled into him, guiding him somewhere only she could take him. Away from everything that came before this moment.

He tugged his lips from hers and worked kisses down her cheek, then neck. Jesus, every part of her was sweet.

When he reached the top of her chest, he gripped the hem of her top and pulled it over her head. Her pale pink bra called to him. And the way her nipples pushed against the thin fabric set his blood burning through his veins.

Fucking gorgeous.

He dipped his head and took one of those nipples between his teeth, sucking and running his tongue over the tip, the material a thin barrier between his mouth and her flesh.

She whimpered, her fingers fisting in his hair. He continued to play with her as he reached down, unfastening the button of her jeans and running down the zipper. When he slipped a hand inside both her jeans and panties, her sharp intake of air cut through the room.

Then he stroked her clit.

Another quiet cry from her, and his blood pumped faster.

He switched his mouth to her other breast, sucking and tugging, continuing to run circles over her clit with his thumb, listening to her changes in breath and learning what she liked.

This woman was a goddess, so fucking perfect that she deserved to be worshiped. Deserved for every inch of her body to be touched and kissed and adored.

He slipped the cup of her bra down, and this time took her bare nipple between his lips. She arched and cried out, her breaths now coming out in short pants.

"Jace…I can't hold on!"

Good. He wanted her to break. To fall off that cliff and trust him to catch her. "Then don't."

He thrust a finger inside her, and her entire body tensed. He moved back up her body and caught her lips just as she broke, swallowing her cries, fucking drowning in them.

Her walls pulsed around his finger, her soft hums and moans burning him.

His mouth was still on hers, his finger still inside her, when the shout of his name sounded. "Uncle Jace? Are you in here?"

Shit. Avery.

Elle gasped, and he slowly slipped his finger out of her before pressing one more kiss to her lips. He grinned at her as he whispered, "Got to go, Tink. But just so you know, that wasn't an accident or a mistake or a one-time thing."

Her eyes flared, pink tinging her cheeks. "Go," she whispered, shoving his chest.

He chuckled as he lifted off her.

Fuck, this was not a good time. He adjusted himself, hoping like hell that helped, before casting one more glance at Elle as she madly straightened her clothes.

That definitely wasn't a friend move…but he couldn't seem to care.

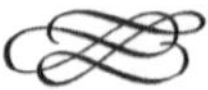

lle wiped down the counters, a small smile playing at her lips. Over the last few days, she'd seen a lot of Jace. He came into the café in the morning. He stopped in most lunchtimes. And after work, they'd either go to his place or hers to eat and talk and watch crappy movies.

It was exactly as it used to be. Comfort. Friendship. They hadn't kissed since that day in his old bedroom. In fact, her sexual frustration was reaching an all-time peak because she *wanted* to kiss him. She wanted to feel him press her to the mattress again, feel him *touch* her.

But it was *her* who'd put in the friendship boundary, and, other than the family dinner, he'd been really goddamn good at sticking to it.

Her cheeks flushed at the memory of how easy it was for him to bring her to climax in his old bedroom.

Argh. Stop it, Elle. You're friends right now. And that was your choice.

"Elle?"

Her head shot up at Molly's voice. She hadn't noticed her returning to the counter after seeing out the last customer.

"Everything okay?" Elle asked.

"Actually, I wanted to apologize."

"For what?"

"For hitting on Jace at the bar the other week."

Elle's fingers tightened around the cloth in her hand. "You don't need to—"

"I do. I should have seen what was right in front of me. You like him, and he likes you. You have this super strong connection, and I had no business going there."

"I didn't tell you how I felt."

"I know. But I still should have seen it." Molly lifted a shoulder. "You two are good together."

"We're just friends."

Molly laughed. "Nope. I am *not* falling for that again. He walks you in here every morning. He goes to lunch with you every day. Then he comes in here when you finish, and you do God knows what together after work. That's not just friendship. And don't even get me started on the way he looks at you."

"The way he looks at me?"

Molly gave her a knowing smirk. "Okay, my shift is finished. Do you want me to help you clean up?"

Today it was just her scheduled for cleanup while Molly finished at closing time. "No, it won't take me long. Go home. Relax."

Molly grabbed her bag. "Easier said than done with the customers we've had today."

She wasn't wrong. They'd had some very demanding customers in the café, mostly tourists whose coffees had been too hot or too cold or not made right. One man complained his sandwich didn't have enough mustard and demanded a refund, but of course, he'd only told them after he'd eaten three quarters of the thing. And then there was the woman who'd wanted a whole new croissant after eating half of her first one, claiming it was too hard.

"You handled them well," Elle said with a grin.

"But I was one step away from throwing in some curses and kicking everyone out." She pushed the door open. "I'll see you tomorrow."

"See you tomorrow, Molly."

Once the counters were clean, Elle mopped the floors. She was just putting the mop away in the small storage closet when the bell on the door rang. She smiled as she stepped back into the café, expecting to see Jace.

The smile dropped. Not Jace. Not even close.

She slipped behind the counter, nerves trickling down her spine at the sight of the bald man with the snake tattoo on the side of his head.

What was he doing here? Was he here to see *her*?

Discreetly, she slipped her phone from her pocket, hiding it below the counter. "Hi. We're closed, sorry."

He scanned her face as he moved toward her, his steps slow, almost predatory.

She tapped a few keys on her cell—only glancing down for a second to make sure she hit Jace's number—silenced her side of the call and put it on speaker before looking up again.

He stopped opposite her. "I was in the mountains and heard people talking about the café."

She frowned. He had a Boston accent mixed with…something else? Italian?

One side of his mouth lifted. "Any chance you could make me something? A sandwich, maybe?"

There was something about his voice that made nerves trickle into her belly. Not his words, because he wasn't saying anything wrong or bad. He just made her feel…uneasy. Or maybe it was the way he was looking at her. So closely that she wanted to turn. Run. Get away. "I'm sorry. I've packed everything up."

He pressed his hands to the counter. Hands that had more snake tattoos running down his fingers. "Come on, honey. One sandwich. It doesn't look like there's anyone else here for you to serve?"

Was that his not-so-subtle way of highlighting that they were alone?

She slipped her phone onto the shelf beneath the counter and inched back a step. "Everything's been put away and cleaned. But if you come back tomorrow, I'll make you that sandwich."

He leaned over the counter, a smile on his face that almost looked predatory. "Darlin', if I wanted a sandwich tomorrow, I would have come in tomorrow."

"I'd like you to leave."

He pulled back as if surprised by her words. "But I only just got here."

"*Now.*"

* * *

JACE STEPPED OFF THE SKYWALK. The last person had just left the walk, and he was running late to meet Elle at the café before her finish time. It wasn't an official thing, just something he'd started doing because he couldn't get enough of her. He wanted to be with her every second he could. They'd slipped into this easy routine lately, and he fucking loved it.

The only problem was, he was having a damn hard time keeping his hands off her. Every night, they'd sit together at her place or his, watch some shitty movie, and all he wanted to do was touch her. Kiss her. And yeah, sometimes he'd slip an arm around her shoulders, but so far that was it. He didn't want to cross that line again. He wanted *her* to initiate it. He wanted to know that she wanted him, *needed him*, as much as he needed her.

He was walking toward the café when his phone rang. His lips stretched into a smile when he saw Elle's name on the screen.

Looked like she was thinking about him too.

He pressed the phone to his ear. "I know I'm late. Almost there."

A muffled noise sounded, then a voice. A *man's* voice.

"I was in the mountains and heard people talking about the café."

Jace stopped. Who the fuck was that?

He glanced at his cell again to make sure it was Elle's name he'd seen on the screen, before putting it back to his ear.

"Any chance you could make me something?"

Then he heard her voice. "I'm sorry. I've packed everything up."

She sounded shaky…scared…and it made dread twist in his gut.

Fuck.

Jace dropped the phone to his side and started running. Pumping his arms and his legs, letting the wind slap him in the face. He'd always thought the café was close to the skywalk, but right now, it felt too damn far.

He forced his body to move faster, ignoring the branches slapping his arms and the loose dirt sinking under his feet. When he hit the deck of the café, his steps were loud, but he didn't care. He pushed inside, and the air hissed from his teeth at what he saw.

Elle, looking so uneasy her face was white, inching back as the asshole started to round the counter.

The guy glanced up at him, eyes narrowing.

Jace was across the room in a second.

"What the fuck—"

The asshole's words were cut off when Jace grabbed him by the shirt and threw him against the wall. "Who are you?"

"Get your fucking hands off me!"

"Like hell I will. This is the second time you've scared my woman, and I want to know what the fuck you're doing hanging around her. *Who are you?*"

The slow smile that spread across the guy's face had fury burning in Jace's blood. "I'm no one. Just a guy visiting your small town, looking for a sandwich."

Yeah right. "She told you she was closed, so what the fuck are you still doing here? Or better question, why are you stepping behind the counter?"

He lifted his hands. "I'm not here for trouble, bro. I'm just hungry."

"*Bullshit.*" His muscles ached to swing. Throw a fist into the asshole's face. Maybe Elle saw it, because her soft voice sounded.

"Jace."

He looked at Elle to see her pleading gaze. She didn't want to see a fight, and he didn't want to start one with her so close.

"Come on, *Jace*," the guy drawled. "I didn't do anything. Maybe you should just let me leave."

Like hell he would. "Maybe. Or maybe I should call the authorities and tell them that the asshole driving the stolen car is here."

The guy lifted a brow, grinning. "You looked into me?"

"No. The sheriff of this town looked into you, and I don't think he'll be letting you go in a hurry."

The smile dropped from his face. Then he swung.

Jace dodged the punch easily, immediately grabbing his wrist and twisting his arm behind his back. The guy was quick, jabbing an elbow into Jace's gut. He only eased his hold for a second, but it was enough for the guy to twist out of Jace's grip and attempt a kick at Jace's shin. He sidestepped the kick and was about to move forward and pin the jerk again when the guy suddenly pulled a pistol.

Elle gasped, and Jace instinctively stepped in front of her, blocking her with his body.

"Put the goddamn gun down," Jace growled, his muscles itching to attack, but no way was he moving away from Elle.

"Why would I do that?"

"Because I was stalling. I've *already* called the sheriff. He's on his way." It was a lie, but this asshole didn't know that.

"All I wanted," the guy said slowly, breaths whooshing from his chest, "was a goddamn sandwich."

"And yet you brought a gun," Jace seethed. "Go. Leave before the sheriff arrives and you do something that gets you serious time."

He scowled, inching backward toward the door, keeping the gun trained on them until he stepped outside.

Even after he disappeared, neither Jace nor Elle moved. They just stood there, almost expecting him to return. Thirty long seconds passed before Jace crossed the space to the door and flipped the lock. Then he called his brother.

Eastern answered on the second ring. "Jace. Everything okay?"

"You know that asshole with the stolen car? He came to the café while Elle was alone. Scared her. He and I threw a few punches, then he pulled a pistol on me."

"Fuck. Be there in ten."

Even though his brother couldn't see him, Jace nodded before hanging up and turning to look at Elle. Her eyes were wide, her complexion still pale.

"Do you think he's gone?" she asked quietly.

"I don't know." He closed the space between them and cupped her cheeks. "Are you okay?"

"I'm fine." The words came too quickly. "Are you?"

"No. I'm pissed. The guy scared you. Pulled a fucking gun while you were in the room."

"I'm okay though." She touched his chest before her gaze shifted to the door again. "I don't understand what he was doing here or what he wanted."

"He didn't say anything before I got here?"

"No. He just kept saying he wanted a sandwich, and on about

the third time of me asking him to leave, he started rounding the counter."

A visible shudder rolled through her body, and Jace immediately wrapped her in his arms. "Thank you for calling me."

He had no idea who the guy was or what he'd wanted, but his intentions hadn't been friendly.

CHAPTER 18

*E*lle watched the trees fly past the car window. Jace was behind the wheel, and her car was still at the visitors center. He'd asked if he could bring her home and stay with her at her place. Well, *told* more than asked. He was still angry, while she was somewhere between confused and shaken.

Who *was* that guy? Had he actually been after her in the street the other day, and Cody had just opened the door at the right time? After today, her gut said yes.

But that didn't make sense. She was nobody. And as far as she knew, she'd never pissed anyone off. At least not to the extent that someone like *him* would want to harm her. She didn't know the guy. Hell, she didn't even know anyone *like* him...someone dark and dangerous.

Jace pulled into the parking lot in front of her building. The entire walk to the door, he kept his arm wrapped tightly around her waist, his gaze continuing to move, scanning the trees and the cars like he was expecting company.

Maybe she was in shock, because she didn't feel fear right now. But then, Jace tended to have that effect on her. The part she'd hated the most had been the danger *he'd* been in. He'd stood in front of a gun for her. Shielded her.

What if the guy had pulled the trigger?

Her blood ran cold, and she forced that thought to the back of her mind as they rode the elevator up to her apartment. It was only once they were inside that she took her first deep breath.

Home. Her little sanctuary.

She crossed to the kitchen, moving on autopilot as she opened the fridge. "Leftover pizza okay? I can heat it up."

When he didn't answer, she was about to turn when strong arms wrapped around her waist, making her gasp.

"Are you really okay?" he whispered, his breath brushing her neck.

He'd asked her that a few times. Once before Eastern got to the café, once during his interview, and again after. And each time, she'd answered the same. That she was fine.

This time, she just couldn't give the same lie.

"You stepped in front of a gun to protect me," she whispered.

His lips lowered to the crook of her neck. "And I'd do it a hundred times over."

She turned in his arms, and he lifted his head. "I didn't like that. I don't like you being in danger."

"I will *always* protect you."

"I was scared for you."

"Don't be." He slipped a lock of hair from her face. "If it's a choice between saving you or me, I'll always choose you."

Her heart twisted. "I need you to be okay."

He lowered his temple to hers. "I will be. As long as you're safe."

She scrunched her eyes against the building tears. "It's getting harder and harder to fight this thing between us." So hard that some days she wanted to lose herself in him and say to hell with the risks to her heart.

"Then stop fighting."

His whispered words slipped into her blood, causing it to rush through her veins. She looked up at him, and all she saw was the best friend she'd grown up with. The first man she'd ever loved. The *only* man she'd ever loved.

"Okay." The word fell into the room like a small bomb detonating at their feet.

His brows flickered. "Okay?"

"I'll stop fighting." Slowly, so slowly that she had time to see a million emotions pass over his face, she brought his head down.

At first his mouth was gentle on hers, almost hesitant. Then she ran her tongue over the seal of his lips. The growl from his throat was so loud that she felt it everywhere. In her mouth. On her skin. In her head.

He lifted her to the small kitchen island and stepped between her thighs, his kiss deepening, his hands exploring her waist as he tangled his tongue with hers.

Every kiss with this man had been hot and important and intense. But this felt different, almost desperate. Like everything they'd both denied themselves for so long was exploding in this moment.

She grabbed at his shirt and tugged it over his head. The second it was gone, he did the same to her, but he didn't stop there. He reached behind her and unclipped her bra. It fell to the floor with a soft thud, then he was cupping her, an entire breast held in the palm of his big hand.

She groaned, pushing against him.

"So fucking beautiful," he said quietly before his lips left hers and his mouth found her nipple.

She cried out and grabbed his shoulders, trying to hang on to something, anything, as he flicked her hard peak with his tongue.

Her head flew back, her lower belly throbbing with desire. It was torture and bliss rolled into one. It was a thousand sensations, all of which she had no idea what to do with.

He continued to hold and massage her other breast, his thumb finding her nipple, rolling it.

"Bedroom," Elle gasped. "Now!"

The word had barely left her lips when he lifted her like she weighed nothing, his mouth rising to hers, nipping her lips as he crossed her small apartment to her bedroom.

Gently, he laid her on the bed, propping himself above her as he undid the button of her pants before dealing with the zipper. He moved down the mattress, dragging her pants with him. Instead of returning to her when he was done, he kissed her ankle, then her calf.

Slowly, he made his way up her bare legs, every swipe of his lips, every touch, making her core throb.

His hot breath brushed over her flesh as he whispered, "I've dreamed about these sweet thighs."

Her heart thumped. She'd always thought her thighs were too big. Too jiggly. But when he kissed them reverently, they suddenly felt like the most beautiful part of her.

When he reached her panties, she couldn't breathe. It was like the air physically couldn't make it into her lungs.

He slipped them down her thighs until she was completely bare beneath him. A part of her, the self-conscious part, wanted to cover up. Shield herself from him. But before she could move a muscle, he was between her legs and running his tongue over her clit.

She cried out, her back arching as a fire built deep inside her. He did it again and again, and she fisted the sheets beside her. She screamed his name as he sucked her clit; as his fingers moved to her entrance. When he pushed inside, her entire body tried to lift off the bed, but he held her in place easily with a single arm.

"Jace!" This time his name was somewhere between a moan and a desperate plea. "Please, I need you."

Finally, his mouth lifted, and he kissed up to her hip bone and across her stomach. He sucked her nipple as he passed. And the entire time, his fingers remained inside her, moving in and out in a rhythmic motion.

She was panting and on fire and throbbing all at once.

She grabbed at his head and dragged his mouth to hers before whispering, "Now."

* * *

THAT ONE WORD hit him like a grenade.

Fuck, she gutted him. He continued to pump his fingers inside her, wanting her right on the edge, just like him.

Her nails raked down his chest, only stopping when she reached the waistband of his jeans. She popped the button, then undid the zipper. It wasn't until she'd slipped her hand inside his briefs that he froze. His entire fucking world stilled. Her fingers grasped his cock, and he couldn't move. She kissed and nipped at his lips, but all he could do was breathe. Close his eyes and tell himself, *plead* with himself, to hold it together for her.

"Mm, I like touching you," she whispered, her breath brushing his lips with her quiet words as she began to pump him, moving her hand from base to tip and back again.

He was fucking sweating, his muscles so tight they might snap.

Her soft kisses moved over his cheek before she nipped the lobe of his ear.

He growled and grabbed her wrist. "I need you to stop, Tink."

She pouted, and it was so fucking cute he almost let her go. "You got to touch *me*," she complained.

He gently rolled her nipple with his thumb. "Because I can't seem to stop myself." He lowered his head, sucking on one perfect breast, loving her cry, before he rose and pushed down his jeans and briefs. He lifted his jeans back up to find the condom in his wallet.

She gasped quietly, and his gaze shot back to her to see her staring at his hip bone.

"What's that?" she whispered.

He didn't need to lower his gaze to know what she was looking at. "Your words. They kept me sane while I was away."

Her brows flickered. "It's my handwriting too. I don't understand."

"I read your letter every day, Elle." He tore open the foil and covered himself before climbing back over her and cupping her cheek. "I read it so many times the paper got ratty and fragile, and I knew I wouldn't have it much longer. But I *needed* it, because every time I read it, I saw you. I heard your voice. And I didn't know when I'd have that in real life again."

Tears gathered in her eyes. "I thought you forgot about the letter."

"Nothing about you, or the effect you've had on me, could ever be forgotten."

A tear slid down her face. "It's still true. You *are* too loved to lose."

"You were with me every day, even though you didn't know it." He lowered his head, kissing the tear. Then his mouth moved over to her lips. It was a slow kiss this time. Gentle. He slipped his tongue between her lips, tangling it with hers before positioning himself at her entrance, only to pause and look at her.

"Tell me you're mine, Tink. Tell me this isn't a one-time thing."

"I've always been yours, Jace. Always."

The sigh hissed from him, and he lowered his head to kiss her again as he sank inside her.

She groaned, her back bowing off the bed. Even when he was seated deep inside her, he was unable to move.

Fuck, she was tight.

She wrapped her legs around him and tugged him closer. That was all it took to pull him out of his stillness. He lifted his hips and thrust back into her. She cried out, the sound so sweet, it punched him in the chest.

He did it again.

Her fingers curled into his hair, tugging at the roots. Her exhale rained over his face, so damn soft.

He thrust again and again, and it was fucking ecstasy. It was everything he'd always known it would be and more. *She* was everything he'd known she would be.

He cupped her breast, palming her and stroking her nipple as he lowered his head and sucked her neck. He wanted all of her. Every sound. Every movement. Every inch of flesh. He wanted every part of her to belong to him.

He reached between them and swiped her clit. She groaned, and her fingers scraped down his chest, almost breaking skin. So damn responsive. He did it again, this time rolling his thumb over her clit in circles.

"Jace…I can't…I'm…"

He bit her earlobe before whispering, "Fall for me, Tink."

The second the words were out of his mouth, she screamed and arched, her entire body convulsing as she broke. He kept pumping, wanting to stretch out this moment. To keep her there just that bit longer.

But at the feel of her walls pulsing around his cock, he couldn't hold on. Two more thrusts and he lost himself. The shatter hit him so fucking hard, his world narrowed to just her and this moment.

He stayed inside her until he had nothing left. Until they were just a mess of heavy breaths and tangled limbs. Then he lowered his head to the nook of her neck and just breathed her in.

After a few beats of silence, her fingers began a slow trail up his back to his hair, and when he finally had the strength to look at her, she gutted him. The gray of her eyes. The way she pierced his soul with a single look.

The corners of her lips twitched. "Why the heck did we wait so long to do *that?*"

He laughed. God, this woman was something else.

He dropped to her side, tugging her against him. "I have no damn clue, Tink. But we're not waiting that long again." No way in hell.

You're too loved to lose.

Elle traced the inked words with her eyes. It was *her* handwriting. *Her* words. And Jace had tattooed them to *his* body.

That was permanent...which was nuts, right? That the man had permanently inked her words to his flesh because the letter had become ratty and old?

His heart beat into her ear as she lay sprawled over his chest, his breathing even and deep while he slept. She'd woken a while ago but hadn't been able to get back to sleep. She also hadn't been able to get up, not while cocooned in his arms.

She'd had *sex* with Jace. A year ago, she would have laughed in someone's face if they told her this is where she'd be right now. She'd loved him for so long, but she'd always told herself that he would never be hers, not in the way she wanted him to be. So she'd forced herself to move on.

But this tattoo, like the candy, was another sign that he hadn't forgotten her. He'd carried her with him, even when he'd cut off contact.

Unable to keep her hand to herself any longer, she traced the letters with a finger. She could still remember writing those words. The tears that had filled her eyes. The heartache that had seized her lungs. Because she'd been on the precipice of losing her best friend. Something inside her had known that once he was gone, nothing would ever be the same.

When the hand on her hip smoothed up her back, her gaze shot up to see Jace's blue stare boring into her, his lopsided grin hitting her in the chest.

"Morning, Tink."

God, even the rasp of his voice made the fine hairs on her arms stand on end. "Hey."

"Did you sleep well?"

"Honestly? No."

The smile dropped. "Why not?"

She lifted a shoulder. "Because I'd wake up, feel you around me, remember what we did, and then I had to remind myself I wasn't dreaming. That we've finally found our way to each other."

If possible, his frown deepened. "I'm sorry it took me so long to get here."

"I'm the one who's been fighting it since you got back." She looked at his tattoo, once again running her finger over the letters. "Can I ask you something?"

"Anything."

"Why did you lose contact with me? Why did you stop replying to my messages and visiting me when you were back in town?"

His intake of breath was loud, and when she looked up, there was pain woven through the depths of his eyes. "There were a few reasons. I told myself I had to let you go, otherwise I'd never give myself fully to the Air Force. And so that you could find someone better. Find a better man, even while I was trying to become a better man *for* you." His fingers tightened on her waist. "But really, I think it just became too hard to have you in my life while not having you the way I wanted. So I tried to let you go."

"Yet here you are."

"Yet here I am." His hand began to caress her back again, moving from her hip bone right up to between her shoulder blades. "I think we both know we were always going to find our way back to each other."

She snorted. "*You* may have known. I certainly didn't. I always felt...*less than* around you."

His brows knitted together. "What are you talking about?"

"Jace...you were the best-looking guy in our class. Heck, maybe even the whole school. And you were funny and smart, and you had these dimples that made people stop and stare. Whereas I...I was so ordinary."

For a moment, he was silent. Then he shook his head. "It's wild to me that you don't see it."

"See what?"

"How beautiful you are, inside and out. How beautiful you've always been."

Her pulse sped up, but she shook her head. "People reminded me every day that you were out of my league. They didn't even know why you were friends with me."

At the flash of anger on his face, she almost wanted to take the words back.

"I didn't know," he growled. "If I had, I would have kicked their asses."

Exactly why she'd never told him what anyone had said. "We should get up. We both have work."

He groaned and rolled them over until he caged her body to the bed. She laughed as he nuzzled her neck.

"I don't wanna get up," he complained, his hands roaming her body. "I want to stay in bed with you."

She gasped and grabbed his wrist when he cupped her breast.

"Jace. I have to get to the café, and you have a rappelling session this morning."

Another groan as he continued to palm her.

She moaned and squirmed. "Jace…" His cell rang, and she grabbed his chin, nudging his head up. "Another sign to get up. Answer the call."

"They'll leave a message."

"Go." He tried to lower his head again, but she tugged his face back up. "Jace."

"Mm, even your authoritative voice is sexy as hell." One more kiss, and he finally rolled over to grab his phone from the side table. A crease formed between his brows before he answered it. "Eastern. You got anything?"

At the narrowing of Jace's eyes, Elle's belly clenched. She sat up, pulling the sheets with her. Was this about the guy who'd pulled a gun on them at the café yesterday? Had Eastern found out who he was?

Jace nodded. "Got it. Thanks for looking into it. I'll make sure she's not alone in the café again."

Another twist of her belly.

Jace hung up but didn't immediately turn to her.

She touched his shoulder. "What is it? Did Eastern find something?"

"The stolen car was dumped last night. They looked it over and found prints from a guy by the name of Darcy Boyd."

"Who?"

"He's a criminal who's done time in prison for battery and assault."

Her skin chilled. "Okay. But why would he be after *me*?"

"I don't know, Tink. Maybe he just saw you and took an interest. We'll find out. But until we do, you stay with at least one other person at all times. No closing the café on your own. No solo walks."

She sucked in a sharp breath. She didn't like it. But she also didn't like how vulnerable she'd felt yesterday alone at work. "I'll have to work with Tilly and Molly to adjust the schedule…but okay."

* * *

JACE STEPPED out of the café onto the deck. He hated leaving Elle, knowing some asshole thug was hanging around town.

Why? What the hell did he want? Was it just that he'd seen her and randomly decided to harass her?

His hands fisted as he headed toward the skywalk. He'd asked Kayden to set up his rappelling gear so it was ready to go for this morning's session. Kayden would run the session with him, because there needed to be two supervisors at all times and his brother was a former PJ in the Air Force, so he knew what he was doing when it came to rappelling. He'd completed some of the most dangerous rescues in the deadliest terrains.

Kayden met him halfway to the walk. "Hey."

Jace dipped his head. "Hey. All ready to go?"

"Yeah, everything's set up." Kayden studied him. "You and Elle okay after yesterday?"

He'd texted Kayden about last night. Having as many eyes as possible looking out for Elle wasn't a bad thing. "Not really. I need to know what the asshole wants and whether he intends to stick around Misty Peak and harass her more or get out of town."

"I'm sorry I wasn't around to help. I can't believe the son of a bitch pulled a gun on you."

Jace didn't care so much about the gun being pulled on *him*, more that Elle had been confronted with a firearm. "Eastern will get him."

As they neared the skywalk, he saw a group of five guys standing around, no doubt their rappelling group. He frowned when he realized he recognized them as guys he'd gone to high school with. A couple had been in his grade, while two others were a year ahead of him.

When the last guy turned, Jace nearly stopped in his tracks.

Casper White. The guy who'd been an asshole to everyone around him—particularly Elle. The night of his last party before leaving for basic training popped into his mind. Of Casper touching her, refusing to leave her alone. He ground his back teeth together. He still regretted not nailing the guy that night.

Casper grinned at him. "Jace Walker. Good to see you, man!"

Jace stopped in front of him. "I thought you left."

"I did. Moved to the Big Apple. I'm home between jobs though. Heard about the new skywalk and the rappelling sessions and thought I'd give it a go."

Jace would have preferred he hadn't.

Kayden held out a hand. "Kayden Walker."

"Older brother, right?" Casper asked, shaking his hand.

The men went around the group, introducing themselves. They made jokes here and there about shoving each other off the skywalk. Jace didn't so much as crack a smile. But yeah, he could see why Casper was friends with these guys. It sounded like none of them had changed since high school.

"Safety's important today," Jace said, a bit too much force behind his words. "So if we tell you to do something, we need you to listen."

He started going through the safety aspects of the session, but when he saw Casper muttering something to the guy beside him, he stopped. "You got something to say, White?"

"Nope." A cocky grin spread across his face. "Nothing at all, Walker."

"Good. Then shut up and listen."

The grin dropped.

He was probably being a dick to the guy, but he couldn't bring himself to care. He felt Kayden's questioning eyes on him, but he ignored his brother while he finished the safety instructions.

Then the group put on their harnesses before stepping onto the skywalk.

"You okay?" Kayden asked quietly beside him as they led the group. "Because if you're not, we can cancel this session."

"I'm fine. I just hate that guy."

Kayden shot a quick glance over his shoulder. "The blond with the smug smile?"

"Yeah, him. He was an asshole to Elle in high school." He was an asshole to a lot of people, but he specifically recalled the guy being a dick to her.

"I'll set him up."

Probably a good idea.

Kayden fell back to talk to some of the guys as they headed toward the rappelling location. It was in the center of the skywalk beside a huge tree. It was the only part of the skywalk where the railing had a gate that opened against the tree they'd be rappelling down.

They were almost there when Casper fell into step beside him.

"So, you still good friends with Elle Marshal?" he asked.

Jace's hands fisted. "We're dating."

"No fucking way." Casper shook his head. "Not that I'm surprised. I've been back a few times over the years, and she's turned into a babe. Nothing like what she looked like in high school."

Jace swung around and stopped, blocking the guy from moving forward, and Casper almost walked into his chest. "You don't talk about her like that."

Casper's brows shot up. "It was a compliment. Am I wrong?" Then he had the fucking balls to laugh. "I mean, *you* saw her in high school. It's why you didn't date her back then, right?"

It took a lot of self-restraint to not hit the guy, and the *only* reason Jace stopped himself was because they were so far off the ground. Instead, he inched closer. "If I *ever* hear you talk about her being anything but beautiful again, I will hit you so hard you won't get back up. Got it?"

Casper's mouth opened and closed before a hint of anger entered his eyes. "I can say whatever the hell I want. But I'm not surprised that Jace fucking Walker still thinks he can dictate what others can and can't do."

Jace inched another step forward, but suddenly Kayden was there, stepping between them, facing Casper. "It's time for you to go, man."

Casper glanced up, red shading his cheeks. "What? No! I've paid for this. I'm doing my fucking session. *He* can go."

"You can either leave by yourself," Kayden said firmly, "or I can make you. Your choice."

The red darkened, the anger in his eyes swirling. "Fuck you!" He looked at Jace. "Fuck *both* of you." Then he stormed off down the skywalk, heading back the way they'd come.

CHAPTER 20

"So this place offers Pilates and yoga?" Elle asked as she climbed out of the car and looked down the street toward the studio.

Sadie nodded and rounded the car. "Yeah, reformer Pilates and mat yoga. I booked us into a Pilates class today. I hope that's okay."

"I haven't done reformer Pilates before."

"Me neither. That's why I thought it would be fun."

Elle's lips twitched because although she'd never done a class, she'd heard it could be hard. "It's a beginner's class, right?"

"Um, I think so?"

Not reassuring at all.

Sadie bumped her hip. "Tell me what's going on with you and Jace."

She bit her bottom lip as they headed toward the studio. It had been a few days since that first night together, and even though they'd spent every night together since, she was still in a state of semi-disbelief.

"We slept together." The words dropped from her lips without thought.

Sadie stopped and turned. "You *slept* together?"

"Mm-hmm."

Her friend's mouth spread into a smile, then she smothered Elle in a huge bear hug. "That's amazing! You fit so well together."

Elle hugged her friend back. "Thank you. I'm just grateful we've finally made it here."

Sadie pulled back. "And here you'll stay."

Hopefully. The single word was a whisper in her head.

As they continued toward the studio, Sadie shot her a look. "I hope it's okay to ask…but I kind of overheard Eastern talking about some guy who came into your café and threatened you?"

"You did?"

"Are you mad?"

"No. Of course not. It's actually pretty strange. I saw this guy twice. The first time, he made me feel uneasy. The second time, at the café…I was scared. So I called Jace and put him on speaker. The next minute, Jace is in the café, and then they're throwing punches before the guy pulls a gun."

"*Jesus*."

"Yeah. I haven't seen him since though, and he dumped the stolen car he was using." Since then, Eastern and his team hadn't been able to locate him.

Sadie touched her arm. "I'm so sorry, Elle. Is there anything I can do?"

"You're already doing it by keeping me distracted with things like Pilates. Plus, I'm on strict instructions not to go anywhere alone, and I go stir-crazy if I spend too much time cooped up in my apartment by myself, so you being with me helps a lot."

Sadie linked her arm through Elle's. "Glad to be of service. And great that the guys are meeting us after so we can walk to Sugar and Spice."

"Yeah, I like that part too, considering I'll probably need the sugar hit."

They both laughed as they stopped in front of a small business. Through the glass, Elle could see a line of reformer machines to one side and mats to the other. The place had a Mediterranean feel to it, with beige concrete walls and lots of potted plants.

They stepped inside, and floral essential oils scented the air.

"Wow, this place is beautiful," Elle whispered. She felt like she was in a spa rather than a workout area.

Sadie leaned into her. "I heard the owner just got back from teaching at retreats in Bali."

There were five reformer machines, and the end two were already taken. Sadie and Elle moved to the two near the front, Elle taking the one by the window. She'd just slipped off her shoes when a door at the back opened and a beautiful woman with long hair pulled up into a ponytail stepped out. She wore yoga pants and a sports crop.

The woman's eyes pinged straight to her and Sadie, and she crossed the room. "Hi. I'm Callie Ward."

"Elle Marshal."

Sadie smiled. "Sadie Sandler."

Callie clapped her hands. "Well, welcome to my new studio. Have either of you done reformer Pilates before?"

"No," Sadie answered. "But we're super excited to learn."

"Great. We do bare feet or grip socks. We sell grip socks if you need some. Make sure you have no zippers on your clothes, then take a seat at one of the reformers. This class isn't easy, but I promise you'll feel great after."

Not easy? Said by a woman who had an eight-pack? That did *not* fill Elle with confidence.

When the door opened and another client stepped in, Callie turned toward her.

Elle glanced at the woman and frowned. She'd seen her before. She was pretty sure she'd come into the café after doing a tour with Jace.

Callie and the lady spoke for a few seconds before the woman nodded. The woman's gaze landed on Elle for a moment, a strange look coming over her face. She gave her a tight smile and went to the last remaining machine.

Elle was still frowning when Callie stepped in front of the class, introduced herself, and got them started.

The second the warmup was over, Elle couldn't think about anything but getting through the exercises without dying. Literally dying. Her butt hurt. Her thighs hurt. And when they started the ab exercises, she began to wonder what the heck she'd signed herself up for.

* * *

"Uncle Jace?"

Jace glanced down at his niece. She held one of his hands and one of Eastern's as they walked toward the Pilates studio to pick up Elle and Sadie before they headed to Sugar and Spice.

"Yeah, Ave?"

"Now that you're dating Elle, will you have babies?"

Who the hell told Avery he was dating Elle? The kid had already admitted to wanting cousins. He looked at Eastern, who was clearly holding back a laugh.

"Not just yet," he said, looking back to his niece. "People often like to date for a while before having kids."

Avery frowned. "Okay. So in a couple months?"

He laughed. Who was this young lady, and what had they done with his baby niece?

Immediately, the thought made guilt fill his chest that he hadn't spent nearly enough time with her over the last eight years. He'd been in active service her entire life and had barely made it back, but the few times he had, the kid showered him in love.

He tightened his hold on her hand. "Maybe not in a few months, but I would love to give you cousins one day."

She beamed at him as they stopped in front of the studio. He scanned the interior through the glass. "This place looks nice."

"Do you know who opened it?" Eastern asked.

Jace shook his head. "Should I?" Then his gaze caught on a woman near the front who looked oddly familiar. "Where have I seen her before?"

"Lock's ex."

What had her name been? Callie? He'd seen her with his brother when both he and Lock had been home at the same time. From memory, she'd lived here with her father, and Lock had met her on one of his trips home. "They didn't date for long, did they?"

"No. And I don't know why they broke up. Lock wouldn't talk about it. Maybe long distance got too hard. She only saw him a few times a year when he came home or she went up to him. But after they broke up, she left town."

Jace's brows flickered. So there was a story there. "Now she's back."

"Now she's back."

Another woman inside caught his attention. He recognized her from a skywalk tour a couple weeks ago…the woman Ali had encouraged him to talk to. What was her name? Stephanie?

For a few days, he'd wondered if she was Dean's sister from Charlotte, but Eastern had pulled up the woman's driver's license and it wasn't her.

The door opened, and Elle and Sadie stepped out, both with flushed cheeks. Sadie hugged Avery and kissed Eastern, while Elle fell into his arms. He just caught her.

"Hey. You okay?"

She shook her head. "No. I'm dying. Or maybe I'm already dead. That class killed me. Do I still have legs? I can't feel them."

He chuckled. "I can carry you to Sugar and Spice if you want?"

"As tempting as that sounds, it might be less embarrassing to struggle my way down the street."

He wouldn't find it embarrassing at all. Still, he slipped an arm around her waist and she leaned into him, allowing him to shoulder a lot of her weight.

"So the class was a good one?" Eastern asked as they started toward Sugar and Spice.

Sadie nodded. "Yeah. It was hard, but I loved the burn."

Elle groaned.

"This is reminding me of the time I dared you to do a workout with me in high school," Jace said with a grin.

"Oh my God, I remember that because the pain is ingrained in my soul." She looked over at Sadie, Eastern and Avery. "I called it the circuit of hell. It involved a million squats, ten million sit-ups, and don't even get me started on the pull-ups he made me attempt. I say attempt, because I couldn't do a single one independently."

Jace remembered that day well because he got to put his hands on her lush hips and assist with those pull-ups.

Avery studied him. "Yeah, Uncle Jace *is* pretty strong. But Daddy says he's stronger."

Jace reached out and punched his brother in the shoulder. "He could only dream of being the gladiator that I am."

Avery frowned. "What's a gladiator?"

"You're looking at him, sweetheart."

Elle laughed and shook her head. "You're already making me feel better after that torture session. Thanks."

They were just nearing Sugar and Spice when three guys rounded the corner across the street. They were laughing and shoving one another's shoulders.

Jace's jaw locked. They were three of the guys who'd booked that rappelling session, and one of them was Casper White.

"Casper," Elle said quietly. "I heard he was back in town for a bit."

He looked down at Elle. "When was the last time you saw him?"

"Maybe six months ago? He returns a few times a year, and he always makes crude, stupid comments. I heard he got let go at work though, so this stay will probably be longer."

The muscles in Jace's arms tightened. "What kind of comments does he make?"

She opened her mouth, only to pause before shaking her head. "Nothing. He's just an ass. It's strange how he hasn't changed at all since high school. Most people experience *some* growth."

"I'm not surprised."

Casper was just about to climb into the back of a blue Corolla when he saw them. He frowned, clearly taking in the way Jace held Elle close. A stupid half grin spread on his face, and even though he was still a distance away, Jace didn't miss his eye roll.

What the fuck was his deal?

Jace was tempted to go over and ask him just that, but the guys climbed into the car and drove away.

They reached the doors of the bakery, and the women went inside with Avery first. Jace was about to step in when Eastern touched his shoulder. "What was that?"

Of *course* his older brother noticed. Not only was he a former Navy SEAL, he was the town sheriff; he saw everything. "Just some asshole from high school who never grew up. It's nothing."

And it had better stay nothing.

CHAPTER 21

Elle threw back her head and laughed at Jace's impersonation of Jimmy Fallon. They stood at a table in Meridian, with Tilly and Kayden. Cody and Harper were working the bar, but they came over whenever they got a chance.

Jace, of course, was the life of the party.

She playfully thumped his shoulder. "Stop, I'm laughing so much my stomach hurts."

His arm slid around her waist. "Well, my darling, I'll just have to kiss it better."

She shook her head. It was nice to see him so relaxed after the Boyd stuff. He'd been on edge for the last week. When he lowered his head and kissed her cheek, she all but melted into him.

"You two are so good together," Tilly said softly.

Kayden lifted his beer to his lips. "Yeah, just lay off the PDA."

This time, it was Tilly who shoved Kayden's shoulder. "Don't listen to him. Kiss. Cuddle. Do everything." She sipped her own cocktail. "Kayden said you were friends growing up?"

"Best friends," Jace confirmed, his thumb grazing her side. "And we still are."

Elle's belly did a little somersault. She'd been fighting against those words for so long, but she didn't need to fight anymore.

As the guys started talking about the things that needed fixing at Jace's house, Elle's gaze roamed the bar. It was busy, but that wasn't a surprise, it was Saturday night.

She had been the one who'd pushed to go out. Jace hadn't wanted her to go anywhere until they found Boyd or had confirmation he'd left town. Hell, he didn't even want her going to work, but she'd started going stir-crazy staying home every night. There was only so much of the walls of her apartment she could take.

He'd agreed to go out on the condition that it was at Cody's bar and they invited another of his brothers. It felt like overkill to her, having two former special operations brothers here, in addition to Jace, but at the same time, she loved that he got to spend more time with his family. He'd missed them. He hadn't said it out loud, but she could tell by the way his energy changed when he was around them. It became lighter, and he smiled more, and God, she loved that smile.

"Hey." She glanced up at Tilly's voice. "Do you want to go get another drink with me?"

"I wouldn't say no to another strawberry daiquiri." Apparently, they were a new addition to the menu, and she hoped they remained. She was a sucker for a good daiquiri.

She went to step away, but Jace grabbed her arm. "Where are you going?"

"To get another drink. Do you want one?"

He shook his head. Not a surprise; he'd been nursing his one beer all night. His gaze moved around the bar like he was searching for danger.

She touched his chest. "It's fine. We're just going to the bar, and Cody's there."

He tugged her toward him and hovered his lips over hers. "Come straight back." Then he pressed another kiss to her lips, and even though it was probably the tenth kiss since stepping into the bar, she wasn't sick of them. She didn't think she *could* get sick of them.

The second his hand dropped, she wanted to snatch it back. To pull him to her again. Instead, she exerted a little thing called self-control and headed toward the bar with Tilly.

Tilly leaned her head into Elle's. "You two are so perfect for each other."

"Thank you. You and Kayden are pretty great too."

Red flushed the woman's cheeks. "Thanks. It was a tough road getting to where we are, but I'm so glad we got here."

"I'm sorry it was hard."

She lifted a shoulder. "A lot of people disliked me when I first returned to Misty Peak, and Kayden definitely didn't trust me. But he does now, and the other locals are slowly coming around."

Elle nodded. She knew all about what Tilly's father had done, everyone in Misty Peak did, but unlike a lot of locals, Elle never blamed Tilly for that. She wasn't the one who'd done anything wrong. "I'm glad people are finding some sense."

They stopped at the bar, where Harper stepped in front of them and smiled. "Hey! More daiquiris?"

"You read my mind," Tilly gushed. "They are amazing. Please tell me they're a permanent addition to the menu."

Harper was just responding when a group of guys approached the bar, standing beside Elle. She was going to ignore them, but when the closest guy bumped her shoulder, she turned—only to groan.

Casper. Lord grant her patience.

His mouth spread into a wide smile. "Elle Marshal. You are looking *hot* tonight."

She scrunched her nose. She wore jeans with heels, and a tank top that showed maybe an inch of midriff. It wasn't the sexiest outfit she'd ever worn, but then, whenever this guy came home for a visit and bumped into her, he loved to make comments about her appearance.

"Thanks."

She turned back to the women, only to have Casper lean into her side. "Ya know, every time I come to town, you get hotter."

Was that supposed to be a compliment? "Please don't do that."

"What?"

She looked back at him. "You and I aren't friends. In fact, you've always been a huge, gigantic ass to me. So don't comment on the way I look, and don't stand so close to me."

"Can't a man change his mind when a woman becomes hot as fuck?"

Becomes? Argh. If there was a king of the pigs, it would be him.

"Everything okay, Elle?"

She turned back at Tilly's voice, just as Harper set the drinks onto the bar.

"Yeah, let's go back to the guys." She was not going to let this jackass affect her mood tonight.

She went to reach for her card, but Harper shook her head. "No money needed."

"Thanks."

Elle grabbed her drink and started to follow Tilly away, only to have her arm yanked back. She gasped as the drink spilled onto her top.

"What the hell is wrong with you?" she shouted.

"Me?" Casper asked. "You're the one acting like a bitch. What? You think you're too good for me now you're not packing the weight anymore?"

She moved on instinct, throwing her drink into his face. "Don't *ever* talk to me like that again. Or better yet, don't ever *talk* to me again."

Red tinged his cheeks and anger darkened his features. Then he reached out to grab her.

* * *

"You can't stop touching her," Kayden said quietly the second the women stepped away.

"I know. I feel like I've been fighting my feelings for her my entire life, and now that I've finally allowed myself to have her, I need to make up for lost time."

He watched as Elle and Tilly stopped at the bar.

"What changed?" Kayden asked.

Jace looked back to his brother, having to roll the question over in his head a couple times before he could figure out his answer. "A few things. I don't think I have anything to prove anymore, whereas when I was a kid, I felt like I had to do something big and important to be good enough for her."

Kayden frowned. "You were always good enough."

"I'm starting to believe that. And I guess, being back and around her all the time, my feelings have just become so intense I can't fight them anymore. And I've lost so many people in my life that I know tomorrow's not guaranteed. If I want something, I have to take it."

"You're not wrong." Kayden was about to sip his beer when he stopped, eyes narrowing on the bar. "Who the fuck is that leaning over Elle?"

Jace's gaze shot up—and anger punched through his veins. What the fuck? Some asshole was leaning into Elle's side, his head low, presumably to talk into her ear.

Jace was stepping around the table when Elle turned away from the bar and started walking back to him. She only got a few steps in before the asshole turned and grabbed her arm to swing her back around.

Casper.

He stormed across the floor, reaching them just as Elle threw her drink in his face. Jace would have been proud if the asshole's eyes didn't blacken with rage. He lunged to grab her, but Jace stepped between them, shoving him away.

"What the hell are you doing?" Jace shouted.

"What am *I* doing?" Casper sneered. "She threw a fucking drink in my face."

"I know. I also know she wouldn't have done it without a reason. So what did you do to make her throw it?"

"We were having a damn conversation, but that bitch decided to act like an animal—"

Jace grabbed him by the shirt and shoved him hard against the bar before shouting, "Did you not hear me last time? You *don't* fucking talk about her like that. Do you understand?"

Casper's eyes widened, his expression changing to one of fear.

When he didn't respond, Jace yanked him forward and shoved him again. "I said, *do you understand?*"

A small hand touched his shoulder before Elle's voice sounded. "Jace. It's okay."

It wasn't okay. Not even close.

Suddenly, Kayden was beside him. "Jace. Let him go."

"Not until he tells me he gets what I'm saying."

The expression on Casper's face shifted back to anger. "I understand," he seethed.

Jace didn't believe him for a second. Still, he released his shirt. "Get out."

Casper's eyes narrowed. "You don't have the right to—"

"But I do," Cody said, crossing his arms from the other side of the bar. "Leave."

Casper's jaw clicked, his gaze shifting from Jace to Cody. "You're shitting me, right? *I* get a drink thrown in my face and I'm the one who has to go?"

"Damn straight," Cody said. "Get out."

Casper scowled as he looked back at Jace. "You're gonna regret this, Walker."

Then he shoved past Jace and stormed out of the bar. Jace

waited until the door closed behind him before turning to Elle and studying her face. Her body. Searching for any sign that she wasn't all right. That he needed to go out there and beat the fucker.

He gripped her arms. "Are you okay?"

She nodded. "Yeah, he was just an ass, as per usual. I probably shouldn't have thrown my drink in his face. I'm—"

"*Don't*. Don't apologize for that sack of shit. What did he say to you?"

"He…" She paused and frowned. "It was nothing. Nothing important or that I care to repeat anyway."

"Elle—"

"Really, I'd rather not focus on him or any stupid thing he said."

Jace wanted to push. He wanted to know every word the asshole had said. Instead, he cupped her cheek. "You sure you're okay?"

"Yeah, but I think I'm ready to go home now."

Thank fuck. He was past ready to have this woman home, in bed and in his arms. "Your place or mine?"

"Anywhere there's you and a bed, I'm good."

His lips twitched. He was ninety percent sure she hadn't meant that to be sexual, but with her, he couldn't help but go there.

He turned to see Kayden and Tilly behind them, and Cody and Harper on the other side of the bar.

"Everything okay?" Kayden asked.

"Yeah, now the asshole has left."

Cody's gaze shifted to the door and back. "Who is he?"

"A jerk Elle and I went to high school with. He lives out of town now. Hopefully he heads back soon."

"Can I make you another daiquiri, Elle?" Harper asked.

She shook her head. "No, I think we'll head out. Sorry about the last one being wasted."

Harper snorted. "That was *not* wasted. Seeing that jerk get nailed in the face with a drink was the highlight of my week."

Tilly touched Elle's arm. "I'm sorry I just kind of walked away from you there."

Elle shook her head. "You didn't know he'd grab me. *I* didn't know he'd grab me. Besides, if he'd tried anything before Jace got to me, I still had the glass to throw at him."

Despite everything, Jace's lips twitched. He would have liked to watch that.

He slipped an arm around her waist. "I wouldn't have let it come to that. Come on, let's go home."

After a quick goodbye to Cody and Harper, Kayden and Tilly walked out with them. Both he and Kayden scanned the surroundings. It wasn't until he and Elle were in the car that she touched his thigh. "You asked me if I was okay, and I am...but are you?"

Was he? He was angry. Hell, angry didn't even cover it.

He covered her hand with his own. "Yeah, I'm okay, Tink. And I'll be even better once we get home and I get you all to myself."

CHAPTER 22

*E*lle set the mop back into the bucket. Done. The floors were clean. "That was a busy day."

Molly nodded from where she was still cleaning behind the counter. "No shit. Every time I thought we were gonna have a lull, more people came in."

"Word must have gotten around town about how good our coffee is."

Molly laughed. "*Your* coffee is good. I'm still perfecting mine. I think my strength lies more in my impeccable customer service."

"You're right, that is your strength." It was no secret that Molly was good with customers. It didn't matter if those customers were locals or tourists, she could talk the ear off anyone about anything.

"All right. Done. I've got an appointment I've got to get to. Strange that Jace isn't here yet."

Elle tugged her phone out of her pocket to check the time. "You're right, he's usually here by now."

"I'll walk you over to him."

"It's okay, I'll lock up after you leave and wait here for him." Jace didn't want her in the café by herself, but she couldn't ask

Molly to stay behind after her finish time, especially if she had an appointment, and a locked door should keep her safe.

Molly shook her head. "Don't be silly. I don't mind walking you. Jace said you couldn't walk alone. Plus, I'm tough as an old boot, so no one will mess with us."

"Tough as an old boot?"

"Eh. My granddad used to say it. Don't ask me why I repeat it. Should we go?"

Elle checked her phone again. Still no word from him. And Boyd hadn't been seen in town, by her, Eastern, or anyone else, since that day here in the café. It should be fine.

She grabbed her keys and bag and stepped outside with Molly.

"That guy hasn't been back, has he?" Molly asked as Elle locked the door.

She shook her head. "No. Is it overly optimistic of me to hope he was just a random tourist with a criminal record and he's passed through town now?"

"Nope. There's no such thing as too optimistic. I think he saw you, got some weird obsession with you, but then Jace scared him off with his big intimidating I'm-former-special-forces vibe."

"Um, I don't know if my looks alone incite that kind of behavior in men."

"You're joking, right?" At Elle's frown, Molly's jaw dropped. "Oh my gosh, you're not. Do you not see how beautiful you are?"

"Molly…"

"I'm serious. You are *gorgeous*, Elle. Stunning. How you could think anything else, I have no idea."

She lifted a shoulder. "Confidence has never been my strong point."

Molly grabbed her arm and pulled her to a stop. "Then let me confirm something for you. You are beautiful both inside and out. It's a natural beauty that most people would kill for, me included."

She snorted. "You? Molly, you are the definition of beautiful."

"I don't have your cheekbones. Or your perfect button nose or your stunning gray eyes."

Elle's cheeks warmed. "Thank you."

"Anytime you need a boost, just let me know. I'm all for women supporting women. We need to remind each other how beautiful we are. In fact, I—"

A crackling noise sounded from somewhere in the trees behind Molly. Elle frowned and looked over the other woman's shoulder, and Molly turned her head.

"It was probably nothing," Molly eventually said. "But let's walk a little faster to Jace." She linked her arm through Elle's, and they continued toward the skywalk.

"I might try and call him." Elle tugged out her phone and dialed his number.

He answered on the second ring. "Hey. Sorry, I got held up. A teenager decided to climb a fucking tree while I wasn't watching and got stuck."

"That's okay. Is he all right?"

"Yeah, Kayden and Hendrix are here. They're getting him down now."

"Great. I'm just walking to you."

There was a small pause. "Alone?"

"No, Molly's with me."

Another pause. "I'll leave Kay and Hendrix to deal with this guy and meet you halfway."

"Oh, no, you don't have to—"

"I'm coming back, Elle."

Honestly, she was glad. "Okay."

She'd just hung up when another crunching noise sounded behind them, this time louder. Elle turned in time to see something swing toward Molly. She didn't have time to warn her friend before the rock hit Molly in the head and she dropped to the ground.

Elle gasped and fell back a step, her gaze moving from Molly, head bleeding as she lay still on the ground, back to the tattooed guy.

Boyd.

He cocked his head. "Finally got you alone."

A part of her, such a big part, didn't want to leave Molly here alone. But then the guy took a step toward her, and suddenly, it was fight or flight.

She ran.

"I fucking love a good hunt!" Boyd yelled.

Her feet pounded the dirt, air soaring in and out of her lungs. Fear was all she felt. It ran through her veins, heating her blood. Fear for herself. For Molly, that she wasn't okay and needed help. She hated leaving her, but she couldn't help her *and* fight the guy off.

When the start of the skywalk came into view, Elle's gut twisted. She didn't want to step onto it. No part of her wanted to be anywhere near the thing. But Jace was there. He said he was coming back to her, so he couldn't be far, and if she just kept running into the woods, Boyd would catch her and Jace wouldn't know where she was.

With a sick feeling in her belly, she ran onto the skywalk. Her heart jumped into her throat.

Don't look down, Elle. Do not look down.

The words screamed in her head again and again.

Panic tried to choke her. Cut off her breath in her throat. But then she heard the pounding feet behind her, and suddenly getting away took up all her attention.

She ran, ignoring the fear and the tremble of her limbs, her body and mind prioritizing the bigger threat—Boyd.

She was just nearing the part of the skywalk where Jace led rappelling sessions when she noticed the gate beside the tree was open. *Wide* open.

Why? Surely Jace wouldn't have left it unsecured?

The steps behind her grew nearer, the air wheezing through her chest louder. She was just nearing the tree when a hard shove hit her in the back. She gasped and fell forward, her head hitting the skywalk hard. She tried to push up, but a kick landed on her ribs, sending her back down, closer to the edge.

"You made this hard for me, lady, but we got here in the end. And you ran straight where I wanted you."

One more kick and she fell off the side of the skywalk, right where the opening was.

* * *

JACE MOVED QUICKLY down the skywalk. He didn't like that Elle and Molly were walking on their own. That asshole Boyd hadn't shown his face for a while, and maybe that had given Elle a feeling of safety. He didn't trust it. There was something in his gut, some sick, sinking feeling telling him to get to her. To protect her.

Why the fuck had the damn kid climbed a tree and made him late?

He sped up into a jog, moving his feet faster, needing to get to her. Have eyes on her.

He'd just rounded a bend in the walk when every muscle in his body froze.

Boyd stood over Elle as she lay on the walk—the gate to the rappelling station wide fucking open.

And in one life-altering moment, he kicked her, and her body flew over the edge.

Jace's world stopped, the air hissing from his chest as his stomach convulsed.

No!

He sprinted forward, feet pounding against the walk. "Get the fuck away from her!"

Boyd's head whipped up. Jace pulled his gun from his concealed holster.

The guy sped off in the opposite direction.

Jace fired, nailing Boyd in the shoulder, making him stumble. Before he could fire a second time—he glimpsed Elle's fingers.

They were just visible at the edge of the skywalk.

Alive. She was alive!

The air whooshed into his chest.

Forgetting about Boyd, who'd already disappeared, Jace dropped to his knees, quickly lowering the gun and grabbing her wrist before pulling her back up. The second she was in his arms, he felt like he could breathe again.

She was *alive*. She hadn't fallen. She hadn't died.

He closed his eyes, letting the pain, that for a split second had crushed him, slip out of his body. No, it wasn't just pain. It was a devastation so physical and intense that he'd felt it in every muscle. Every limb. Every inch of his body.

Elle shook in his arms, her fingers latching on to him so tightly it was as if she was afraid she'd fall again.

"Jace…" That one whispered word, said with so much fear, cut into his flesh like a dagger.

He opened his mouth to respond when pounding footsteps echoed behind him. He looked over his shoulder to see Kayden sprinting toward them.

His brother came to a stop. "I heard a gunshot. What happened?"

"He fucking kicked her over the edge!" Jace snarled, not a scrap of calm in his voice.

"Who?"

"Boyd, the guy who pulled a gun in the café. I shot him in the shoulder as he ran away, but he didn't stop. I don't know where he is."

Anger twisted Kayden's features. "I'll go after him."

"Molly," Elle gasped, the whispered word barely reaching

them. "Need to find Molly. He hit her on the way to the skywalk and knocked her out."

"On it," Kayden said quickly. "Jace, call Eastern." Then his brother took off.

Jace looked down at Elle, finally focusing on her pale skin. The tremble in her limbs. "Are you okay?" The second the words were out, he wanted to kick his own ass. Of *course* she wasn't okay. She'd almost died. His skin felt too fucking tight at the thought.

"I'm not sure. I…I can't stop shaking."

She was in shock. But then, so was he. He tightened his arms around her. "I've got you. You're safe with me."

She snuggled closer, digging her head into his chest.

He tugged out his phone and hit Eastern's name.

"Jace, I'm just in the middle of—"

"Boyd attacked Elle."

"What?"

Jace tried to get his anger under control, but it was impossible. "He chased her down the skywalk and kicked her off the edge. She almost *died*." Fuck, it hurt even more saying it out loud than it had in his head.

"I'm leaving the station now."

His gaze shifted to the gate beside the tree, already spotting signs that the lock had been tampered with. Boyd had planned this. The asshole had planned to push her off the fucking edge. And Jace wanted to kill him for that.

ace watched the slow rise and fall of Elle's chest. The way the morning light hit her skin so softly and the locks of her hair spread over the pillow.

He'd almost lost her yesterday. For a few agonizing seconds, he'd thought he had. It was the only reason his bullet into Boyd's shoulder hadn't been a kill shot. He *never* missed. But yesterday he had, because for a moment he'd thought the woman he loved had been taken from him.

It didn't feel real. He didn't know a world without Elle in it, and he didn't want to. Even when he'd been in the military, so far from her and so disconnected, he'd still been able to function because he'd known that she was okay. That she was alive and safe, here in Misty Peak.

If he had to wake up and know she was no longer within reach...

No. He couldn't do it. The idea hurt so much, he almost wanted to keel over.

He grazed a swath of hair from her cheek, slipping it behind her ear. Her soft hum slipped into his chest. The sound was everything. *She* was everything. How he'd stayed away for so long, he had no idea.

Never again. Never again would he deny that she was his. That by her side wasn't exactly where he was meant to be.

Her eyes tightened before fluttering open. The air punched from his chest. Because those eyes…so gray they reminded him of the sky during a storm…they were his kryptonite.

"Hey." Her single quiet word barely crossed the distance to him. "How long have you been watching me?"

"Not long enough." But then, no amount of time would ever be enough.

The hint of a smile slipped from her lips. "Are you okay?"

She was asking *him* that? "I'm not the one who almost died yesterday."

"But I *didn't* die. And you didn't answer my question."

"No. I'm not okay."

Her brows flickered and she rolled to her side, placing a hand on his chest. "Why?"

"I almost lost you yesterday."

"But you didn't."

The memory of her going over that edge was so alive in his head, it replayed again and again.

He placed a hand over hers. "I'm sorry."

"For what?"

"Running from this for so long. Costing us so much time."

She shook her head. "You didn't cost us time. You gave us each a chance to grow into the people we needed to become to be what the other needed."

He smiled slightly. "That *does* sound better."

Although, if he'd stopped fighting his feelings a long time ago, he could have saved them both a lot of unnecessary torment. She was being kind, because that was Elle. And he wouldn't take her kindness for granted.

He lowered his mouth, hovered it over hers. "That's why I need you in my life. You make *everything* better."

He kissed her. Let the softness of her lips smooth out the sharp, jagged edges caused by yesterday's terror.

She hummed against his lips, her fingers slipping into his hair, tugging and pulling. He slid the sheets off her and crawled over her body, careful to avoid her bruises before running his tongue across her lips. When they opened, he eased inside, tangling his tongue with hers.

God, she tasted good. And the feel of her body under his was almost enough to heal the trauma he'd felt yesterday. And it *had* been a trauma. Seeing her go over that ledge had been the worst fucking thing he'd ever experienced—and he'd gone through some heavy shit in his life.

He lifted his lips and touched his temple to hers, his breathing hard and fast. "You're here. You're safe. It's something I need to keep reminding myself."

She cupped his cheek. "It's okay. *I'm* okay."

"I can't forget... I can't get the image of you falling off the walk out of my head."

"I'm here, Jace. With you. And I'm not going anywhere."

"Promise me. Promise that you and I are forever."

Her gaze shifted between his eyes. "Until our last breaths."

He kissed her again. This kiss was harder. More desperate. He wanted to drown in her. Let her sweep him away and take him somewhere else entirely, where nothing else existed except the two of them.

It was only the ringing of her cell that had her pausing.

"Ignore it," he said between reckless kisses.

She groaned and turned, reaching for her cell on the bedside table. "I can't."

He knew that. Even as a teenager, she hadn't been able to let her calls go to voicemail.

As she answered the call, he kissed her cheek, then her neck.

"Aunt Jewel? What's wrong?"

He tugged at the bottom of her shirt…well, his shirt. And he fucking loved her wearing it.

"How do you know what happened?" Elle asked.

He kissed up her stomach, ignoring the rage that pummeled his veins at the purple bruising. When he reached her chest, he took a nipple between his lips. She gasped and grabbed his head as he sucked.

"No, Jewel, I'm… Yes, but…"

He ran his tongue back and forth over the hard peak, and Elle arched into him, her fingers threading into his hair.

"Yes," she said, breathless. "Okay. I'll come. Yes, now."

He lifted his head. "Now?"

She covered his mouth with her hand. "See you soon, Jewel." She hung up. "What are you doing?"

He took hold of her wrist and kissed her palm. "Kissing you."

"No. You had your lips around my nipple while I was talking to my *aunt*."

"Hmm, I like hearing you say nipple. It makes me want to taste it again."

He was about to lower his head and do just that, but she grabbed his hair. "I have to see my aunt."

"Why?"

"Because she heard about yesterday. How, exactly, I'm still not sure. Freaking small town."

"You could have said we'd be over *later*."

"Uh, yeah, I could have, but someone was distracting me and I could barely think." The smile dropped from her lips. "We also need to visit Molly, check in on how she's doing."

Something hard lodged in his chest. He hated that someone else had gotten hurt. "Okay. Your aunt, then Molly. But first I need to finish what I started."

She opened her mouth, but before she could get a word out,

he dove, this time taking her other nipple between his lips and sucking hard as she writhed beneath him.

* * *

ELLE STARED through the window as Jace pulled up in front of her aunt's house. She didn't get out right away, instead examining the red trim and the yard that was crowded with plants. It was the house she'd grown up in since she was eight.

When a few seconds passed and she still didn't move, Jace touched her thigh. "Everything okay?"

"Yeah, I just…sometimes when I come here, it reminds me of being eight years old and getting dropped off by my dad, not realizing I'd never see him again."

Her mother had left her and her father when Elle was five, because she'd met some guy and her new life didn't have *room* for kids. Or at least, that's what her father had told her. Her dad tried to do the single-parent thing for a while, but when she was eight, he just gave up, dropping her at his sister's house without looking back. She'd never heard from him again.

Asshole.

Jace squeezed her thigh. "Worst mistake he ever made. You were a huge loss, Tink."

She gave him a small smile. "I'm so grateful that Jewel took me in. She looked after me when I had no one else and she did the best she could, considering she was pretty young. I just felt so abandoned by the two people who were supposed to love me the most. I think that's where this idea that I wasn't good enough first stemmed from. Good enough. Pretty enough. Outgoing enough."

"You are *more* than enough. And Jewel loved you. She still does."

One side of Elle's mouth lifted, and she turned her gaze away from the house to look at him. "She loved you more."

"That's not true."

"Oh yes, it is. I bet you the second we step in there, she'll say a quick hello to me and be all over you. I'll be forgotten."

He leaned over and hovered his lips over hers. "Not gonna happen."

She grinned as she kissed him, because he was about to eat a slice of humble pie.

They climbed out, and her door had barely closed before Jace was at her side. He'd been noticeably different this morning. He was always attentive, but his gaze had been lingering on her longer than usual. His hands always on her or close.

Yesterday had clearly shaken him, maybe even more than her.

She leaned into him as they climbed the stairs to her aunt's front door. She lifted her hand, but her fist hadn't even hit wood before it was tugged open and Jewel stood in front of them.

She gasped. "Elle! You're okay!" She tugged Elle into her arms. "I'm so glad. I was so worried when Marie told me what had happened."

Elle hugged her aunt back. "And how did Marie know?"

"Oh, I'm not sure. She heard it from Fred, who heard it from someone else."

Crazy. This town was *crazy*.

When her aunt pulled back, her gaze immediately shifted to Jace. "Jace Walker. The son I never had." She pulled him into a hug. "It is *so* nice to see you."

Jace hugged her back, his gaze moving to Elle as she mouthed, "I told you so."

One side of his mouth lifted, and even after her aunt pulled away, she grabbed Jace's hand and tugged him into the house. "Come. Eat with me."

Elle swallowed a laugh as she followed them in, pushing the door closed after her.

"I made cucumber sandwiches and carrot sticks," Jewel said as she stopped at the table.

Oh, Lord. She remembered those cucumber sandwiches. They were awful. God-awful. Cucumber, pickled onion and butter... that was it. How her aunt ever thought of those fillings as a good combination, Elle didn't know.

She opened her mouth to tell Jewel she'd just eaten, but Jace got in first. "I'd love one."

Suck up. "Not for me, thanks, Jewel."

Her aunt frowned. "Don't be silly. You just went through a trauma—you need to eat."

Once Jace was seated, Jewel grabbed Elle's shoulder and guided her into the chair beside him. Jace smirked. Okay, here was the Jace she remembered. He *knew* she hated these sandwiches. In fact, he'd often brought two sandwiches to school so she didn't have to eat the one her aunt had packed for her.

Of course, she'd told her aunt a million times growing up that she didn't like them. She'd also insisted on making her own lunch. Neither of those strategies had worked with Jewel. But it wasn't out of spite. Her aunt genuinely thought she was doing Elle a favor by making her lunch.

Jace leaned over. "Maybe this is why I'm the favorite."

She thumped his shoulder as Jewel set plates and coffees in front of them.

"Now," she said, sitting opposite. "Tell me everything, including whether or not you're safe and what I can do to help."

Jace's muscles visibly tensed.

She reached under the table and put a hand on his thigh as she told her aunt everything that had happened, including her run-ins with Boyd before yesterday. Jace was quiet the entire time, and even when Jewel directed questions his way, Elle would often answer them.

To be fair, Jewel had a lot of questions.

By the end of the conversation, her aunt was leaning back in her seat, hand to her chest. "God. I'm so sorry. You should have told me about this Boyd fellow earlier. I'm so glad you were there, Jace."

"Me too," he said, voice quiet but hard.

Elle squeezed his thigh before rising from the table. "I'm just going to the bathroom."

She rose and moved from the table. When she was done, she stepped back into the hall, only to pause at the photos on the wall. They were the same photos that had been on the wall since she was a kid. Some of her and Jewel. Some of the dog they'd had while she was growing up.

Her gaze shifted to the last photo in the line. It was of her and Jace. When Jewel had first put it up, Elle had argued for weeks that it needed to come down. That there was no way she wanted Jace to see it.

She hadn't taken it down. And at some point, Elle had found a comfort in it being there.

They were young, maybe sixteen. They'd just been to the river, and both of them had wet hair, damp clothes, and the biggest smiles on their faces.

God, she'd loved him so much. Even then.

She was still staring at it when two strong arms wrapped around her waist. She smiled and leaned back into Jace's familiar body.

He kissed her cheek. "You looking at us?"

"Always."

"I love that photo. I still remember that day."

"Me too. Although, the old me used to look at it and mainly see my body, and what I didn't like about it."

Jace's muscles tensed around her. "And now?"

"I just see how happy I was to be by your side." It was exactly where she'd wanted to be. Where she'd always wanted to be. She turned in his arms. "We should go visit Molly."

"I don't know if I'm ready to leave Jewel's cucumber sandwiches and all her doting yet."

Elle laughed. "Your ego is big enough. It doesn't need any more doting. And you can take some sandwiches in a doggy bag. Come on."

They said a quick goodbye to Jewel—who *did* give them some cucumber sandwiches in a container—before climbing back into the car. Jace seemed more at ease as they made their way to Molly's house. Elle had texted her that morning. Thank God she just had a mild concussion and nothing more serious.

They were halfway there when a traffic commotion up ahead had Elle straightening in her seat. She gasped at the sight of a crashed Toyota. The entire front of the vehicle was compressed against a large tree.

A few deputy cars and an ambulance were also scattered around the site.

"Oh, God!" Elle gasped. "I hope no one was hurt." But even as she said it, she knew there was no way the driver of the car had gotten out totally unscathed. The car must have been moving at a high rate of speed before hitting the tree.

"Eastern's there," Jace said quietly as he pulled over to the side of the road. "I'm just going to check in with him."

Jace climbed out, and Elle immediately followed. Eastern saw them, an emotion she couldn't place passing over his features before he headed their way.

Jace's arm slipped around her waist. "Is everything okay?" he asked as his brother stopped in front of them.

Eastern's gaze flicked her way before returning to Jace, and for some reason, her belly twisted. She could already tell—everything was *not* okay.

"The driver died on impact," Eastern finally said.

Jace's arm tightened around her. "Anyone we know?"

There was a beat of silence before Eastern answered. "It was Darcy Boyd."

CHAPTER 24

$\mathcal{E}$lle sipped her chai latte. Sugar and Spice was busy around her, but her mind kept flicking back to the same thing.

Boyd. He was dead. Was it an accident? The mechanic told Eastern there'd been a fault in the brakes, so all signs pointed to yes. She should be grateful, right? That he was gone and she didn't have to worry about him?

A hand on her arm caused her to jump. She turned to look at Jace beside her.

He frowned. "Are you okay?"

"Yeah, I just...I keep thinking about Boyd." There was no point in lying.

His fingers tightened around her arm. "He's gone now. You don't need to worry about him anymore."

"I know. I just hate that we don't have any answers. Like why he targeted me. Why he tried to *kill* me." God, even saying those words out loud sounded weird. A guy she'd never met had tried to *kill* her.

Eastern was still looking into him, but so far, he'd found no connection between her and Boyd. He appeared to be just what they already knew he was—a small-time criminal. An abuser. An out-of-towner.

"I hate that too." A muscle ticked in Jace's jaw. "I wish we knew, but I'm not sorry he's gone."

She nodded, shifting her gaze back to the latte. "So I'm safe now, right? He's gone and he was the only threat…" She knew he couldn't guarantee that, but a part of her still hoped he would anyway.

Jace's brows flickered. "I'd like to think so. But I still want you to stay close to me for a while to make sure."

The café was closed for a week, and Jace had taken the week off work to be with her. It also gave Molly time to recover.

When her gaze caught on his phone, she frowned. "You haven't received any more messages from that private number?"

"Not since I blocked them."

That was good. One less thing to worry about.

"You know what we need?" Jace asked.

"A crystal ball that has all the answers we're seeking?"

"Well, that…and cupcakes."

In the glass cabinet at the counter, a dozen different types were on display, and they all looked amazing, especially the pumpkin pie. She sighed. "But how will we ever choose?"

"Why choose when we can have one of each?"

She opened her mouth to tell him that was ridiculous, but he was already up and walking to the counter.

When the bakery door opened, Callie, the new Pilates and yoga studio owner, walked in. The woman's gaze immediately slid to Elle, and she smiled before heading her way.

"Hey, Elle."

"Hey. It's good to see you, Callie." The woman was wearing her usual leggings and sports crop, probably having come straight from a class. "How's the studio going?"

"Great, actually. We've been really busy, which surprised me. I thought it would take a while to build up clientele, but I guess

Misty Peak was ready for a fitness studio." She cocked her head. "You're always welcome to come back for another class, you know."

Elle internally cringed. "Thank you. I think I need some time to summon the courage first. Your class was amazing, but it absolutely destroyed me."

"We have beginner's classes."

"*What*? The class Sadie and I took wasn't a beginner's class? She said it was!"

Callie grinned. "No. It was intermediate. But come by and I can give you a schedule of all the classes so you can see which ones you might like to try. If you want to, that is. No pressure."

She was going to kill Sadie. "Thanks. I'd appreciate it."

Jace returned to the table. "Hey, Callie, right?"

"Yeah."

"Jace."

"I know. How are you?"

"I'm good."

"Happy to be back?"

"I am." He glanced at Elle.

Callie smiled. "Your family's almost all home."

One side of his mouth lifted. "Yeah, don't know if we'll *all* ever be home though. Nylah will likely stay in Cradle Mountain, and I think Lock might be out there for life."

Her smile slipped a fraction. It was subtle, but enough for Elle to notice. Did she know Lock?

"Is he good?" Callie asked, voice sounding strained.

"I mean, from the little he updates us, it seems so."

She swallowed and nodded before stepping back. "Good. That's great. Well, I'll see you both around."

Elle frowned as the other woman walked away. What was her history with Lock? Because there *was* a history. Before she could ask Jace, Mrs. Sandler stopped at their table with two plates, each holding a cupcake, as well as a takeout box.

The store owner smiled at them. "Here you go. Enjoy."

When she walked away, Elle raised a brow at Jace. "How many did you order?"

"I told you, one of each."

"Jace…that's ridiculous and will make us sick."

"The only thing that makes me sick is thinking I'm not feeding you enough."

She sighed. "I'm already gaining inches on my hips from that damn candy you gave me."

Seriously, she'd gotten over her not-wanting-to-touch-it issue, so now every time she walked past the jar, she took one. Not because she wanted it, but because she *needed* it. She was already out of cola skulls and was seriously considering ordering more.

"I love your hips," Jace whispered, his breath brushing over her lips. "They're as beautiful as the rest of you."

* * *

JACE LOOKED up and down the street as he stepped outside. Even though Boyd was dead, Elle was right. They didn't know why he'd targeted her, and that left an uneasy knot in his gut.

His fingers tightened around her hand as they made their way to his car. He helped her in before climbing behind the wheel and setting the cupcakes in the backseat. The second he looked at her, he forced the tension from his features.

"Ready to go home?"

"Now that I'm full of sugar and in serious need of a long nap? Definitely."

Damn, her smile was gorgeous.

He started the car and pulled onto the street before reaching across for her hand. She slipped her fingers through his easily. He needed to be touching her today. Needed eyes on her and to have her close.

He'd only driven down a couple of streets when someone in the rearview mirror caught his attention. Whoever it was drove a red Honda with tinted windows, and they'd been behind him since they'd left Sugar and Spice.

He took another left, then a right.

Elle frowned. "Where are we going?"

The red car reappeared in the rearview mirror.

Jace tightened his fingers on the wheel. The asshole was following them.

"Something's wrong," Elle guessed before he could respond to her.

"Someone's tailing us."

She gasped and started to turn, but he grabbed her arm.

"Don't." He hit the Bluetooth on the steering wheel.

Eastern answered on the first ring. "Jace. Everything okay?"

"I've got a tail."

"A tail?"

"A red Honda Accord. Plate numbers are TCA 4832. Can you run them?"

"Hang on." There was the sound of typing. "It's a rental car. I can contact the business and see who rented it, but it'll take me a few minutes."

Fuck. If he was alone, he'd lead the car into a dead end and approach them, but no way in hell was he doing that with Elle by his side. They could be armed.

"Do it," Jace finally said. "I'm gonna lose them."

"On it."

The second the call ended, Jace shot a look at Elle. "Hold on, Tink."

She gripped the grab handle, and he pressed his foot to the floor. They immediately sped up, and he took a hard right.

"Where are we going?" Elle asked.

"To Eastern." He wasn't sure if their tail would follow; it

depended on how stupid he was or whether he knew this town well enough to know where they were headed.

His tires squealed as he took a right, then a left. He knew these roads like the back of his hand.

A few minutes later, he shot a glance in the rearview mirror to see that the road was empty. Were they gone?

He slowed the car to a normal pace.

"Did you lose him?" Elle asked quickly, an edge to her voice.

"I don't know."

Two more streets and he pulled into the sheriff's office parking lot. No one pulled in after them. Still, he didn't immediately get out, and when Elle put her hand on the door handle, he grabbed her other wrist.

"Wait."

She frowned and looked behind her. There was still no one there.

"I'm gonna come around to your side." He climbed out, his gaze continually shifting around the parking lot before stopping at Elle's door. The second she was out, he slipped an arm around her and tugged her against his side. He didn't let his guard down until they'd stepped into the building, and even then, his muscles remained tight.

The older woman at the front desk looked up. "Hi. Can I help you?"

"I'm here to see my brother."

The words had just left his mouth when a door behind the desk opened and Eastern stepped out. "Come in."

Jace's hand shifted to the small of Elle's back, and they moved into Eastern's office.

Eastern lowered behind the desk. "I contacted the car place and got the details of the woman who hired the car."

Jace frowned. "Woman?"

"Yeah." Eastern clicked a few keys on the laptop. "Alice Kelly."

Kelly...the name felt like a kick to the gut. "Dean's sister."

Something Eastern would already know after looking into the family.

Why the hell would she be here, in Misty Peak, tailing him?

Eastern turned the screen around to show them an ID, and sure enough, the woman on the screen looked just like Dean, only female. Same eyes. Same hair color.

It was his sister.

"It's her," Jace said quietly, pulling the pieces of the puzzle together. "She's the person behind the unknown number."

She had to be. They already knew it had to be a family member, and it was the sister Eastern hadn't been able to track down because she'd been out of town. Now she'd rented a damn car to tail him.

"She's escalating," Eastern said quietly.

"Jace," Elle whispered. "Tell me what's going on."

Jace clenched his jaw. "I blocked her from my phone and she couldn't reach me. Now she's here to mess with me in person."

CHAPTER 25

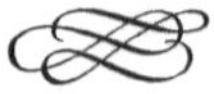

"Elle, I can tell something's going on," Sadie said quietly. "What is it? Are you thinking about the attack last week? Or the person who was tailing you?"

Elle swirled her cup of coffee. It was the first day they were open since Boyd's attack. She was on a break with Sadie, who'd dropped by both for a coffee and to check in. The place wasn't busy, and honestly, Elle was grateful.

She'd told Sadie about the car that had tailed them and the person who'd been identified as renting the car. But even if she hadn't, Eastern would have told her, and Elle was fine with that. "I don't want to make this about me."

Sadie cocked her head. "Make what about you?"

"It's going to sound silly and petty and like a non-issue after everything that's been happening."

"Tell me."

Elle sighed. "Since that car tailed us, Jace has been…distant."

Sadie frowned. "Distant how?"

"It's just little things. He hasn't been smiling or cracking his usual jokes. He used to stay in bed and we'd snuggle in the morning, but he's been getting up early to work out. It kind of feels like he's…pulling away." Man, that hurt to say out loud.

"Oh, Elle…he's probably scared about something happening to you. Someone *did* try to kill you. I know they're not around anymore, but now with this woman out there…it's a lot."

"I know. But I guess a part of me, the insecure part, is worried that…"

"What?"

Elle tightened her hold on the mug. "It just scares me. I've always had this idea that he's way out of my league."

Sadie opened her mouth, but Elle spoke first.

"Jace has done so much to convince me that isn't true. Over the years, I've also done a lot of work on myself. It's just, after these last few days, those old insecurities have started to creep back in."

Sadie reached across the table and slipped her hand over Elle's. "Hey. I've seen the way that guy looks at you. When you're in the room, you're *all* he sees. Trust him to stick around."

"Thank you. I *do* need to trust him. I obviously just like to overthink everything."

"Oh, I know all about that. I'm a queen overthinker. It's a woman's prerogative. Maybe talk to him tonight?"

That was the thing, she'd been *trying* to talk to him. And she always got the same response. That he was fine. That everything would be okay.

Sadie sipped her coffee. "Did Eastern tell you he questioned Alice's family and they told him she was on a retreat?"

"Yeah, but they couldn't tell him which retreat she's on." A retreat would be convenient seeing as she wouldn't be able to answer her phone. She shook her head. "Sorry, we've been talking about me this entire time. Tell me about you. How's it going with Eastern and how's beautiful Avery?"

A soft smile immediately curved Sadie's lips, and for the next ten minutes, Elle listened as Sadie spoke about her boyfriend and his daughter. She was so happy that her friend had found love with Eastern. It was only fitting, seeing as she'd basically nannied his daughter her entire life. They made a beautiful family.

When her break was over, Elle rose and hugged Sadie. "I'm so happy for you."

"Thank you. And I hope your chat with Jace goes well. I think it will."

Elle smiled as she pulled back. "Let's hope so." She watched as her friend left. She was clearing the table when the door opened after Sadie and Casper stepped in.

Oh, Jesus. What the heck was he doing here? Elle almost rolled her eyes. Would the jerk not just leave her alone?

Of course he walked straight over to her. "Hey, Marshal."

"What are you doing here, Casper?"

He cocked his head. "Now, I might be wrong, but this *is* a public café, is it not?"

This time she did roll her eyes as she grabbed the cups from the table. "So you're here for coffee?"

"Sure. Why not?"

She rounded the counter, hearing his footsteps close behind her as he stopped on the other side. Molly was making a bagel at the other end of the counter, and there were half a dozen people in the café, but right now, all her focus remained on Casper.

She put the mugs into the sink before turning back to him. "What can I get you?"

He leaned over the counter. "Dunno. What's good?"

"The coffee. Would you like one to go?"

"To go? You trying to get rid of me?"

"After what you said to me in the bar, you're lucky I'm not kicking your ass out."

"After you threw a drink in my face, you're lucky I didn't press charges."

She scoffed. That comment didn't even deserve a response. "You can have a coffee to go, or you can get out."

An arrogant smile curved his lips. "There you go again, thinking you're too good for me."

She didn't think—she knew. "Is that a no for the coffee?"

"No, I think I'd like one."

She ground her back teeth together and turned to the coffee machine.

Molly came up beside her, bagel in hand. "Hey. Everything okay?"

"Yeah, I'm going to make his coffee and send him on his way. It's fine."

"Okay. Let me know if you want me to take over. I'm great with captain douchebags."

Elle laughed as Molly went out to the floor.

"So," Casper started. "I was wondering. What do you think will happen if you put the weight back on?"

Her back stiffened, and she turned to glare at him. "Excuse me?"

He lifted a shoulder. "Well, he had years to get you into bed. You were obviously obsessed with him. He wasn't interested in you in that way back then. And it wasn't because he didn't like to date. Fuck, he had a new girlfriend every week, and he flaunted every one of them in front of you."

She grabbed the cup and poured milk in, anger rolling over her flesh. The milk was probably still cold, but she didn't care. "Why are you saying this to me?"

"I'm just looking out for you, Elle."

She snorted as she pressed the lid to the cup and turned. "You expect me to believe you have my best interests in mind?"

"Of course. I mean, we all saw how pathetically into him you were in high school. You loved him, right? But did he keep in contact with you when he left?" At her silence, he offered a sympathetic look. "Didn't think so. And once he gets bored, or you put on a few pounds—because people *always* regain the weight—he'll probably leave you again. And even if you don't, he gets bored pretty easily, doesn't he?"

"Don't presume to know him *or* me." She hit the amount into the digital cash register a bit too roughly, then put the coffee in front of him.

He swiped his card before lifting his cup. "I don't need to know either of you well to know how this ends. He'll leave you, you'll go back to looking like the ugly duckling, and then you'll be heartbroken."

"Get. Out."

He smiled as he straightened. "Give me a call when you need that shoulder to cry on. I'll try to muster up some sympathy. Or at least an 'I told you so.'"

* * *

"You still haven't been able to make contact with the sister?" Jace asked, fingers tightening around the phone he pressed to his ear.

He needed to find this woman. Figure out what the hell her end game was here in Misty Peak.

Eastern's exhale was loud over the line. "I'm doing my best, but her phone always goes to voicemail, and her family can't confirm which retreat she's supposedly at."

Bullshit. All of it.

Anger pummeled his veins, but it wasn't Eastern's fault. "I appreciate the time you're spending on this."

"You doing okay?"

He looked out over the trees below the skywalk. Usually when he came up here, the view allowed him to let go of any other shit he had going on in his head. Today, it wasn't so easy. Hell, this last week hadn't been easy. "It's just bringing it all back up, man."

There was a pause from Eastern. "Your teammate's death?"

"Yeah. I feel like I was just getting to a good place. A place of accepting that his death wasn't my fault. Allowing myself to move on. And now with his sister likely targeting me, probably because she blames me…" Fuck. He'd blamed himself since the day Dean had died. Granting himself peace hadn't been easy.

"Jace, you're right when you say his death wasn't your fault. And if those messages on your phone were her, and she's gotten it into her head that it was your fault, then that's *her* trauma speaking. It has nothing to do with you."

"But Elle could get hurt in the crossfire." And that would confirm everything he'd felt for most of his life. That people in his orbit got hurt. His best friend growing up. Both his parents. Dean.

"Hey! Stop it. I can almost hear you blaming yourself," Eastern said firmly. "We're going to figure this out together. You hear me?"

He ran his fingers through his hair. "Yeah, I hear you."

"Don't shoulder blame for anything that isn't yours to carry."

His jaw clicked. "Thanks, brother." But it was easier said than done.

When he hung up, he didn't move right away. Instead, he let the breeze run over his skin. Watched the branches move in the wind. He loved being home, but he hated bringing his past here with him. It was starting to feel like danger and loss would follow him forever. Haunt him. Maybe that was why he'd been somewhat withdrawn from Elle the last few days. He didn't want to be, but he also didn't want her to get hurt because of him.

He stepped off the skywalk. He was just nearing the visitors center, passing the parking lot, when he saw Casper in the parking lot.

Jace stopped. What the fuck was he doing here?

When Casper caught his gaze, the asshole smirked at him before lifting a coffee cup in a mock salute, as if to fucking brag that he'd just been in the café with Elle, before climbing into his car.

The *fuck*? Had Jace's warning to stay away from Elle not been fucking clear?

He watched the guy's black Mazda drive away before covering the remaining distance to the café. The second he stepped inside, his focus beamed straight to her. She was standing at the coffee machine, facing away from him.

He crossed the space between them. Not caring that he didn't work here and wasn't supposed to be behind the counter, he stepped up to her back.

"Hey."

She jumped and turned, her gaze colliding with his. "Jace. What are you doing here?"

"It's two, your finishing time."

Her brows rose, and she checked the clock on the wall. "I had a late break and lost track of time."

There was something in her voice. Some sadness he didn't like.

"I'll just finish this coffee order," she said quietly.

She turned back to the machine, but he touched her hip and lowered his head. "Are you okay?"

"Of course."

He didn't believe her. Her voice was too high-pitched, like she was forcing herself to sound okay when she wasn't.

"I saw Casper leaving."

Her body stiffened. He not only felt it beneath his hand, he saw it. "Yeah, he came in."

"What did he say?"

She poured milk into the cup before sprinkling some chocolate on top. "It was nothing."

It wasn't *nothing*. The asshole shouldn't have been here in the first place. "Tink—"

"I need to take this coffee out, then we can go."

He wanted to push. To find out every fucking word that jerk had said. But this wasn't the time or place.

Reluctantly, he nodded and stepped back. He'd stop asking for now, but he *would* find out what Casper had said. That was a guarantee.

She was too quiet. Had been quiet since they'd left the café.

The hum of the engine was the only sound in the car. He hated it. Which was fucking hypocritical, because it was *he* who'd been quiet the last few days while he'd been obsessing over every little thing. But now, with her barely speaking to him, it made him want to take back all those wasted moments. Talk to her about anything and everything.

He slipped a hand over her thigh. He'd already tried to ask about Casper again, but so far hadn't had any luck getting a straight answer out of her. She just kept telling him she didn't want to talk about it. That what Casper had said didn't matter.

But it *did* matter. Everything the asshole said mattered, because it clearly affected her.

He pulled into his driveway. He hadn't even asked her which house they should go to, his or her apartment, they'd just started staying at his place most nights.

He climbed from the car and moved around to her side, scanning the area as he went. He'd been so damn on edge for weeks that keeping his head on a swivel had become the norm even now, when he wasn't deployed.

When they stepped into the house, he turned the lock.

"Hungry?" he asked, moving to the kitchen. "I could make some gumbo?"

Her lips twitched. They'd once attempted gumbo as teenagers, and it had been a disaster, mostly because he'd refused to read the recipe and had thrown in whatever he liked.

"I'm not very hungry." She slipped off her shoes. "I might jump into the shower really quick."

Before he could respond, she turned and headed into their bedroom. He grabbed the edge of the counter, fingers tight as anger swam through his veins. What the hell had Casper said to her?

He tried to busy himself in the kitchen and living area, but his gaze kept shifting back to the bedroom door. Ten minutes later, he gave up.

Screw it.

He crossed the space to the bedroom and walked straight through to the bathroom. The lights were dimmed, and Elle had her back to him, her face turned up to the water as she stood in the shower. He didn't think about what he was doing, just moved on instinct, stripping off his clothes and stepping into the shower behind her.

When he slipped his arms around her waist, she gasped. "Jace! I didn't hear you come in."

"I need to know what's going on in your head, Tink. What did he say? You're killing me with your silence."

She ran her fingers over his arm, taking a few breaths before she answered. "You're going to think I'm being stupid."

He kissed her shoulder. "If it upset you, it's not stupid."

There was a beat of silence as she dipped her chin to her chest. "Casper just made some stupid comments about you and me and…"

"And what?"

"And our relationship in high school. He reminded me of how many girls you dated that *weren't* me, and how I looked back then."

Every muscle in his body grew so tight, it was an effort to remain exactly where he was. To not turn, storm right out of the shower, and go find the asshole.

"Elle, look at me."

She turned, her gray eyes burning into him.

"From the first day I laid eyes on you, I felt something stir inside me. I don't even know how to describe it. It was this need to be around you. It was so strong that you were all I thought about that day. And you've been in my head every single day since. I didn't think I was near good enough for you, but the stupid teenage version of me tried to have you without *actually* having you. That was my mistake. Now that we're together, now that you're mine, I can't let you go. I am literally not capable of it."

Tears burned her eyes. "Really?"

"You actually think I could live without you?"

"But these last few days, you've been so distant."

"I have old insecurities too. About you being better off without me. About the people around me being hurt. But even in my darkest moments, I'm still too selfish to give you up."

A tear fell down her cheek. "I can't give you up either. But I think I get scared that one day I might have to."

"Never. You'll never have to." He lowered his head and kissed the tear from her cheek. "I'd do it all over again, you know."

"Do what?"

"Grow up with you. Torture myself just to be near you. Fall in love with you."

Her intake of breath was sharp. "Love?"

He lifted his head, his gaze colliding with her. "Yeah, Tink. I love you. I've loved you for so long, and that love has become a part of me. I don't know how to be without you in this world."

Her hands moved over his chest, a tremble in her fingers, more tears in her eyes. "I love you too, Jace. I've tried not to love you for so long. I even tried to convince myself while you were gone that I didn't. But I did. I've *always* loved you."

A territorial growl ripped from his chest. He lifted her and turned, pressing her to the wall. "You're the reason I came home, Elle. *You're* my reason."

She cupped his cheeks, pressing her forehead to his. "Thank you for returning to me."

He kissed her. Once. Twice. Light grazes of mouth against mouth. On the third kiss, her lips separated, and he slipped his tongue inside, tasting her. Melding with her.

Her fingers threaded through his hair, her body grinding against him. So soft and all his. She'd become so achingly familiar to him, and as vital as the air he breathed.

He skimmed his hand over her body, finding her ample breast and cupping it. Grazing his thumb in a circular motion over her hard nipple.

She groaned, her core rubbing harder against him.

"I want to slip inside you so bad right now," he whispered, the need consuming him.

She nipped his bottom lip before kissing across his cheek and whispering into his ear, "I'm on the pill. Take me, Jace. I'm yours."

Fuck. With another growl, he positioned himself at her entrance. But before pushing inside, he ran his thumb over her clit.

She groaned, her head dropping into the nook of his shoulder. "Jace…"

He kept rubbing, until Elle tightened her legs around him, pressing his tip inside her.

A low, primal sound tore from his chest. "Elle…"

"Now, Jace. I need you now."

Her words cut through that last bit of self-control, and he snapped, pushing inside her in one deep thrust.

* * *

ELLE CRIED OUT, the sound so loud it echoed off the tiles. It was the first time there was no barrier between them, and it felt raw and intense and right.

She grabbed Jace's shoulders, needing an anchor as he started to thrust. Long, deep thrusts, which pushed her right to the edge.

This wasn't just sex. It was a million things. Love. Connection. A profound need to recapture every lost moment from the years they'd been apart.

Her hands ran up his neck, slipping into his hair and pulling. When he wrapped his lips around her nipple, she moaned, her head flinging back, the air barely making it to her lungs.

"Jace..." His name was a whisper on her lips. So achingly familiar. And hers. *He* was *hers*. And he *loved* her.

She'd told herself, *begged* herself, to let him go. To move on. But she never had. Not really. She'd loved him for so long that the feeling had ingrained itself into every part of her. It was rooted deep in every inch of her skin. This need to be with him and only him.

And finally she was.

His tongue ran over the peak of her nipple, releasing with a pop before moving to the other. All the while, his thrusts never stopped or slowed, the rhythmic motion driving her wild. She couldn't stop the cries falling from her lips, hanging in the air and competing with the sound of water hitting tiles, flesh hitting flesh.

When it became too much, when she needed his mouth on hers, she tugged at his hair and drew him back to her. Immediately, she slid her tongue inside his mouth, her nails scraping at his skin as she tasted him.

He reached between them, once again rubbing her clit.

*Oh, Jesus…*he was everywhere.

Her breathing became choppy, her entire body burning. God, he set her on fire.

His thrusts went deeper. Harder. His thumb still moving over her clit. She wanted to hold on. To have him inside her, a part of her, for as long as possible.

But one more thrust and she fell. Tore apart in his arms while screaming his name.

Her entire body convulsed as he continued to thrust, prolonging the orgasm and forcing her world to narrow to just him.

When she had nothing left, her screams became whimpers, and that's when Jace growled and broke along with her, his head lowering to her neck, his primal sounds so loud they rippled around the room, bouncing off walls, beating into her.

Then, finally, there was stillness, bar the rise and fall of their chests and the water raining down. She wrapped an arm around his shoulders, running her fingers through his wet hair, wanting to stay exactly where she was for as long as possible.

"God, I love you, Tink." His words were muffled against her neck, but she heard them as if he'd shouted.

"Say it again," she whispered.

He lifted his head, the air still rushing in and out of him as his gaze bore into her. "I love you."

The emotion in her chest felt so big that it clogged her throat. She'd waited so long to hear him say that, dreamed about it. And it was everything she'd always known it would be. "I love you too, Jace Walker."

He lowered his head, but he didn't kiss her, he just touched his temple to hers. He was still inside her, linking them in the most intimate way, both taking a moment to recover from what had just taken place. To remind themselves that this was real, and they'd finally found their way to each other.

CHAPTER 27

*E*lle hummed as the warm morning light crept over her face and everything from the night before slipped back into her memory. The shower. The things Jace had said to her.

He loved her. He'd loved her for a long time. She almost wanted to pinch herself to make sure this wasn't a dream.

She rolled, hand feeling the other side of the bed, searching for him…only the sheets were cold.

Her eyes pinged open. The bed was empty.

With a frown, she pushed up. He wasn't here. And by the look of the dark bathroom and walk-in closet, he wasn't there either.

Slowly, she climbed out of bed and grabbed one of his shirts to throw over her body. It dwarfed her, but it also smelled exactly like him. It was a scent she wouldn't even know how to describe, just deep and masculine and so infinitely Jace.

She stepped out of the bedroom and into the living room. No Jace. And he wasn't in the kitchen or dining room either.

God, where was he?

She inspected every room, but when she didn't find him, she climbed the stairs. She was halfway up when she heard it—quiet, repetitive thuds.

Were they coming from the last room at the end of the hall? It used to be a common room when they were younger, where he and his siblings would play video games.

Her footsteps slowed as she neared the door and quietly pushed it open. The room was completely different. The couches were gone. The TV unit with the video game sets were no longer there.

Instead, workout equipment was pushed against every inch of wall space, with a boxing bag centering the room. And punching that bag was Jace.

His back was toward her, but it did nothing to hide the power of his hits. The muscles that flexed across his gleaming bare back with every punch that sent the bag flying.

God, he'd be terrifying to an enemy. One hit and the person wouldn't get back up.

For a moment, she just watched him, transfixed by the power and fluidity of his movements, as if he'd punched a bag a hundred times before. And maybe he had. Probably not this bag, but keeping active and maintaining his fitness had always been important to him, exactly why joining the Air Force had suited him.

He bounced lightly, and was sidestepping around the bag and half turning, when he caught sight of her. Immediately he stilled, his brows slashing together before he tore off his gloves, then took out his earbuds.

"Hey. How long have you been standing there?"

Her gaze lowered to his chest. Man, oh man, there was muscle upon muscle, and right now those muscles were glistening with sweat.

She swallowed, forcing her attention back to his face. "Not long enough. I could watch you do that for hours."

One side of his mouth lifted. "You'd get bored."

"I doubt it." She stepped into the room. "When did you change this to a workout room?"

"It was the first thing I did after the master bedroom. I needed somewhere to work out."

"Because you've been stressed?"

He inched toward her. "Because it took me too long to get my girl."

A hint of a smile curved her lips. "Your girl… I like that."

When he stopped in front of her, she ran her hands down his chest, not caring how sweaty or hot he was, just needing to touch him.

His arms immediately wrapped around her waist. "I can't believe it took me so long to make a move on you." His head lowered and he nipped her neck. "How I resisted for so long, I have no idea."

A shudder rolled down her spine. "But we got here in the end."

"Thank God."

She cupped his cheek so that he looked at her. "When you were hitting the bag, you looked tense." Tense didn't even begin to describe it. But then, he'd looked tense for a while.

There was a flash of emotion across his face. It came and went so quickly that she couldn't quite identify what it was. Then he smiled. "After last night, I'm better than okay."

She frowned. That felt like an easy lie. But she didn't want an easy lie. She wanted the truth, even if it was hard to hear or ugly.

He slipped a lock of hair behind her ear. "Did you mean it?"

"About loving you? Of course I meant it. I've waited a long time to say it, and now that I have, I want to say it over and over again."

"Hm, and I want to hear it over and over again." He lifted her quickly, then she was in his arms, her hands on his shoulders as his mouth collided with hers.

"God, I love you," he said quietly between desperate kisses.

She smiled against his lips. "I should let you get back to your workout."

"I'm done. What are we doing before work this afternoon?"

"Well, I was thinking about doing a Pilates class, but—"

"I'll do it with you."

She pulled back and frowned. "You want to do Pilates?"

"Yeah. Why do you say it like you can't believe it?"

"Uh, because you're into boxing and weightlifting and rappelling off skywalks. They're the opposite of Pilates."

He lifted a shoulder. "I'm always interested in trying new things."

"Call me selfish, but I'm more worried about me. It's a beginner's class and I don't know if I want you having a front-row seat to witness just how bad I am."

"I've never done Pilates before, so I'm sure I'll be worse."

She threw back her head and laughed. "Jace, you've been physically gifted since you could walk. I doubt you'll even break a sweat." Whereas she'd probably leave the class looking like a sweaty newborn giraffe, barely able to walk.

"I think you overestimate me."

She didn't. But she wasn't going to waste time arguing with him. "You can join me. But I want something in exchange."

His brows flickered. "Anything."

"More of those kisses."

He growled and turned, pressing her to the wall and crushing his lips to hers.

* * *

JACE BIT back his smile at the look of annoyance on Elle's face. "You mad at me, Tink?"

"Yes!"

He chuckled and slipped his arm around her waist, tugging her closer as they walked to Sugar and Spice. "Why?"

"You know why. You're good at everything. Everything! Without even trying. While I huff and puff like a pig, needing a break every two seconds." She glanced up at him, brow pinched. "Statistically, *girls* are supposed to be better at Pilates than boys."

"You were amazing."

She scoffed, and the sound was so unladylike, he wanted to laugh a second time. "I was *not* good. I thought with this being a beginner's class, I'd at least get through without feeling like I was dying. And yeah, it was easier than the last one, but it was still hard. My glutes are on fire."

He looked at her ass. "It looks pretty perfect to me."

She hit his chest playfully. "Charmer."

He lowered his mouth to her ear and quieted his voice. "Besides, I wasn't *that* good. I was very distracted."

"Distracted?"

"Mm-hmm. By this beautiful gray-eyed woman. She was wearing these skintight leggings that showed off all her curves, and this short top that made me want to march right over and tear it off her."

Elle's cheeks tinged pink. "Jace, everyone was wearing leggings and a sports bra."

"I didn't see a single one of them. I only saw you."

"Stop."

"It's the truth." He kissed the top of her head as they stepped into Sugar and Spice.

Cody and Harper stood on one side of the counter talking to Sadie, who was behind the display case.

Sadie smiled at them. "Hey, guys!"

The women hugged each other while Jace approached his brother. "Here for a coffee?" he asked.

"Yeah. And a cupcake for Harper."

Harper scoffed. "He pretends it's for me, then proceeds to eat half of it."

"What can I say—they're good." Cody grinned.

"Did you guys just come from a workout?" Sadie asked, inspecting their clothes.

"Pilates," Elle said.

Sadie gripped her chest playfully. "You went without me?"

"Uh, yeah, because I needed a beginner's class and you did *not* take me to one."

"Hey, it was still a good class though, wasn't it?"

"I couldn't feel my legs after!" Elle protested.

"Pfft, who needs legs?" Sadie said with a laugh.

While the women talked about Pilates, Cody asked, voice hushed, "You hear anything on Boyd or the woman in the rental car? Alice, was it?"

Immediately, his muscles tensed. He was trying not to think about either, but the second he'd woken up this morning, it was all in his head. That, and what Casper had said to Elle. Exactly why he'd needed to get up and move. To exhaust his body and try to forget, at least for a moment.

"Eastern hasn't reported finding anything yet."

Cody gripped his shoulder. "He'll get there."

Jace knew that. His brother never left a case unsolved. But his question was…when?

He was just glancing toward the window when two guys passed outside the bakery.

One of them was Casper.

The words the asshole had said to Elle yesterday came back to him. The hurt in her voice when she'd finally told him. The way a part of her had believed what he'd said.

Jace was moving before he could stop himself. Storming toward the door, ignoring Cody calling his name.

He stepped outside and shouted, "Casper!"

The guy was a few shops down, but he turned, a stupid fucking grin on his face. "Jace. Hey. What can I do for you today, old friend?"

He closed the space between them. "Elle told me what you said to her."

"What I said?" The frown on his face was the fakest fucking thing Jace had ever seen.

"You told her that I'd leave her?" Jace growled. "Made comments about the way she looked in high school."

"Oh, yeah. You know, I don't see a problem with anything I said. You were best friends, then you left her basically without a word for years. It's not out of the realm of possibility to think you'd leave again." Casper lifted a shoulder. "And she wasn't exactly a stunner in high school. People like her always put the weight back on. I can't see you sticking around if she looked like she used to."

Jace swung without pause, nailing the asshole in the face.

Casper's friend gasped and stepped back as Jace peeled Casper off the ground and shoved him against the nearest building. "Either you're stupider than you look, or you can't take a fucking hint. I've told you more than once, you *don't* talk about her like that."

Casper grabbed his face, blood pouring from his nose. "You broke my fucking nose!"

From his peripheral vision, Jace saw Cody running toward him, but he ignored everything but the asshole in front of him. "The next time you say something like that to her—shit, the next time you so much as *look* at her, I will do a hell of a lot more than break your nose."

"I'm gonna charge you for assault, asshole!"

"Jace. Let him go," Cody growled.

Jace leaned in so close that he could see every fucking pore on the guy's face. "You stay away from Elle."

Casper's eyes narrowed, his hand dropping from his face. "Or what? What're you gonna do? Kill me? This isn't the fucking military, Jace. You lay another hand on me and you're done!"

Cody grabbed his arm. "Jace! *Step back.*"

Jace remained exactly where he was. "I can do a hell of a lot worse than kill you. Stay. Away. From her."

He shoved Casper hard before stepping away and storming back to Sugar and Spice, where Elle and Harper were now standing out front watching.

CHAPTER 28

"Are you sure you don't need me to tail you home?"

Elle smiled up at Kayden. It was midafternoon and usually Jace drove home with her after she finished at the café, but today Eastern had called him into the office, hopefully because he'd found something on Boyd or Alice. Another week had passed, and there'd been no signs of Alice or any kind of danger, but Jace was still on edge.

Before he left, he'd asked Kayden to walk her the short distance to her car. Kind of overkill in her opinion. "I'm sure. I'm going straight to Jace's house."

Kayden stopped beside her car, his gaze moving over the parking lot. "I only have one tour left for the day. I can ask one of the guys to—"

She touched his arm. "Kayden. It's fine. Thank you for walking me to my car."

A muscle ticked in his jaw before he nodded. "Straight home."

"Straight home."

With a goodbye, she slid behind the wheel. Before starting the car, she hooked up her phone to the car charger. It had died about an hour ago. Usually, she brought a spare charger in her bag, but today she'd left it at Jace's house. With half her things at her place, and the other half at Jace's, life felt kind of chaotic right now. Not so much in a bad way, just an everything-is-everywhere way.

Pulling out of the parking lot, she waved to Kayden as she went.

Today hadn't been busy, and usually that meant her day dragged by, but Molly had filled a lot of the silences with talk and laughter. She'd joined the dating app that Elle had used, and while the awkward dates made Elle cringe, Molly found humor even in her worst ones, making for some hysterical stories.

Thank God she had Jace, because she *was not* cut out for online dating. Or any kind of dating in this day and age, unless it was with a certain man she'd known and been in love with since she was a kid.

Her mind flicked to Jace and what his meeting with Eastern may involve. It had to be about Alice, right? Either that, or they'd finally figured out why Boyd had targeted her.

A shudder coursed down her spine at the thought of Boyd. At least she didn't have to worry about him anymore.

She was almost at Jace's house when she realized her phone had turned itself back on, and she'd missed a call and voice message from her aunt. She frowned. Her aunt had also texted her just before her phone died, asking for Jace's address. Something about delivering a package.

Using the car Bluetooth, she hit play on the voice message.

"Elle..."

Her fingers tightened around the wheel at that single word— at her aunt's high-pitched voice. She didn't sound like herself, and there was a shake in her tone as she said Elle's name.

A few heavy breaths sounded across the line before Jewel spoke again. "I should be calling the police or an ambulance, but I think I'm going to pass out again and I need you to be okay!"

What the hell was she talking about?

"Someone broke into my house. A woman. She…" Her aunt paused to breathe, and Elle's skin chilled. "She was asking questions about you. I refused to say anything, and she pulled out a gun and hit me in the head."

Elle's heart started to pound, her attention barely on the road.

"I woke up and she was gone, but Elle, I'm scared for you. Find Eastern Walker. Now!"

Her hands shook, fear rushing the blood in her veins. She turned onto Jace's long driveway, cutting the wheel toward the lawn so she could turn back around and head toward her aunt's house to check that she was okay—

When a car suddenly slammed into the back of her, sending her straight into a tree.

The airbag exploded, and she hit it hard. A buzz blasted between her ears, so loud it was all she could hear. Almost numbly, she reached for her seat belt. She'd just tugged it off when her door was opened and rough fingers wrapped around her upper arm. She cried out as she was yanked from the car, groaning at the tight squeeze of those fingers.

"Elle fucking Marshal."

Casper?

She looked up. It was definitely him. There was a bandage over his nose, but it was his wide pupils and glassy, bloodshot eyes that had her belly dropping. She'd seen the look often when he'd been high on drugs during high school.

"Casper?" she gasped. "What are you doing?"

"What am I doing? That asshole Jace always thought he could tell me what to do, and he's *still fucking doing it*. He wants me to stay away from you? Well, guess what—he doesn't get to dictate my fucking actions." He pinned her against the car and leaned into her, smelling her neck.

She shoved at his chest, but he didn't budge. "Get off me!"

"You're not, you know." His hand slipped under her top, sliding up her waist.

She grabbed his wrist, trying to stop him. "Not *what*?"

"Too good for me like both of you think."

When his lips touched her neck, she reacted on instinct, throwing up a knee hard between his legs. He groaned and doubled over, and she immediately followed up with a knee to his injured nose.

A sickening crunch sounded, but she ignored it, shoving him hard and running around the car into the trees that surrounded the drive.

"You bitch!" Casper shouted.

She'd just reached the tree line when, simultaneously, a heavy weight fell on her back and a gunshot exploded through the air.

She cried out as she hit the ground, the weight of Casper's body pinning her. For a moment, she didn't move, confusion clouding her head.

Who had fired the gun? Casper?

But he was on top of her. It didn't make sense.

She tried to shove him off, but not only was he too heavy, he wasn't moving.

Why was he so still?

Her breathing became labored, her limbs shaking. It took her three tries to shove him off and roll behind the closest tree.

Popping noises sounded around her as puffs of dirt exploded near her feet.

Shit. There was someone else here.

She shot a look around the trees to see a flash of a person. A woman.

That's when Elle's mind cleared and she realized what was happening. Someone was firing a gun at her—and they'd already shot Casper in the back.

* * *

JACE SLAMMED his car door shut. He didn't want to be here. He wanted to be with Elle, making sure she got home safely. But whatever this was, Eastern had said it was important.

He walked into the sheriff's station, nodding toward the lady behind the desk before stepping into Eastern's office. He stopped at the sight of a woman sitting in front of the desk. She turned—and recognition hit Jace hard in the chest.

Alice Kelly.

Before he could open his mouth to ask one of the million questions in his head, Eastern spoke.

"Alice got back from her retreat, and her parents got in contact to let her know what's been happening here. She also got my messages."

Alice rose. "The second I got Sheriff Walker's messages, I knew I had to come."

Jace crossed the room slowly. "What do you mean, you had to come? According to the car rental company, you've been here for weeks."

She shook her head. "No, I haven't. And I didn't rent that car."

What was she—

"I didn't realize she'd do this," Alice whispered. "I'm so sorry."

Iciness slipped over his skin. "What are you talking about?"

The woman swallowed, dropping her chin to her chest before looking up again. "My best friend's name is Stephanie Whales. She and Dean had this on-and-off relationship. She always struggled with her mental health, and he seemed to be the only person who could pull her back from the edge on her bad days and make sure she was okay."

His brows flickered. "What does any of this have to do with me or the rental car?"

Alice sucked in a breath. "Before I left for the retreat, I told Steph about the trip and asked her to come with me. It was a grief recovery retreat, to help me deal with losing Dean, and I thought she could use that too. While she was at my place, she found the letter you wrote to my family."

A sinking feeling churned in his gut.

"I stepped out of my bedroom," she continued, "to find Steph hysterical. Saying that Dean shouldn't have died. That...that you killed him by not protecting him. I told her that wasn't true. That he was killed by a foreign enemy, but she wouldn't listen. It was like she *needed* someone to blame, and once she'd read that letter...that person became you."

The air quickened in Jace's lungs.

"The next day, I couldn't find my driver's license." Alice lifted a shoulder. "I didn't think anything of it at the time, just assumed I'd lost or misplaced it, so I got a new one before my trip. But after talking to your sheriff, I'm pretty sure Steph took it."

Eastern cleared his throat. "They look similar. It's possible this Stephanie used Alice's ID to rent the car that tailed you that day."

"Do you have a photo of her?" Jace asked, the dread now spidering through his gut.

Alice looked to Eastern, who turned the screen of his computer.

Jace leaned forward to study the screen. "It's her." He looked up at his brother. "She did a tour of the skywalk, then went to the café. She also did a Pilates class with Elle."

She was also the woman who'd been hovering around the skywalk when he'd first started. He'd told her about the tours.

Fuck. She'd been in town all this time.

"She's unstable," Alice whispered. "I don't know exactly what her diagnosis is. She never wanted to share it, but she was on medication. If she's off that medication..."

Jace stepped back, tugging out his phone to call Elle. He needed to hear her voice. Needed to know she was all right.

By the fourth ring, he knew she wasn't going to answer.

Shit.

He called Kayden, and his older brother answered immediately. "Jace. Everything okay?"

"Is Elle still there?" A part of him already knew. She'd finished half an hour ago, so she'd be gone, but he needed Kayden to say it out loud.

"No. I walked her to her car like you asked about fifteen minutes ago. Why?"

Jace cursed and looked up at his brother. "I need to get to her."

He hung up and without a word, ran out of his brother's office and toward his car. He heard Eastern call after him, but he didn't stop or slow. Eastern would follow, but Jace didn't care about that. He was armed, and he just had to hope like hell that Elle had made it to his place safely.

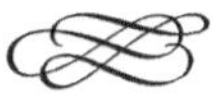

CHAPTER 29

*E*lle's feet pounded the dirt. Fear coursed through her blood, making her fast but unsteady.

Casper had been *shot*. It didn't feel real. Who'd shot him? Who *was* this woman? The same person who'd attacked her aunt? Why? All she'd seen was a flash of denim jeans and a white T-shirt on a slim silhouette. Not enough to identify her.

Distant footsteps sounded behind her. The person wasn't close, but they weren't far either.

Air soared in and out of her lungs as she neared the house. She didn't have a key or her phone, but Jace's words slipped back into her memory. About the lock on his old bedroom window still being broken. Was it possible he still hadn't fixed it? Could she get inside and hide in the house? Maybe find a phone or a weapon?

She focused on *that*, and not the person behind her. Not the gun that had fired or the bullet that had hit Casper.

A sob tried to crawl up her throat, but she swallowed it. She didn't like Casper, but he didn't deserve to be shot in the back.

Instead of running toward the front of the house, she ran around it as quietly as possible, toward the back, near where

Jace's old bedroom was. The shooter might expect her to run to the front, and then she'd be open to a bullet.

As she neared the back, her run slowed to a fast walk, and she used each tree as a shield, sneaking from one to another. She couldn't hear the footsteps behind her anymore. Was that good or bad? Had the woman changed direction?

When she was opposite the window, her hands suddenly felt clammy and her throat tight. To get to the house, she had to leave the protection of the trees.

Three breaths, each one long and drawn out, steadying her… reminding her that she was strong and she could do this. She'd climbed through his window a hundred times before, never making a noise. She could do it again.

One final breath, and she crept forward, keeping low as she crossed the backyard. When she reached the window, she nudged it open, a relieved cry almost slipping from her throat when it moved.

Still broken…thank God.

She pushed it the rest of the way, cringing as a small creaking noise sounded. Quickly, she scrambled through and slid down the wall, finally sucking in a lungful of air.

She wasn't safe yet, but if the woman hadn't seen her access the house, then she'd surely assume Elle was still outside. And that was Elle's advantage.

Remaining on the floor, Elle crawled across the room and out into the hall.

Phone or weapon. She needed one of them. Jace didn't have a landline, but he might have an emergency burner. And he'd definitely have a gun hidden somewhere. In his bedroom?

It took her longer than it should have to make it to his room, and her heart pounded the entire time. Dammit, the windows were huge in here.

Staying low, she crawled across the room to his bedside table. She opened the first drawer and rummaged around. Nothing.

She checked the second drawer, which was filled with books and notepads, then the third, which had some odds and ends.

No gun. No knife or phone. Nothing.

Shit.

She opened the drawers again, this time feeling carefully to see if anything was strapped to the underside. When she didn't find anything there either, she checked under the bed.

Every second felt like ten and made her chest grow tighter. Was it possible he didn't have a weapon in here?

No. He had to. He was too safety conscious.

Think, Elle. If anyone knew him well enough to find it, it was her.

She crept into the walk-in closet and searched every shelf. She looked behind clothes and shoes. After a few minutes, her skin started to feel clammy. She grabbed a stool and looked on the top shelf. She was pushing blankets aside when she saw it. A box. No, not a box. A safe.

It was here. She didn't know that for sure, but she felt it. It had to be.

But the safe was locked with a code.

Crap.

She tried Jace's birthday first, but it didn't work. His mother or father's birthday? She closed her eyes, trying to remember the dates. When she did, she quickly typed them in. But neither worked. She tried a few more combinations before an idea came to her.

She typed in the six digits of her own birthday—the safe popped open.

And inside, there was a handgun.

She'd just wrapped her fingers around the grip of the weapon when glass shattered in another room. Her gaze shot toward the door and she bit back a gasp. Quickly, she climbed down and hid behind the door of the closet.

She stood and waited, gun raised, ready to shoot.

* * *

JACE PRESSED his foot to the floor of the car. He was driving more than twice the speed limit, and it still didn't feel fast enough. He needed to get to Elle. He'd tried her phone half a dozen more times, and she hadn't answered a single call.

Something was wrong.

When he finally got to his street, he saw two cars pulled to the side of his driveway, the first being Elle's, the second a vehicle he'd seen once before—Casper's black Mazda.

His eyes narrowed on her open door. On the way the Mazda had crashed into her car.

Son of a bitch.

He was scanning the line of trees that bordered his drive when he saw the body. Not Elle's body—a man's.

He stopped behind the cars and grabbed his Glock before climbing out. Keeping the gun raised, he eyed the trees around him, searching for any movement or sign that something wasn't right. When he reached the body, he knelt and checked for a pulse.

There was a heartbeat, but it was faint.

He turned the man over to see Casper.

What the hell was going on? Had Elle shot him? No, she couldn't have. As far as he knew, she didn't even own a gun.

He checked her car, spotting her phone. She wouldn't have willingly left without it. Someone else had been here. Someone who'd shot Casper. But what had happened to Elle?

At the sound of a car pulling into the driveway, he rose and turned his Glock on the newcomer, only to lower it at the sight of Eastern. His brother climbed from the car, his own pistol in hand as he jogged toward Jace.

"Next time, you wait for fucking backup," Eastern growled as he stopped beside him. "Who is that?"

"Casper White."

"Dead or alive?"

"Alive. Just."

Eastern lifted his radio and called for an ambulance before glancing around. "She's not here?"

"No."

Eastern's radio squawked. "Sheriff, a deserted car's been reported on Flint Matthews's property. It's the rental car you were looking into."

Jace's gut clenched. Flint's property bordered his own.

"She's here," Jace said, more to himself than his brother as he searched down the drive. "Stephanie's here and she's after Elle." He started to move forward, but Eastern grabbed his arm.

"Wait."

"She's in trouble. I'm *not* waiting for backup!"

"I don't expect you to wait for backup, but we have to be *smart*. The woman's armed and not afraid to shoot. We can't save Elle if we're dead. We go toward the house from separate directions through the forest. I'll take the back of the house and check outside first. You take the front, and the second one of us sees her or needs backup, we call for it. Got it?"

"Fine." He tugged his arm away and started running through the trees, while Eastern went in the opposite direction.

The same questions ran through Jace's head the entire time he ran toward the house. Was Elle okay? Had she gotten away? How had Casper gotten caught in the crossfire?

He forced himself to move faster, pounding his feet into the earth as branches raked his skin. When he neared the house, he slowed his steps.

Keeping the Glock raised and his eyes moving, he slipped from the trees to the house. He'd deployed on so many dangerous missions. Put his life on the line again and again, but this felt different. Harder. More perilous. Because this was Elle, the woman he'd been in love with since he was a kid. The girl he'd *grown up* loving.

His eyes narrowed on the open front door. The long, narrow glass window beside it had been shattered to gain entry. Had that been Elle or Stephanie?

He didn't make a sound as he slipped inside the front door. The quiet of the house was loud, punching him in the gut and making him question if he was too late.

No. He wasn't too late. He was here, and so was she. He just needed to find her.

Keeping his back to the wall, he stepped into the living room, searching for Elle or Stephanie. There was nothing.

He made his way into the kitchen, quietly checking cabinets and around corners. Checking under anything capable of hiding a body.

When still he found nothing, he moved down the hall and into his bedroom.

Little things immediately pinged his attention. The way the drawers on his bedside table weren't completely closed. The sheets on his bed were tossed up at one corner.

Someone had been in here. Someone had searched this room.

Quietly, he inched forward, first checking under the bed, then stepping into the connecting bathroom. When both proved empty, he focused on the walk-in closet, eyes narrowing on the half-closed door.

His steps were silent as he inched forward, closing the space between him and the closet. Then in one swift move, he swung the door around and aimed his Glock behind it.

Elle gasped, hands shaking as she thrust his gun forward and aimed it at his chest.

Her eyes widened as they took him in. "Jace!"

She was alive... *Thank God!*

He lowered his hand and tugged her into his chest. Holding her. Breathing her in. Fucking drowning in her. "You're okay." He wanted to repeat those words again and again to convince himself they were true.

"I'm okay," she whispered.

For a moment, neither of them moved. It was like they couldn't. Then a noise sounded in the hall. It was the smallest creak of a floorboard. Elle stiffened, while Jace pushed her behind him and stepped back into the bedroom, Glock once again lifted.

Stephanie stepped into the room, her own gun raised. Anger narrowed her eyes as she flicked her attention from him to Elle before returning her gaze to him.

"Jace. I should probably be pissed that you're here. I'm not. Because now you can watch as I destroy your life—like you destroyed mine."

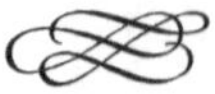

CHAPTER 30

Jace remained perfectly still as Stephanie aimed her gun at his face. At least it was pointed toward him. He took another step forward, making sure to shield Elle with his body.

"It won't bring him back," he said quietly. "No matter what happens today, Dean will still be gone."

"Shut up!" she shouted. "Don't talk about him. Don't even say his name!"

"Why not?"

Her eyes darkened. "Because you *killed* him!"

"That's not true. I didn't pull the trigger on the gun that took his life."

"No, but you should have protected him and you *didn't*, which is as good as pulling the trigger. You wrote it in that pathetic letter you sent his family." She stepped forward, a wild look in her eyes. "I didn't actually come here to kill you, you know. I didn't have a plan at all. I just had to see the man Dean worshipped. The man who was right there when he died but did nothing."

"So what changed?" he asked, needing to keep her talking until his brother found them.

"What *changed* is that I saw you with *her*. I saw the way you looked at her. The same way I looked at Dean. And it made me angry. So fucking angry! Because you got to keep the love of your life, while mine *died* because of you. That's not fair!" she screeched. Then she took a deep breath, like she was trying to calm herself.

"Did you hire Boyd?" Jace asked.

Her eyes flared, and he had his answer before she said a word. "I found him through a friend. He did odd jobs for money. After I saw you together, I wanted you to feel the pain of losing her like when I lost Dean. But the moron fucked up. I knew he was right on the verge of being caught. I couldn't risk him outing me, getting me arrested before *she* died. So I tampered with his car."

"What about Casper?" Jace asked. "Why kill him?"

"I was aiming for *her*. He'd just smashed into her car and was chasing her into the woods. It would have been an easy out for me." She shrugged. "He got in my way."

"Don't do this," Elle whispered from behind him. "They'll know it was you."

She straightened, seeming to pull herself together. "I don't care. I don't care if I die or if I'm arrested. I just care about getting justice for Dean. I owe him that."

Jace shook his head. "I tried to protect him, but an enemy combatant appeared from the other direction and—"

"And you let him die!" she yelled. "He was a *person*. A son. A brother. And I *loved* him. I really loved him…" Tears gathered in her eyes. "And he loved you. He *trusted* you. You should have had his back."

"I think about that moment every day," Jace said softly. "And every day I wish I could have protected him."

Surprise flickered in her eyes before she blinked, her expression switching back to anger. "But you didn't."

"I couldn't. It will be a permanent scar that I carry for the rest of my life. I'm sorry."

This time she shook her head vigorously, tears rolling down her cheeks. "*Don't*. I don't want you to be sorry. I want you to *pay*. To feel the pain that I felt when I lost him. I want you to feel like your insides have been torn out and the ground beneath your feet has crumbled. I want you to *hurt* like I hurt!"

"I feel all of that," he whispered. "I watched him die, and a piece of me died with him out there."

More tears poured from her eyes. "It should have been you."

"It could have been me. It could have been any of us on our team. There are no guarantees on a mission. Every time an airman leaves base, we know we might not come home. And Dean was aware of that."

Her bottom lip trembled. "But he counted on you. He looked up to you. To all of you."

"And he was like a brother to me. I lost a brother that day."

The gun in her hand began to shake.

Eastern stepped into the room behind her. "Put the gun down, Stephanie."

She jumped at the sound of Eastern's voice but didn't lower her weapon. She shook her head. "No. I need to finish what I started. I need her to die like Dean died. It's the only way for me to get closure." There was less conviction in her voice now though.

"You don't need to do anything," Jace said quietly. "Dean's gone, and no matter what either of us do, nothing will bring him back or take away the pain of losing him."

She frowned, and it almost seemed like she was stuck, unsure what to do.

He stepped forward. "Dean wouldn't want this. You know that. Lower the gun, Stephanie."

Her chest started to tremble, the air loud on every inhale and exhale.

"Dean would want you to put the gun down," Jace pleaded.

One more beat of silence…and her face crumpled before she dropped to her knees and began to cry. Loud, pained sobs. The second the gun left her hands, Eastern holstered his weapon and moved forward.

As he handcuffed Stephanie, Jace holstered his own Glock and turned before taking the gun from Elle's fingers and setting it back in the safe.

Then he cupped her cheeks. "Are you all right?"

She nodded quickly, her gaze flickering between his eyes. "Are you?"

Hell no. He didn't feel close to all right. But she was alive.

"I will be." He tugged her into his chest, letting her breathe a semblance of peace back into him.

* * *

ELLE LEANED against the back of the ambulance as a paramedic checked her cuts. She wasn't focused on what he was doing though. All her focus remained on Jace, who stood several yards away with two officers.

He was giving his version of events. She'd already told hers. It felt surreal, like she was retelling a story that wasn't her own. Because this sort of stuff didn't happen to her. She didn't get run off the road and attacked and shot at. That was the stuff of movies.

Except today it wasn't. Today it was her life.

She'd told the officers about her aunt, and Eastern had sent a deputy over to her house. They'd found Jewel passed out with a head injury, and she was now in the hospital with a concussion and lots of bruises.

Guilt swamped Elle. Guilt and worry. All she wanted to do was go to her. Make sure she was okay.

"Okay, Miss Marshal, cuts have been cleaned and bandaged. You're okay to go when you're ready."

She gave the paramedic a small smile. "Thank you." She'd known she was fine, but after crashing her car, Jace and Eastern had pushed for her to be looked over by paramedics for the small scrapes and bruises.

She itched to go over to Jace, but he was still talking to deputies, so instead she moved to the steps at the front of his house. The second she started walking, Jace's gaze shifted to her. It was so intense that she swore she could feel it.

As much as today had been a lot for her, it had been even more for him. He'd had to relive one of the hardest moments of his life—losing a teammate.

God, her heart hurt for him when Stephanie had accused him of killing Dean. When he'd revealed what Dean's death had done to him, and his wish that he'd been able to do more. She'd known, he'd said it before, but today there'd been so much raw emotion in his words.

It wasn't his fault. It had never been his fault. And she'd remind him of that every day if he needed her to.

The ambulance left, and Elle watched as Jace shook the officers' hands before they left too.

She rose from the steps as Jace made his way toward her. Immediately, he pressed his temple to hers, closing his eyes and taking a deep breath. "I'm so glad that's over."

She studied him. "I'm sorry about everything."

A muscle pulsed in his jaw. He was still hurting. Would probably hurt for a long while.

She cupped his cheek, needing him to look at her. When those beautiful blue eyes collided with hers, she frowned. "You know that she was in pain, right? She needed someone to blame, and you were the easiest target. Nothing about what happened to Dean is your fault. It's *never been* your fault."

He turned his head and kissed her palm. "His death will

always feel like a wound I can't stitch back together. And for a long time, that wound hurt more because, just like Stephanie, I needed someone to blame, and that someone was me." His gaze bored into her. "But you're right, his death wasn't my fault. It was a tragedy…but it wasn't my fault."

Thank God. She wrapped her arms around him, holding him close.

He held her back, his chin resting on her head.

"I'm so glad you're okay," he whispered.

"Me too." Glad they were *both* safe. "I need to get to the hospital to see Aunt Jewel."

He nodded before lifting his head, studying her. "I'm so fucking angry about Casper."

She swallowed. Jace was with her when she'd told the officers about Casper crashing into her car. About the things he'd said… the way he'd tried to touch her.

She hated to think what might have happened if Stephanie *hadn't* shot him.

"He was high on something. I'm not saying he deserved what happened to him, but he certainly didn't do himself any favors."

It was kind of strange how Stephanie had inadvertently ended up saving her from him. The fine hairs on her arms stood on end. She didn't want to think about any of that.

Jace's arms tightened around her, his eyes narrowing at her shudder. "Maybe we should leave the visit of your aunt until tomorrow. Rest for a bit."

She shook her head. "No. I need to see her. Besides, as long as you're by my side, I'll be just fine."

He frowned. "Are you sure?"

"Yes. All I need is you, Jace. All I've ever needed is you."

CHAPTER 31

*E*lle had one hand out the window, letting the wind slip through her fingers as they drove down the street. Jace's fingers felt warm on her leg. He'd barely stopped touching her in the weeks that had passed since Stephanie's attack. And she wasn't complaining about that one bit. She needed his touch as much as he needed to touch her. She needed the reassurance that they were both okay, alive and breathing.

"What are you thinking, Tink?"

She turned her head to study him, a small smile curving her lips. "How lucky we are to have each other."

His fingers tightened around her thigh. "I think about that every day."

"So it was a good decision to come home?"

"The best decision I've ever made. Other than the one I made as a kid to be your friend, that is." He lifted her hand and kissed the back.

Her heart gave a little pitter-patter as she looked back out the window.

"But that's not all you were thinking about."

Elle frowned as she turned back to him. He was right. "What do you think will happen to Stephanie?"

His muscles visibly tensed. She probably shouldn't care. The woman had tried to kill her, both by her own hand *and* by hiring someone to do her dirty work, and in the process, she'd killed Boyd and shot Casper. Whatever happened to her, she'd brought on herself.

"It depends what her psych assessment ends up looking like, but regardless, she'll likely be shut away from the public for life."

Elle nodded. "Is it strange that I kind of feel sorry for her?"

"Not strange, Tink. You have a big heart. But she can't be around people. It sounds like she wasn't in the best mental state even *before* Dean died, and his death tipped her over the edge." He flicked his gaze to her before looking back at the road. "I hope she gets the help she needs though."

"Me too."

Jace turned right, and she saw Meridian up ahead, a few cars parked at the curb.

"You think we're the last ones to arrive?" she asked, even though she already knew the answer.

He chuckled. "I know we are. You can blame me."

It was definitely his fault. He'd decided to interrupt her shower and, well, then it had taken three times as long to get out of the house.

They were meeting his brothers, their partners and Avery at the bar. It was a Monday night, so the bar was closed, which meant they'd have the place to themselves while they ordered takeout for dinner.

Jace pulled up in front of the bar before looking at her. "Ready?"

"With you? Always."

She climbed out, and Jace was by her side in seconds, slipping his arm around her waist and tugging her close.

When they stepped inside, it was to see the guys standing by the bar, and the women and Avery sitting around a table. Everyone looked up and greeted them with smiles. It felt warm and comforting...like family. Not just Jace's family, a found family.

Elle made her way around the room to greet everyone, then Jace kissed her cheek before moving to the bar, while she took a seat beside Sadie.

Sadie grinned at her. "How are you doing?"

The woman had checked in on her every day over the last couple weeks, always with cupcakes and coffee in hand. She knew exactly how she was doing. "I'm really good, considering. Jace has been...God, I don't even have words. Amazing. Loving. The best partner I could ask for."

Sadie's smile softened as she looked at the men. "They're great guys, aren't they? Strong. Protective. And man, do they love hard."

That was exactly what the Walker brothers were. "I feel so lucky to have him," she whispered. "For so long, I thought I had to let go of the idea of him and me together. I thought he'd never return my love in the way I needed."

Sadie bumped her shoulder. "Yet he did. And I think he was always going to come back for you."

Thank God for that.

"Sadie!" Avery yelled. "Tell them about the cookies we baked yesterday."

Sadie looked at Avery, love in her eyes as she happily obeyed.

For the next hour, Elle tried to concentrate on the women around her, but she couldn't stop staring at Jace.

She loved him. She loved him so much that sometimes when she wasn't with him, she ached. And now he was hers, and she was his. She didn't know what she'd done to deserve him, but she wasn't going to question it...just appreciate every moment she got with him.

* * *

"You look happy, brother."

Jace nodded at Cody, who stood behind the bar with Eastern beside him, while Kayden sat on a stool beside Jace. It felt good to be with family. It was only over the last few days that he'd started feeling like himself again, but being here, surrounded by the people he loved, helped a lot.

"I am," he finally said. "There are moments every day where I think back to seeing Elle's crashed car in the driveway, not knowing where she was or whether she was okay. I remember that fear, and it drives me crazy for a second. But it also drives me to love her harder and reminds me to never let her go."

Not that he needed reminding. Every time he looked at her—hell, *thought* about her—he knew there was no way in hell he could *not* be with her. He'd done that already. For years he hadn't even been close to her, and those years had been the hardest of his life.

Kayden clenched his shoulder. "I know that feeling. When I almost lost Tilly, I thought I'd lose my mind."

"It's a hell no one should have to live," Eastern said quietly.

Jace's gaze returned to the women. To Elle. Focusing on the way she lit up when she smiled. The warmth on her face when she laughed.

"I knew you two would end up together," Cody said as Jace turned back. "I think I even made a bet with one of you. It's time to pay up."

"What the hell are you talking about?" Kayden said. "*I* was the one who made that bet. If anyone's paying up, it's you."

"Hell no, it was me," Eastern interrupted. "I said it the first time I heard her sneak through his bedroom window."

The *first* time? "You knew she snuck in?"

Cody laughed. "We all knew. Even Dad."

"Just like we knew you'd end up together," Kayden added.

Jace shook his head. "It seems everyone knew but me."

"A part of you *did* know, though, didn't you?" Cody asked.

Had he? "I *wanted* to be with her. I loved her for so long that I forgot what *not* loving her was like, but there was this block. This voice telling me I couldn't have her. That I had other shit to do first."

"I'm glad you came out the other side of that," Eastern said.

"Me too."

Over the next hour, they pulled tables together, ordered pizza, drank beer and cocktails—mocktails for Avery—and talked and laughed. He slipped an arm around Elle's shoulder and pressed a kiss to her cheek.

She sighed. "This is nice."

"This is everything."

She turned to look at him, a soft smile on her lips. "Thank you, Jace."

"For what?"

"Coming home to me."

He leaned in and hovered his lips over hers. "Something tells me it was always going to end this way."

"Thank God."

He kissed her, and the second his lips touched hers, he felt that thing he'd spent years chasing. The high. The adrenaline. The pumping of his blood.

He vaguely heard the *click* as the door to the bar opened, but it wasn't until he heard a few loud gasps that he lifted his head and turned to find the *last* person he expected to see—their last remaining brother.

Lock.

CHAPTER 32

_L_ock Walker strode down the street toward Meridian. The streets were dark, only the glow of the streetlights illuminating the path in front of him.

He stared for a moment at the front of the bar. A bar he'd spent so many hours in with his father growing up.

Cody ran it now. His brother had mentioned they were all meeting up there tonight, but they had no idea that he intended to join them. Or that he was even in town.

He shot a glance at his watch. He'd been here for less than an hour. Wasn't it supposed to feel like home the second he stepped foot in Misty Peak? It didn't. But then, nowhere felt like home. It hadn't for a while.

The familiar facade of his dad's old building grew closer, and fuck if the memories didn't hit him hard. Of his dad pouring drinks. Of the noisy nights with his family.

There were also other memories. Ones that were harder for him to think about. Of his father getting sick. Of Dad looking less and less like the strong tower of a man who'd raised him every time Lock came home for a visit.

He stopped in front of the doors and took a deep breath. He

couldn't go in yet. Because for a single second, he felt stuck. Rooted to the spot.

Why was it so hard? Why was being here *so* fucking hard?

It shouldn't be. *None* of this should be. Not leaving the military, or coming home, or trying to figure out who the fuck he was and what the hell he was doing with his life.

His gaze moved down the street, a street where so many more of his childhood memories lived, before looking back at the door.

Do it, Lock. Step inside. Tell your brothers you're home for good.

One more beat of stillness—and he forced himself to push into the bar.

They were all there. His four brothers. Their partners. His niece. Nylah was the only one missing.

Cody was the first to look up, a frown creasing his brow. Then Kayden. Then Eastern and finally Jace.

At first no one spoke, outside of a few gasps, and a quiet slipped over the room, so heavy it thickened the air.

Then a wide grin spread across Cody's face. "Lock Walker. What the *fuck* are you doing here?"

His brothers rose to their feet and, one by one, embraced him. He returned their tight hugs, then lifted his niece into his arms. She was too damn big. A hell of a lot bigger than he remembered. He knew she was eight, but in his head she was still a toddler, inciting chaos.

Then he was introduced to their women, each as beautiful as the next. But it wasn't just that they were beautiful. Each of them had a smile that lit up the room…and when his brothers looked at their women, there was love in their eyes. Real fucking love.

Shit, he'd missed *a lot*.

Cody pushed a beer into his hand, and Eastern shoved him onto a stool at the bar.

"Talk," Kayden said.

Lock raised a brow at his oldest brother. "What do you want me to say?"

Jace crossed his arms. "Don't screw with us. Are you on leave?"

His next breath was heavy. "Actually, my Ghost Ops team disbanded, and we were all discharged. I'm home for good."

There was that thick beat of silence again. He didn't blame them. He'd barely come home over the years, so they probably thought he'd never return, even if he left the military.

"You're screwing with us, right?" Cody asked.

"Nope."

"Hell yeah!" Jace shouted.

Kayden gripped his shoulder. "In that case, it's good to have you home."

Lock dipped his head. "Thanks."

"If you need somewhere to stay, the place upstairs is empty," Cody said.

Lock shook his head. "I've got somewhere."

He didn't say more than that, and he could see the questions on his brothers' faces, but they didn't voice any of them. He'd owned a place here in town for a while.

Over the next few hours, everyone around him talked while he mostly listened. Watched. Observed the dynamics of his family.

It wasn't until Sadie asked Elle a question that his attention shot over to them.

"Are you coming to Callie's class with me tomorrow?"

Lock's heart stammered at the sound of her name.

Elle shook her head. "Absolutely not. You go to your intermediate classes. I'm switching to beginner's yoga."

He didn't have to ask to know which Callie they were talking about. The same Callie who lived so damn deep inside him that he could barely *think* about her without his entire body reacting.

Jace turned to him and lowered his voice. "Did you know she was back?"

Lock's fingers tightened around his beer. "Eastern mentioned it."

All his brothers knew about his relationship with Callie. It was short and they'd only seen each other when he'd made it home or she'd gone to his base, but it had been intense…and it had changed him.

He cleared his throat. "Is her new studio doing well?"

Jace nodded. "It seems to be busy."

Of course it was. Everything that woman touched did well. She was smart and hardworking and had this smile that turned heads.

Kayden turned toward him and shoved Lock's shoulder. "You're the last Walker sibling left single."

"How long he lasts is the question," Jace said with a grin.

Cody nodded. "Yeah, there's something about this town… people don't stay single for long."

His brothers talked and laughed, but Lock barely paid attention. It still felt too surreal to be home, like he wasn't really here.

Eastern was the first to leave because he needed to get Avery home to bed. Then one by one, Kayden and Jace headed out with their women. When it was just him, Cody and Harper left, Cody gripped his shoulder.

"You sure you don't need a place to stay? If you don't want to stay in the upstairs apartment, we have a spare room at our place."

Harper nodded. "You're more than welcome."

Lock shook his head, standing. "Thanks, but I've got a place."

Cody watched him closely. "Okay. Well, it's great to have you home. Call if you need anything."

"Thanks."

He told them both goodbye and drove the short distance to the house. It was a place he'd owned for a while now, yet still hadn't told anyone about, not even his brothers.

He parked in front but didn't get out right away. Instead, he sat, studying the rotting wood and broken decking. To anyone else, this place would look like a piece of shit, yet he'd bought it in this condition, because to him, it was so much more than that. It was the place where he was supposed to start his new life. The house he was supposed to turn into a home.

He hadn't.

Would he finally get that chance now?

He'd come home not just because his Ghost Ops team had disbanded...but for her.

For Callie.

To get her back.

To build the life with her that he was supposed to have built years ago.

Order book five in the series, RECKLESS LOVE, featuring Lock and Callie, NOW!

Declan

Cole

Ryker

BEAUTIFUL PIECES

Erik's Salvation

Erik's Redemption

Erik's Refuge

SHORT CHRISTMAS STORY

Hidden Shadows

RECKLESS SERIES

Reckless Hope

Reckless Trust

Reckless Fall

Reckless Faith

Reckless Love

JOIN my newsletter and be the first to find out about sales and new releases! CLICK HERE

ABOUT THE AUTHOR

Nyssa Kathryn is a romantic suspense author. She lives in South Australia with her daughter and hubby and takes every chance she can to be plotting and writing. Always an avid reader of romance novels, she considers alpha males and happily-ever-afters to be her jam.

Don't forget to follow Nyssa and never miss another release.

Facebook | Instagram | Amazon | Goodreads

www.ingramcontent.com/pod-product-compliance
Lightning Source LLC
Chambersburg PA
CBHW061543210726
48287CB00006B/2064